SIGN OFF

Caught Dead In Wyoming
Book 1

Patricia McLinn

Divorce a husband, lose a career ... grapple with a murder.

TV journalist Elizabeth "E. M." Danniher will tell you she committed two sins—she didn't stay young, and she made an enemy of a powerful news executive—her ex. She used to break national news. Now her top story as the "Helping Out!" reporter at dinky KWMT-TV in Sherman, Wyoming is getting a refund for a defective toaster.

But the case of a missing—or has he been murdered?—sheriff's deputy is about to introduce her to what happens when people are Caught Dead in Wyoming...

Caught Dead In Wyoming Series

Sign Off

Left Hanging

Shoot First

Last Ditch

Dear Readers: If you encounter typos or errors in this book, please send them to me at: Patricia@PatriciaMcLinn.com. Even with many layers of editing, mistakes can slip through, alas. But, together, we can eradicate the nasty nuisances.
Thank you! – Patricia McLinn

Cover design: ArtbyKarri.com
Cover Art: Deb Dixon
Photo Credits:
Truck (manipulated) © Bonita Cheshier | Dreamstime.com
Landscape (manipulated) © Dary423 | Dreamstime.com

Chapter One

IN JOURNALISM, it's called a tick-tock.

It's a piece that recaps a big, ongoing story by hitting each important date and occurrence in order to bring the audience up to date to that very moment.

Tick.

Spewing blood from a battered nose and curses from a mouth of ill repute, Sheriff's Deputy Foster Redus climbed into his brand new forest green Ford pickup outfitted with flared fenders, chrome brush guard, skid plates and Holley headers and drove into the Wyoming gloaming last fall. It was the Monday after Thanksgiving. That was the last anybody in Cottonwood County admitted to seeing him.

Tock.

That same week, in a land far to the east where the canyons are concrete and the herds are SUVs, I finally opened my eyes to the fact that my divorce decree covered not only a man, but a career.

Tick.

A week before Christmas, the Cottonwood County, Wyoming sheriff arrested Thomas David Burrell, who'd caused the aforementioned spewing of blood and curses, and charged him with murder, though neither Foster Redus nor his pickup had been found.

Tock.

I spent that week in my Illinois hometown with my family, which was evenly divided among considering me a marital failure, wanting to kick some ex-husband butt, and assuring me this would all turn out for the best because I could now get out of that nasty city and nastier business. That three-way split was not *among* the members of my family, it was *within* each and every one of them old enough to put sentences together.

It made for a trying week, since I never knew which one-third of a relative I was going to encounter at any given moment.

Tick.

On New Year's Eve day the Cottonwood County prosecuting attorney dropped the charges against Burrell without prejudice for insufficient evidence.

Tock.

I signed off for the last time from a New York newscast that night. That's right, after two weeks of vacation, the schedule required me to return for one last shift—why waste a precious commodity like New Year's Eve off on a has-been?

On April Fool's day I arrived in Cottonwood County, Wyoming— no cracks about the timing, please—and went on the air the following week as "KWMT-TV's 'Helping Out' reporter E.M. Danniher."

The gap between New Year's and April Fool's Day?

Not a thing happened officially on the Foster Redus case. As for my life, no comment.

That brings you right up to a particular crisp morning in early May in Sherman, Wyoming.

Tick.

Tock.

I'd heard about the Redus case—it was hard not to in KWMT's newsroom—but it didn't occupy a lot of my attention. I had my own concerns.

Concerns like figuring out how come LL Bean and Harry and David had no trouble with my change of address, but my ex-husband's lawyer couldn't master the concept. Like finding more congenial surroundings (no matter how temporary my stay in Wyoming might be) than the hovel masquerading as a house that I was renting. Like adjusting to a landscape that looked as if it came out of the head of a science fiction writer. Like acclimating to co-workers who treated me either as visiting royalty or a particularly nasty-tempered shark circling their very private swimming hole.

As eighteen second-graders from Lewis and Clark Elementary School and three harassed adults scattered through the KWMT-TV newsroom's maze of dented desks and mismatched chairs, I was specifically contemplating how to handle anchorman Thurston Fine, who'd botched the intro to my package the night before.

Twice.

At five and ten. Who needs DVR when you have Thurston Fine?

Fine was KWMT's star—of the variety used for a kindergarten pageant. A pattern traced out on cardboard, covered in tin foil and pinned up—glossy, neat and flat. He so obviously ascribed to the shark school of thought that I found myself looking around for Roy Scheider and Richard Dreyfuss whenever we met. Fine hadn't stuck a javelin down my throat—yet—but I figured he was looking for the right opportunity.

As a stop-gap measure he had undermined me, on air and off for the past month.

Last night he'd pulled one of the oldest tricks, stopping, as if he'd decided to leave off the last line of his script, then stepping on my first words as I tried to launch into my intro to the piece.

A good news director would have handled it.

KWMT's news director was Les Haeburn.

Insert philosophical shrug.

"Helping Out" wasn't Emmy material. It wasn't even material enough under Haeburn's dominion to keep me fifty percent occupied. Maybe I would change that, or maybe I would decide I liked it like this. More likely, it would become moot before long. In the meantime, I had plenty of free time to contemplate the niceties of taking a hunk out of Fine's leg. Figuratively, of course.

That's what I was doing when a thin girl with wispy brown hair falling straight at either side of a square face stepped in front of my new professional home, third battleship-gray desk from the windows. Sitting on a chair that only swiveled to the right put me eye-level with this detachment from the second-grade horde.

"Everybody went that way." I pointed toward the control room door. She wouldn't want to miss the comedy of Les Haeburn's steady-hand-at-the-helm routine. Though it might take a somewhat more jaded outlook than a second-grader possessed to see the humor.

"I know."

Her voice was assured. Her eyes, so dark brown they seemed to be all pupil, stayed on me.

Apparently, she had a need other than reattachment.

"Uh, the bathroom's over there." I pointed again.

"I know." She didn't move.

Enough of my contemporaries had beaten the biological clock lately that I knew the ground rules about diapers and babies, but where in the developmental continuum trips to the bathroom became a solo venture remained foggy.

"I'll get your teacher and—"

"You're Miss Danniher."

Being recognized is not necessarily the thrill some people imagine. This time, however, a reprieve from potential bathroom duty offset the discomfort.

As my ex-husband took to saying, everything's a trade-off.

"Yes, I am."

"On TV. Mrs. George from next door said you're a consumer advocate." The girl said the final two words carefully. "So I watched."

That surprised me. From the little feedback we'd gotten to "Helping Out," I didn't think it had any viewers, and here was evidence of two.

When I'd received the assignment, I checked with a few connections, who all said the consumer affairs beat was hotter than ever. But in the four weeks I'd been on-air, I'd gotten a grand total of seven phone calls from viewers, and four were from Ed Radey, who didn't like his wife's cooking and wanted me to "help out." I could come cook or I could take them to dinner, he wasn't particular.

The girl's stare intensified, and her thin body leaned over the desk toward me, turning down the corners of the *Sherman Independence* where it extended beyond the edge. "You help people. You got that man to fix that woman's toaster."

"Yes, but not everythi—"

"You told people with problems to tell you and you'd help them."

The segment tag actually says "KWMT-TV will consider your problem as a potential topic for 'Helping Out.'" I opened my mouth to educate this girl in the denim blue sweater and faded red plaid shirt on the importance of qualifiers such as "will consider" and "potential." She didn't wait.

"You're going to help me." Not a single qualifier.

"What we do in 'Helping Out' is look into your problem and—if we can—we try to find a solution that's satisfactory to you and the other party."

"You're going to help me."

"Now wait a minute—"

"You're going to help me keep going to the Circle B and seeing Daddy. He needs me."

"Someone's trying to keep you from seeing your Daddy? Who?"

I am not a softy. It was simply the reporter's instinct to ask questions kicking in.

"Mom and Mr. Haus. He's her lawyer."

"Are your parents divorced?"

A solemn nod. "But Mom wants Mr. Haus to get the judge to say Daddy can't see me anymore."

Her dark brown eyes might not show color, but they revealed emotion. Mom better not be hoping for roses this Mother's Day from this offspring—maybe thorns, but definitely no roses.

"Why do you think your mother doesn't want your father to see you?" Possibilities arose in a mental film clip of too many horrifying news stories. But this child wasn't wary or withdrawn. And the only fear she seemed to harbor was of not seeing her father.

"She's mad at him. She's always been mad at him. Even when I was a baby."

A woman using a child to punish an ex-spouse? Not unheard of. But why move to cut visitation now if she'd been angry all along?

"Your mother and Mr. Haus think they can get the judge to say your father can't see you?"

"Yes." After the single word, her teeth clamped over her bottom lip. Not to stop trembling—it wouldn't have dared—but to prevent something from escaping.

Nothing gets a reporter's juices going like somebody keeping a secret. Even somebody younger than my favorite pair of jeans.

"Why do they think that?"

Not a flicker of reaction.

"You know, I can't help if you don't tell me the whole story. Just like Mrs. Atcheson with the toaster. She told me everything—when she bought it and where and how much she paid." A wary blink. "But if you're not going to tell me, I guess you don't really want my help. Of course you said you wanted my help, but that's up to you—"

"He didn't kill him."

"What?" If Mrs. Atcheson's toaster had turned into a Veg-o-Matic before my eyes, I couldn't have been more surprised. "Who didn't kill who?"

(I know, I know—it should be *who* didn't kill *whom*—so shoot me.)

"They said he did and they put him in jail, but the man said they couldn't say Daddy did, so they let him go. But Mom said they couldn't say Daddy *didn't*, so maybe the judge will say Daddy can't see me. Ever."

On the edge of my consciousness the sound of a door opening registered, but my attention stayed on the intense, square face leaning toward me.

"Let me get this straight. Your father was accused of killing somebody. But he was released. And your mother's using the accusation to try to get the judge to rescind his visitation—" *Remember the audience.* "—to say he can't see you anymore."

"Yes. So you have to stop her and Mr. Haus."

"But who—"

"Tamantha Burrell! What are you doing? The rest of the class is on the bus. You know you're supposed to stick with the group."

The least harassed looking of the three adults (likely the teacher since teachers build harassment immunity while parents move on to the germs of a new age) swept up to the thin girl. Smiling at me, she snagged my visitor—Tamantha Burrell, by name, and that information filled in several gaps—in obvious preparation for a speedy exit.

"You tell this nice lady how sorry you are for bothering her and how much you've enjoyed seeing how people like her work behind the scenes on a television station."

Teacher clearly hadn't followed Tamantha's lead in watching "Helping Out" and didn't have the foggiest who I was. She started drawing the girl away.

Tamantha held back long enough for parting words—not the ones her teacher had recommended but a repetition of her unequivocal order:

"You do it."

"YOU'RE NOT."

The unexpected voice from over my left shoulder made me jump, and the clip I'd been reading fluttered onto a stack of manila-foldered brethren. The amused disbelief in the voice made me irritable.

"There are a lot of things I'm not, Paycik. Including in the mood for a chat with KWMT's 'Eye on Sports.' Go away."

He didn't budge.

I stared at him. An attractive man, with the kind of strong bones cameras like, and great hair. Thick and just enough wave to look casual on air without requiring a lot of effort. He wore a crisp soft yellow shirt that would look fine on-air, and jeans battered to the point of fraying, because the news desk masked from the ribcage down.

I should have heard him coming. He wore cowboy boots—honest to goodness cowboy boots. No spurs to jingle-jangle, but clunky heels that should have made plenty of noise. Unless a man took special effort to be quiet.

I don't ascribe to the theory that jocks are stupid per se. Some are, some aren't. Limited observation of Mike Paycik nudged him provisionally toward the latter category.

For one thing, he'd taken time to get a degree while he was playing college football.

For another, he'd saved money from pro ball to buy a tidy spread, as it was universally described in these parts.

For a third, when doctors said quit torturing those knees or don't ask them to hold you up, he'd quit.

And for a fourth, when he'd retired last winter, he'd returned home to Cottonwood to start his broadcast journalism career, coming to the spot where he would be forgiven all flubs. When he does burst onto the national scene—and he will, oh, yes, with that voice and those looks, he will—there will be no beginner's gaffes to pollute the audience's perception.

A smart move.

However, at the moment, Mike Paycik's apparent inability to understand English had the "stupid" arrow slipping closer to "is."

"You're studying the Burrell case because of what that kid said to you?"

Who'd had time to study? I'd barely confirmed the bits and pieces I'd heard since coming to town.

Burrell acknowledged fighting with Redus the night the deputy was last seen—accounting for bloodstains found in Burrell's house that matched Redus' type but not Burrell's—though the clips didn't say what the men had fought about. Burrell swore Redus was alive and kicking when they parted, but no one admitted to seeing the alleged victim since.

The clips had explained one mystery Tamantha had left behind.

Going to the Circle B referred to her father's ranch. When the *Independence* said Redus had been in Burrell's ranch house, it wasn't talking about house design.

"Eavesdropping?" I asked sweetly, leaning against a file cabinet at one end of the windowless cave KWMT grandly called the library. Except for a battered table against one long wall, file cabinets encircled the room. Old tapes occupied shelves above the cabinets. Freestanding shelves down the middle were backed by more filing cabinets. On top bulged cardboard boxes with labels too faded and dusty to read. The only open floor space was a narrow rectangular aisle around the room.

"Maybe you got in the habit of listening in on the other team's huddle in football, but in the real world it's not polite to eavesdrop on a colleague's conversation with a source."

His grin widened. "I played offense, so the other guys mostly eavesdropped on us. And I'm not sure you can consider anyone under the age of reason a source, can you?"

"That's the thing about sources, the age of reason is a sliding scale, not an absolute number."

"Now, see, that's the sort of insight I was hoping I might learn when Les announced that Elizabeth Margaret Danniher was joining our little family."

I could hear Haeburn using exactly that phrase, and grimaced. Mike's grin reached his eyes, and for a second we connected, at least on the level of mutual distaste for our mutual boss.

Then Paycik ruined it.

"I'd heard of you, of course," he said earnestly, "but when Les said you were coming here, I did some checking, all the way back to when you did newspaper work."

The guy was a good decade younger than me, but *all the way back?* "You mean before I joined up with Edward R. Murrow in reporting the London Blitz?"

He waved that off—not generally a smart move when making reference, even obliquely, to a woman's age. Especially a woman on the camera side of television. Especially a woman recently booted out of a prime spot in front of that camera.

I would've expected better from someone so obviously practiced in charming females, but his earnestness had blossomed into full-blown enthusiasm.

"You did some great stuff. Investigations. Exposes. You really stick with a story and dig."

I was tired of bantering. I was tired, period. I'd looked up the file simply to satisfy a curiosity that had nibbled at my concentration on important matters like hobbling Fine, through a less-than-busy afternoon. But since I'd been off officially for twenty minutes, I was wasting precious time—my own.

It was a commodity I'd forgotten about in all those years with the network. And for the rest of the KWMT staffers it appeared as much of a rarity as in any other newsroom, maybe more. KWMT wasted no resources on up-to-date equipment or extraneous personnel. Which made it all the odder that Haeburn had me doing so little. Granted, the network was picking up my sizable salary—another of my sins when they could sign up fresh blood for much less—but it was still odd.

But who was I to complain?

"Oh, go away."

"It's a great story. Biggest around here I can remember." He looked at me with speculation. "Thurston Fine grabbed the story when it broke, you know."

And turned it into mush, no doubt.

I said nothing.

That didn't stop Paycik. "He didn't let anybody else touch it. But all he's done is report the company line from Sheriff Widcuff."

I hadn't met Sheriff Robert Widcuff. As with jocks, I make no assumptions about politicians or law enforcement professionals—although anyone who would run for an office that combines two of the more thankless jobs around does nudge the "stupid" arrow. Reading between the lines of the clips, Widcuff had pushed it even closer to "is" by charging Burrell when he didn't have a tight case and the prosecuting county attorney was out of town.

That meant the prosecuting county attorney, a man named Ames Hunt whose political ambitions had already reached my ear, had nothing to lose by acknowledging there wasn't enough evidence to keep Burrell in jail.

Releasing Burrell took no skin off Hunt's ambitious nose, but it made Widcuff look bad.

I closed the heavy metal drawer.

"I could go away," Mike said, retreating to his bantering tone. "I could go away and you could go on reading that skinny file. But I've got a better idea—we'll go get a drink and I'll tell you all about Tamantha Burrell's daddy."

Half turning, I got a better look at his face. Despite his light tone and the returning grin, he was serious.

"Why would I want to hear what you have to say? The file's the official information."

"That's exactly why you want to talk to me. There's a lot about this case that won't get in any official document. The whole thing's pretty interesting, don't you think?"

It sure beat Mrs. Atcheson's toaster. But I wasn't admitting that to him. Not yet.

"How would you know any unofficial information other than gossip?"

He grinned. "Welcome to Cottonwood County, where the people are few and the gossip is plentiful. But this goes beyond basic gossip. My aunt's a dispatcher for the sheriff's department over in O'Hara, where Redus had been stationed. She doesn't believe in keeping secrets from family. And she's inclined to agree with Tamantha—Tom Burrell didn't kill anybody."

Mike Paycik repeating his aunt's theories, which were probably based on overheard sheriff's department gossip and personal prejudices.

On the "how-reliable-is-this-source?" scale it ranked with a congressman running for re-election.

"Sorry, I have other plans for the evening."

Paycik quirked a brow. "Washing your hair?" he asked politely.

Oh, yes, the guy had talent. That didn't mean I had to applaud.

I answered with equal seriousness. "Grocery shopping."

Besides, how hard could it be in a sparsely populated county to track down a sheriff's department dispatcher who also happened to be Mike Paycik's aunt, and talk to her in person?

That is, on the off chance that a little girl's order, the potential to put Thurston Fine's nose out of joint and the effort to keep myself from going stir-crazy caused me to do something as out of character as asking questions.

Chapter Two

I WAS SENT TO SHERMAN, Wyoming for my sins. On that, everyone agreed.

The exact nature of those sins rouses wide differences of opinion. But the result is not open to debate. After anchor stints in Dayton, St. Louis and Chicago, and network assignments as a correspondent in London and Washington before New York, I am riding out the end of a network contract in Sherman, Wyoming doing a two-times-a-week segment called "Helping Out."

If I were doing the stand-up on the Elizabeth Margaret Danniher story, I'd start the next sentence with "Ironically." As in "Ironically, E.M. Danniher's former spouse sent her to exactly the sort of life they'd once envisioned together."

Long ago and far away. Now he viewed it as sentencing me to a tour in hell.

As I headed west on U.S. 27 from KWMT toward what center the town had, the sky suited hellfire's palette. The nuns who'd spent so many Saturday morning hours teaching me my Catechism probably wouldn't have approved of the sentiment, but hell-fire was damned spectacular.

In hopes of attracting Yellowstone or Grand Teton-bound tourists, Sherman's Chamber of Commerce liked to say it sat at the foot of the Rockies. Only if the Rockies had very long feet.

But the location did let KWMT boast the largest broadcast area in the state. In fact, it was challenging Billings' stations for a chunk of Montana.

A victory there might nudge it up a spot in the rough and tumble competition of the country's Bottom 50 television markets.

At the moment, Sherman's location east of the mountains offered another advantage; the mountains blocked less of this sunset than they would have if we'd been farther west. And as long as I wasn't getting singed by the flames, I enjoyed hell-fire's display.

As I pulled into the parking lot of the Sherman Supermarket, on the western fringe of downtown, it crossed my mind that it was a heck of a lot easier to sidestep the flames out here where the buffalo used to roam than where bulls and bears stampeded through Wall Street. Not only did the parking lot take up enough real estate to make Trump swoon, but each spot was sized for a limo . . . or a pickup truck.

My penchant for grocery stores used to drive remote crews crazy, but give me an hour with the grocery store and the local paper, and I can give you the broad strokes of a community's character.

Take the Sherman Supermarket. From generous parking spaces to the straightforward name—no deli, gourmet or health food pretensions here—to wide aisles that accommodated cart-to-cart fraternization, to the preponderance of fifty-pound bags of potatoes and the dearth of cutely packaged single-sized portions or trendy vegetables, Sherman Supermarket proclaimed itself a habitat of a sociable but wide-flung, family-oriented society.

This is not to say that outside influences hadn't seeped into the shelves lining the black and white-tiled floor. By careful selection, I'd loaded my cart with low-fat, low-cholesterol, low-sodium goodies. Then, in a symbolic act of solidarity with my new home, I added a thick steak and a bag of potatoes.

Finally, I topped it off with a package of Pepperidge Farm Milano cookies.

I deserved them.

Just before leaving the station, I'd been having a pleasant enough conversation with Jenny, a young production assistant, in the ladies room—as the sign on the door describes a cubicle with two stalls, two sinks, one foggy mirror and a sliver of aged floor.

Then she said something odd.

Standing beside me as we combed our hair, I saw her examining my reflected face with great interest. Fearing she sold cosmetics packaged all in lilac on the side and was about to give me the pitch, I hurriedly stowed my comb and prepared to depart.

"You don't show any signs of it. You're really lucky."

Assessing stares were nothing new in this business. Besides, I *do* show signs of my years—crows' feet, laugh lines, slippage under the chin, somewhat plumper pillows under the eyes—I'd never tried to deny it. Saying I didn't, while flattering, didn't seem a good way to sell cosmetics.

So it was probably curiosity that made me slow enough to let her add, "I had a friend, her skin got real dried out and grainy. A strange kind of color, too, like bleached cement, you know?"

"No, I don't know. What are you talking about?"

"Drugs," she blurted out.

"Drugs?" I stupidly repeated.

"Isn't that why you left the network? I mean, he said it was like that Savage woman." Dawn was breaking. Years back, a book and cable movie detailed how Jessica Savitch, a pioneer woman in network news, had her career unravel because of cocaine addiction. She'd appeared to be getting her life back in order when she was killed in a car crash. "The same thing. Promoted real fast and all the pressure. He said you just—"

"Who said?"

"Uh, Thurston."

Ah, Thurston.

So, Thurston Fine wasn't going to be satisfied with the usual elbow-digging of professional jockeying for position. He'd bombed Pearl Harbor, and I hadn't even known it.

It seemed extreme, but the "whys" rested inside Thurston Fine's head, and I doubted we'd ever be chummy enough for me to delve into his mysteries.

I also understood one other thing. I must never, under any circumstances, tell Jenny something I didn't a.) want her to tell everyone she spoke to, and b.) want her to tell everyone she spoke to that I was her source.

Drugs. Of all the vices, that was one I'd missed. Heck, I did one better than Bill Clinton. I not only didn't inhale in college, I didn't smoke. I hate the smell of marijuana, and smoke makes me cough.

Now, I will admit, on occasion, to having more alcohol than was strictly good for me. But these days, my major vice centered on the cookie aisle at the Sherman Supermarket.

Hence, the Milano cookies.

My willpower thoroughly undermined, I was reaching for the Seville box when a voice from over my shoulder made me start for the second time in two hours.

"I figured it out."

You do not live in the cities I've lived in and report on the things I've reported on without reacting when someone accosts you from behind in a public place. Instinctively pivoting, my mind had already recognized the voice and ordered a call-down of the red-alert troops.

My elbow didn't catch on as fast. When it contacted a semi-solid, it jabbed like hell.

Unfortunately, what it jabbed wasn't some vulnerable part of Mike Paycik's anatomy, but a box of Southport selection.

"Jesus, Mary and Joseph, Paycik!"

He looked as if he wanted to laugh, but knew better. Instead, he bent down and retrieved the box that bore a deep, rounded dent over a picture of a Tahiti cookie from atop the pointed toes of his boots.

"Sorry, Elizabeth."

He started to return the box to the shelf. I snatched it and tossed it into the cart. Just what I needed, a box of cookie crumbs. I don't even like Tahitis. But Catherine Danniher's children were raised with clear rules—you break, you buy. Even cookies.

"I didn't mean to spook you. But why're you so jumpy?"

I glared at him. "I am not *jumpy*. What are you doing here, Paycik?"

He practically beamed, but cut the laser show short when I rolled the grocery cart half an inch from his toes. It would have been half an inch *on* his toes if he hadn't moved an inch. Although considering how pointy the boots were I probably would have had to go back another two inches to actually get toes.

"I came to tell you I figured it out."

Figured what out? I'm not stupid; I didn't ask.

It didn't stop him. "I was having a beer over at the Stockman when I figured out what you were up to."

Since I'd kept the cart going, he said this to my back. He trailed behind as we passed white cheddar-flavored popcorn, ranch-flavored chips and onion-salted pretzels. Sure, *now* I could hear the *thwack, thwack* of those solid heels.

"You're waiting until you can get the story from primary sources. That's why you didn't want to hear it from me. I should have figured you'd want to question Aunt Gee. That's pretty basic."

I made good time down the aisle packed with canned vegetables, so his words were fainter. But the cart didn't corner worth a hill of beans, and he caught up.

"I'll call Aunt Gee and set up a time tomorrow, then you can drive up to O'Hara Hill, and I'll tag along. Smooth things over, and at the same time see how it's done—"

"No."

Add together Mike Paycik's patent ambition and his attitude toward me (he hadn't gone as far as bowing but he certainly fell into the treating me as "visiting royalty" camp), and that equaled a clear view of his motive.

Paycik wanted to learn tricks of the trade from somebody who'd been trading a while. I couldn't blame him. I would have tried the same thing in his position. But I *wasn't* in his position. He wanted to build a career. I wanted to retrieve one. Being a mentor didn't fit in. Besides, if I'd wanted to be a teacher, I would have learned to make lesson plans.

He was smart enough to play stupid. "Well, I'll drive then, and you can relax on the way up—"

"No. You won't drive. I won't drive." At least not together.

I saw my opportunity and took it, diving down the aisle discreetly labeled feminine hygiene. He wouldn't follow me here. The longer my refusal stood, the stronger it grew. He'd back off, and—

"Why?"

All those years in locker rooms must have dulled his male sensibilities. He slipped past the cart and stood squarely in its path. He wasn't even looking sheepish or shifting from foot to foot.

"Why would I spend my Saturday driving God knows how long to God knows where to hear a story about somebody who might or might not have disappeared six months ago?" I leaned over the handle of the cart. "Maybe I don't care."

He grasped the front of the cart and leaned toward me. "You should."

That's all he said while we stood a grocery cart away from being nose to nose.

Oh, yes, he'd be very, very good someday. I could feel words being dragged out of me by the vacuum of dead air.

"Why should I?"

A glint of self-satisfaction gave him away, but I'd been looking for it. Most wouldn't have caught it.

"Because it's an interesting case. Because it's an unfinished story. Because it's tearing this county apart. Because nobody's reporting it worth a damn. Because Fine never will." He looked at me almost defiantly. "Because a little girl asked you to."

The itch that unfinished stories can lodge under your skin is an occupational hazard. But it wasn't *my* unfinished story. And I wasn't seeking to grab a story or glory away from Thurston Fine.

On the other hand, it didn't seem likely that he would show me the same *laissez faire* courtesy, judging from his antics so far.

And there was the matter of Tamantha.

I couldn't see Tamantha Burrell being satisfied with Fine's approach to a story, which seemed to consist of letting it age as long as brandy.

"Humpf. You were the one laughing at me for looking up the clips."

He grinned. "Just yanking your chain. I was really pleased to see you had the file."

"Why?" After I asked it, I realized how interesting a question that was. "Why are you so interested in this?"

"Ah, now that's a long story. I'll tell you on the drive to O'Hara Hill tomorrow."

O'Hara Hill was in the northwest corner of Cottonwood County, tucked up against the rising wall of the mountains. I hadn't been to that area yet.

Not that I intended to explore every notable corner of the county like some tourist with a Frommer's guide to Manhattan. That wasn't why I'd come to KWMT. Acquiescing to the network's holding-my-feet-to-the-fire interpretation of my contract by coming here was meant only to buy me time.

Glaring, I yanked the cart out of his grasp, swept past and headed to the safety of the checkout. Safety, because after five weeks in town, I knew that Penny Czylinski ruled the solitary Sherman Supermarket checkout register operating at this hour, and Penny didn't let anybody get a word in except Penny.

I reached the lane as the previous customer popped out the far end of the chute, suitably bagged, receipted and talked into oblivion.

"'Bye now. Well, hi there." Penny dismissed the audience she'd used up and moved on to fresh meat with no fuss, and barely a breath. Her solid, worn hands moved even faster than her mouth.

"Well, you do buy—" Oranges and celery rung up. "—the strangest things." Laundry detergent and the first box of cookies. "Haven't seen you—" And on, and on. "—since last week. And you bought entirely different things then, didn't you? All those pretzels and popcorn. I just knew you were depressed. Some folks crave the sweets when they're blue, some crave the salts. I could tell you were a salt first time you came through my line. But this—" A low-sodium, low-fat, no-cholesterol balanced meal in a box passed under her hand. "—looks like you're taking a different view of things." She looked at Mike, still glued to my shoulder. "That's good, that's real good. I was worried about you—shopping Friday nights when a pretty thing like you should be out on the town. It's nice to see you have other plans—" Steak and potatoes were toted up. "—for the weekend."

Penny looked from Mike to me with significance dripping from her watery blue eyes. Mike gave her his best smile. I glowered at them impartially.

"Folks can talk all they want about beauticians knowing what's going on around here, but I could tell you tales just from the items I see pass by this register. Why, I knew Hannah Trusett was expecting her third long before Lloyd or the doctor did, because she started buying that pistachio pudding mix she'd craved with the first two. And I told Reverend Boone he needed to check up on old Mary Ferguson when Bill didn't buy Comet two weeks running. Mary scoured everything under the sun, and she wouldn't have let Bill get away without her Comet no matter how she was ailing. Sure enough. Mary'd died three weeks before, and Bill was so cut up, he just kept pretending she was taking a lot of naps. Poor soul.

"Course there're some cases aren't that obvious," Penny went on. Mike made a noise. I refused to look at him. "Like the fella who came in back at Thanksgiving and bought our last two turkey basters."

"Twins?" I suggested under my breath. Mike made that noise again, but Penny kept right on.

"And Gina Redus starting to want only that Grey Poupon mustard last fall—" She swung a loaded paper bag into the cart and began filling the last one. "—when plain old French's had been good enough for her from the time she was knee-high." She hit the total, put the last bag in the cart and took my money, in one continuous motion. "Come to think of it, she's been buying only bakery bread 'stead of Wonder since last fall, too. Gettin' real choosey."

Penny handed me my change, but her eyes were already on the next person in line, a robust woman in corduroy with an adolescent in tow and a cart mounded with canned goods, meat and potatoes. "'Bye now. Well, hi there."

Fighting the lethargy you feel after coming out of a stiff wind, I gave the cart a good push and got a few feet ahead of Paycik. But I had to wait for the automatic door, and he was at my shoulder as I reached the parking lot.

"You know who she was talking about?" he demanded.

I would not ask. But I did let him load a brown paper bag into the back seat.

"That last person she was rattling on about? Gina Redus? That's Foster Redus' wife. His estranged wife."

"Or widow."

"Or widow," he agreed, wisely showing no triumph. "Sounds like she's had more money to spend since last fall. Same time her husband disappeared."

He closed the car door and looked at me. I knew I was licked, but sometimes if you don't admit it—

"Eight o'clock? I can come by for you, get an early start."

"You do, and I'll use the shotgun that came with the house."

He grinned. "See you tomorrow."

"I am not going anywhere with you tomorrow, Paycik. I have plans."

Still grinning, he waved over his shoulder as he headed off.

I DID SEE PAYCIK THE NEXT DAY. Fortunately for his hide and my clean criminal record, it was well after eight a.m.

Chapter Three

"I HEAR YOU'RE DOING a story on the Foster Redus case."

I had just slid the fork into the tip of a piece of the chocolate pie that had made the Haber House Hotel's dining room famous when the man stopped at my table.

Sure, I had all those groceries I'd bought the night before, but I'd earned a break after spending Saturday afternoon examining wallpaper samples in search of something dynamic enough to enliven the bathroom in the house I rented.

Cozy two-bedroom with all the necessities. Neutral interiors. Storage space galore. Spacious grounds. Other amenities.

That's what the ad had said.

Real estate ads in New York are notoriously inflated, but somehow I hadn't expected that in Sherman. Clearly this ad-writer had trained in Manhattan.

Cozy meant tiny. *Two bedrooms* was true only if you didn't use the second one as a closet. *All the necessities* meant a roof and floor. Walls and windows were debatable. They let so much wind in that the house sounded like an oversized kazoo. *Neutral interiors* meant dismal beige with sparks of mud brown. The *storage space* was in a ramshackle frame structure only the generous would call a detached garage that was nearly twice as large as the house. Its north and south walls listed toward the west. *Spacious grounds* . . . now that one was accurate. The house was surrounded by space that was almost all ground—no flowers, few bushes, sparse grass and a couple of stunted trees.

I knew this wasn't because nothing would grow here. The yards on either side of this house and across the road had patches of lawn in front and pleasant gardens in back, with natural areas kept neatly in the more distant reaches of their yard.

I was at a loss over the *other amenities* unless it referred to the ghost in the backyard. The four-legged ghost that dematerialized any time I was around was possibly a tallish dog that could have been in training for becoming a fashion model. Except this stick figure's moves were all slink, no strut.

Maybe it wasn't fair to lay all the fault with the ad-writer. I hadn't questioned a thing, just rented the house sight unseen and at the asking price. I hadn't cared—until I saw the place.

I'd unpacked only enough to get me through a few weeks.

I figured by then I would have made up my mind about staying in Sherman through the final months of my contract. If I did that, I had to find somewhere else to live. If I didn't . . . well, then I'd be search-ing out real estate someplace entirely different.

But even staying here a few more weeks would finish driving me around the bend if I didn't do something about the bathroom.

Jenny-the-production-assistant would be sure about that drug rumor if she ever saw my face reflected in the medicine cabinet mirror in that bathroom.

I almost believed that rumor when I contemplated my image that morning. And that was despite deliberately staying in bed well past Paycik's threatened arrival time. I'd decided I would not answer the door under any circumstances.

And then, the pain in the ass didn't show up. Not at eight. Not at eight twenty. Not at eight thirty-eight. Not at eight forty-seven. Not at nine oh-nine.

That's when I gave up on sleeping and contemplated the horror that was my bathroom.

Black and deep purple cabbage roses swarmed over a background of vile green, which matched the tile in the bathtub surround. In an apparent attempt to color coordinate, the glass of the light fixture had been painted over in the same vile green.

Natural light might have helped, but the window, which was in the shower area, boasted multiple layers of paint, presumably for privacy.

I had spent two hours this morning chipping paint off one side of the light fixture. I broke for lunch, experiencing a trickle of accomplishment.

I rewarded myself by putting leftover ground beef and crumbled up bread in one bowl and water in another and setting them out for my four-legged ghost on the ragged stump that was the closest the backyard came to outdoor seating.

The accomplishment trickle dried up when I returned to the bathroom, flipped on the light and assessed my handiwork.

Now, when I looked in the mirror, one side was stark white and the other was ghoulish green.

That's when I decided new wallpaper had to be the answer. So what if I left it behind in a few weeks. It would spare me weeks of looking like an extra in a remake of *Night of the Living Dead.*

The first blow at the supply store that stocked paint in one corner was that there were only two books of wallpaper samples. The second was that the man and woman behind the counter gawked at me when I asked about hiring someone to hang wallpaper.

Apparently in the West, one took care of one's own problems, including replacing black and purple cabbage roses.

I have never hung wallpaper, but I'd been shot at on assignment and I'd ad-libbed an entire segment when a fired technician sabotaged the Teleprompter before he left the building. So how hard could wallpaper be?

It might not matter. After page after page of pink and blue bunnies with an occasional red and blue railroad train thrown in for variety, I realized both sample books were for nurseries.

After that, I deserved a treat for dinner, and my cooking didn't qualify. So here I was in the Haber House dining room, where I'd had a salad and burger as a prelude to chocolate pie.

"I'm Ames Hunt, county prosecutor."

He didn't have to tell me that. I'd seen his picture and name in the files the day before.

He also didn't have to tell me how he'd heard about my supposed interest in this case. Along with the green flakes, paint chipping had loosened up some of my brain cells. It was entirely too convenient that Penny had just happened to bring up the topic of Gina Redus' buying habits. Mike must have primed the pump with her. And he'd either done the same with Hunt, or Penny had passed on a grain that had snowballed into a boulder by the time the breakfast dishes were cleared around town.

"Nice to meet you, Mr. Hunt." I half meant it. As county prosecutor he could be a good source to cultivate. Especially if the rumors about his running for the state senate were true. On the other hand, my taste buds were salivating for chocolate pie. "I'm Elizabeth Danniher."

"Oh, I know that," he said with a practiced lifting of finely cut lips. "Your reputation precedes you. We're honored to have you here in Sherman."

His hand was cool and dry as he shook mine—firm, but not painful. He had a good start on politicking.

"Thank you. But I think you've been misled. I'm not doing a story on Foster Redus. I'm the consumer affairs reporter, so unless he has a faulty blender and can't get a refund . . ."

He timed his laughter nicely so I didn't have to finish. He adjusted his wire-rimmed glasses on a straight, blunt nose that matched his other pleasant, regular features. A cartoonist would hate him—no identifiable characteristic to exaggerate.

"Well, if you should come up with anything concrete," he began, with just enough emphasis on *should* to let me know he thought it unlikely, "you will let me know, won't you?"

Come up with anything on what? The blender? I kept my sarcasm to myself, along with the contradictory urge to make Ames Hunt eat, as a second course to a heaping serving of crow, his skepticism that I could possibly come up with something. I'd been the one to dismiss the possibility. His only crime was agreeing with me. So, I smiled brightly and said, "Of course."

"Good, and in the meantime, if you have any questions on consumer protection, please feel free to give my office a call."

He handed over a business card and, after a few more pleasantries, left me to enjoy my chocolate pie in peace.

Peace lasted two blissful mouthfuls.

"Ames Hunt tell you anything interesting?"

The chocolate didn't turn to ashes in my mouth, but the new arrival didn't enhance the flavor, either.

"He told me his entire life story. Exclusive. Now, go away."

Instead, Mike Paycik took off a cowboy hat and hooked it on a chair back finial, slid into the seat, grabbed a fork, pirated a hunk of my pie and eluded retribution, shifting away before my fork could leave a quartet of puncture wounds in the back of his hand.

"Hey, be careful," he mumbled around a mouthful of my pie. "You almost stabbed me."

"I'll do better next time." When he started to grin, I narrowed my eyes at him. "I grew up with three older brothers, so don't think I won't."

"I'll make it up to you if you come with me to the rodeo. I'll buy you a snow cone."

"It's so cold, you won't have to buy it, just hold a cone out and catch the stuff as it falls," I grumbled.

I kept grumbling as he raided several more forkfuls of pie before it was gone. I'd never admit it to Paycik, but he'd earned points by not showing up this morning.

"Besides," he said, "you should be up for a late night after I let you have your beauty sleep this morning."

There went the points.

He narrowed his eyes at me in a way that would give him wrinkles someday—and only look the better for it, damn him.

That dropped him into points deficit.

"Although you do look a little—"

The pit of points bankruptcy yawned at his feet.

"Say it and die," I muttered.

He stepped back from the precipice.

"—like someone who could use some fun at the rodeo."

Oh, yes, the man was quick with the ad lib.

Besides, I was intrigued by the idea of going to the rodeo.

Sherman's rodeo is held nightly all summer, with one night a week reserved for pros, and the others open to all comers. Tonight was the exhibition opener, to work out kinks before the regular season began in two weeks, and it was free to the locals.

For getting to know a community, sporting events rank with grocery stores and local papers.

After an hour in the stands, I had learned several items about my new home.

First, most of the people were smart enough to wear winter jackets on a night like this, even if the calendar did say May. Unlike certain newcomers.

Second, chaps might have been designed to protect cowboys' legs from brush and other dangers while riding, as Mike informed me, but they have an interesting side effect of showcasing the buns for the viewing pleasure of anyone who happens to sit behind the chutes where the bull riders and bronc riders mount up.

Third, the smart women sit behind the chutes where the bull riders and bronc riders mount up.

Funny how quickly a word like *bronc* slid off my tongue. Not even *bronco*, but *bronc*. It just sounded right.

By the time the rodeo ended just short of ten o'clock, I was chilled enough to be glad we were leaving, and mellow enough to be on the verge of thanking Paycik. He made that difficult as he latched one hand around my elbow and steered me rapidly through the crowd.

"Is this supposed to be an example of broken field running?" I asked when a logjam on the stairs allowed me to catch my breath.

"What?" He was looking over the crowd in front of us, presumably seeking a hole to slip through for extra yardage.

Beyond the stairs, traffic thinned considerably as spectators fanned out toward their scattered cars. I was about to steer around two women blocking the path, when Paycik's hand on my elbow braked me to a stop.

"Mona? Mona Burrell, right?"

The nearer of the two women turned to his deep voice like a flower to the sun.

"It is Mona Burrell, isn't it?" Mike asked with a nice bit of hesitation. He took off his hat, holding it against his chest the way he had for the National Anthem.

It should have seemed affected. Just the way his cowboy boots and worn jeans and silver belt buckle should have seemed affected. Instead, they looked as natural on him as they did on the rest of the male population in the crowd, along with easily half of the female population.

Maybe it was just in New York where it looked affected.

"Yes, I'm Mona Burrell." She smiled up at him. She was maybe three inches shorter than my five-nine, despite hefty heels on her cowboy boots. She wore form-fitting jeans over a form worth fitting, and a cropped red leather jacket with black fringe. Unmoved by the wind that stirred my hair into a froth, her artful disarray of streaked blond mane reached her shoulders and framed a face dominated by blue eyes. Her makeup was well done, although harsh overhead lights traced hairline cracks around her eyes and mouth.

"I'm Mike Paycik," he was saying. "You might not remember me, but I remember you."

The tone was pure flattery. Mona Burrell wouldn't have been female if she hadn't preened. And she was most certainly female.

"Why, Mike, how are you? I remember you, big football star and all." She moved her left shoulder forward in a move that resembled a shrug, but that accomplished a whole lot more. It moved her closer to Mike, partially blocked me and released a cloud of scent heavy enough to outweigh the Wyoming breeze and the combined odors of horses, cattle and humans. "I just didn't recognize you at first. I haven't seen you in forever."

"It has been a long time. Mona, I'd like you to meet E.M. Danniher. She's a new reporter with KWMT." Some of Mona's gloss dimmed as she accepted the introduction. It hardened and glittered with Mike's next words. "Elizabeth is looking into the case against Tom."

"What's there to look into?" she demanded. "Tom killed Foster, and that's all there is to it."

"What reason would your ex-husband have for killing Foster Redus?" I asked.

It was an accident asking that question. I didn't mean to. Because I wasn't interested. Not in the answer, not in the case. I had my own concerns, remember?

But have you ever tried to not let your leg jerk when the doctor hits your knee with that little mallet? That's what questions are like for me. Something someone says hits that nerve and *pop!* out comes the question.

"Jealous," she said. "He couldn't stand the idea of me being made happy—fulfilled, if you know what I mean—by another man."

She lavished a look on Paycik that indicated the position was open, and she'd consider his application with favor.

Mike smiled blandly at her right shoulder.

"So you mentioned that to the law enforcement officers when they investigated Foster Redus' disappearance?" I asked.

"Law enforcement?" She gave a snort my mother would condemn as unladylike, but that succinctly conveyed Mona's opinion. "Sheriff Widcuff is too stupid to enforce anything. Why, Foster was practically running the department."

"See, that's the sort of insight I thought you could give us, Mona," Mike said. "Especially Elizabeth, who doesn't know the people involved. How about if we come by tomorrow?"

"No. Tomorrow's not good." Mona Burrell's face and voice said the whole idea wasn't good.

"Monday, then."

"I don't—"

"Seven thirty Monday night," said another voice.

It was Tamantha Burrell. I hadn't even realized she'd joined the group. Or had she been there all along?

She wore a baseball cap drawn as low as her ears would allow. Those ears stuck out through the parted sheet of straight hair. Too-short jeans and an oversized pair of athletic shoes combined to make her exposed ankles appear impossibly fragile.

God, how hard was it going to be for a girl like Tamantha to be the daughter of a woman like Mona, especially when she slid into the orgy of self-doubt and looks-obsession that came in a package deal with adolescent hormones?

Right now, she showed no sign of either disapproval or envy of her mother's flashy looks. She showed signs only of wanting to pin down a time that I could come and interrogate her mother. Which she accomplished while her eyes zapped me with nonverbal messages to get cracking at carrying out her orders.

On second thought, maybe I should have been wondering how hard it was for a woman like Mona to be the mother of a child like Tamantha.

With Tamantha and Mike tag-teaming, the time was firm before Mona or I could demur. After that, farewells were initiated, with Mike getting an invitation to join Mona and the friend she hadn't bothered to introduce for drinks at the Kicking Cowboy.

"Oh, you too, Elizabeth," Mona added half-heartedly.

"Maybe another time. It's getting late. I have to get Elizabeth home," Mike said, making me sound like a doddering old woman.

Before I could do more than grimace, he drew me away.

"You were asking questions," he crowed as soon as we were out of earshot.

"It's reflex." I drew in the first deep breath I'd taken since encountering Mona Burrell's perfume. "I found myself interviewing the clerk in the wallpaper store this afternoon. It doesn't mean he's guilty of taking kickbacks."

I was aware of Mike's considering stare, but didn't return it because I was looking in the direction the other parties to our recent conversation had taken. "Now that's an interesting group."

Mike followed my nod to across the parking area. Mona Burrell and her daughter had just walked up to where Ames Hunt and Thurston Fine stood talking beside a brace of shiny red sedans. Mona hung at the edge of the conversation, and Tamantha waited impatiently three feet beyond. Mona's friend had moved on. Hunt and Fine were so scrupulously careful about not glancing in our direction that I was certain they were talking about us.

"Interesting," Mike said, "but not surprising. Mona and Ames went to school together. And Thurston's a big Ames Hunt backer politically. He even went out and bought a red Buick just like Hunt owns. Thurston thinks Hunt can go far, and that doing the coverage on Hunt's career will take him far, too."

"It can't be far enough," I mumbled.

Almost as if in response to my comment, Thurston Fine's voice reached us across suddenly still air. "I've got a joke for you to take to the Kicking Cowboy, Mona. What's the difference between a pit bull and a woman reporter?"

"I don't know, Thurston," Mona replied with a giggle. "What's the difference?"

"The pit bull has a better hairstylist."

Laughter floated across to us. Mike slanted me a look.

"Don't worry," I told him. "I've been called worse."

On the other hand, I've been called worse by better than Thurston Fine.

Who knows how much of one thing and how much of another shapes our decisions. Was it Thurston taking out his insecurities on me by spreading lies linking me with drugs? Was it Mike Paycik's flattering belief that I could show him something special in the way of investigative reporting? Was it Tamantha Burrell's stern expectation that I would fix her problem as I had gotten Fells' Mart to fix Mrs. Atcheson's toaster? Was it the need to get away from black and purple cabbage roses on a vile green background?

Aiming for a nonchalant, companionable air, I slipped my hand around Mike's arm.

"What did you say your aunt's name is?"

Chapter Four

PAYCIK HAD TO WAIT nearly twenty minutes for me Sunday.

I didn't make him wait purposely, I just run slow in the mornings.

Still, it served him right. If he'd just told me his aunt's name, I could have left for O'Hara Hill in my own good time instead of on his crack-of-dawn schedule. But he'd made me promise we'd go together. And even then he wouldn't tell me his aunt's name. Who would have expected such distrust from a football player?

So he deserved to wait.

Sometimes I wonder if it's out of such evening-ups that we derive true satisfaction in life. Forget accolades or Emmys. It's watching the guy who cut us off a mile back get pulled over for speeding, it's seeing the teenage bitch queen who'd never had pimples develop premature wrinkles, it's making somebody who'd hooked you with your own curiosity wait for nearly twenty minutes in the gray and brown living room of a rental house.

It's not noble, but it's human. And it's a kind of justice.

Paycik didn't complain, and he'd brought coffee.

He was hard to hate.

The caffeine hit my bloodstream, the mists parted, and I realized that having gone some distance west we had turned right off Highway 27 and were now driving north, beside fenced range land dotted with the occasional cow, and parallel to a string of the Rockies called the Absaroka Range. Paycik was talking, which is how I knew the name of the mountains.

"Not to be confused with the range in Montana, of course. Although—"

"Why are you so interested?" I interrupted.

He glanced over from the driver's seat. "The mountains are in Cottonwood County, so they're part of the area we cover. Besides, they've been part of my life since—"

"Not the mountains—Foster Redus. Why're you so interested in his disappearance?"

"I'm not. Not when you put it that way."

"Then why?"

"I'm not interested in Foster Redus' disappearance. I am interested in Tom Burrell being blamed for it."

"He was blamed because they'd been fighting?" I said. When he nodded, I added, "Why were they fighting?"

"Redus was fooling around with Mona."

"They're divorced, so why'd Burrell care?" Remembering Tamantha's comments, I added, "It's not like it's recent."

"No. They've been divorced for years. But Redus was still married—Gina didn't start divorce proceedings until just before he disappeared. So there was talk. A lot of talk, especially with Redus not limiting himself to Mona. Mona was nowhere near discreet, and I don't think Tom liked Tamantha being exposed to that or to the talk."

Which meant Burrell had a motive to match the evidence of the bloodstains in his house.

"But the charges were dropped."

"Yeah," Mike's eyes narrowed as a cloud hurried on and sunlight shafted across the road. "But not the rumors. And you know one result of that from Tamantha—Tom could lose his share of custody. Tom Burrell's family has ranched here for generations. He's lived in this county all his life. He's been respected, liked. Now when he walks in places, half the people walk away. It's got to be hell."

"With no body, people will forget. Besides—"

"Not in this county."

"—if there'd been a body, chances are they'd have found it by now." Mike was shaking his head. "Why not?"

"That's why." He jerked his head to the left, where jagged mountains rose abruptly from the floor of the arid basin we drove along. Behind the first irregular row, a second rank was visible, and a third, and fourth, into misty distance. "There are places up there you could hide a body where it wouldn't ever be found."

He turned left off the highway onto a lesser road that seemed destined to crash headlong into the mountains. In silence, we drew nearer and nearer. At what seemed the last possible moment, the road broke to the right in the first curve of a huge, spiraling S.

At the end of it, we seemed to hesitate an instant. The narrow valley before us was bounded on the east by a trio of buttes that almost appeared flat in comparison to the peaks that crowded in at the west. Yet the buttes were high enough to cut off the town from the open basin to the east. Buildings huddled along the valley as if aware of their insignificance.

The instant passed, and we started a gradual descent. We approached the town of O'Hara Hill from the south, on what appeared to be the only paved road. It shot straight through the relatively green valley and exited at the north end, slipping through a gap. Four abbreviated streets ran north-south within the valley, two to the east of the main road, one to the west. Short cross-roads connected the four north-south arteries, neatly gridding the town.

The sheriff department's sub-office, the fire station, the town hall and a local office of the regional electrical co-op all shared a green-roofed cement-block building about the size of three double-car garages. A rough parking lot surrounded it on three sides. The fourth side backed up to what appeared to be a wall of granite, with scrub pines defiantly growing out of its fissures at peculiar angles.

As we walked toward the entrance, a dark, trim young man in a deputy's uniform left a marked car and reached the door ahead of us. He politely held the door open.

"Mike Paycik, isn't it?"

"Yeah, and you're . . . Alvaro, right?" Mike flashed a grin. "Janet's younger brother. How is she?"

"Great. She's married, got three kids, living in Denver."

"Three kids? Geez . . ." Mike shook his head in amazement. "This is E.M. Danniher, a fellow reporter at KWMT. Elizabeth, this is . . . Robert?"

"Richard." The young deputy smiled as he shook my hand. "Robert's my next older brother. Welcome to Wyoming, Ms. Danniher."

"Thanks, but please call me Elizabeth."

"So what brings you two to O'Hara Hill?"

Before either of us could answer, a man in his mid-fifties came bustling out of an interior door and into the tiny reception area where we'd stopped.

"Well, well, the press is here. What're you finding to sensationalize here in sleepy O'Hara Hill on a Sunday, eh?"

The man was shaped like a long water balloon squeezed at either end, so the middle stuck out. And he had Jimmy Johnson hair. You know, that guy who coached the Dallas Cowboys to a couple Super Bowl championships in the early '90s whose hair never moved, not even when a tub of Gatorade was upended over his head. They showed instant replays. It never budged.

"Sheriff Widcuff," Mike said in such a neutral tone it could stand as an identification, an introduction or a greeting.

"So, Paycik, you came back home after you were all washed up playing ball, huh?" The sheriff returned the nodded greeting of Richard Alvaro, who disappeared behind the door the sheriff had emerged from, then gave Mike a wide grin that showed tightly spaced teeth. It was hard to tell if he was deliberately being obnoxious or if it was accidental. "And now you've latched on as part of the . . . what is it . . ."

"Fourth estate," I said.

He looked at me blankly. "Media. But you're just a rookie at this game, so you brought the varsity." He aimed that grin in my direction. "You come to see what you can dig up that you can throw a little paint on and present to the public as a masterpiece, huh?"

"We're here to see Mike's aunt."

"Sure you are," he agreed heartily. "You're not here to poke into the Burrell case at all, are you? So whatever I tell you will be a bonus. Out of the goodness of my heart and to show I'm not one of those elected officials who's always blaming the press for their woes. Get along mighty well with you folks, as a matter of fact. So I'll just tell you, Burrell might be free now, but we're not done with this case by a long shot. No sir, not by a long shot."

"That's interesting—" Almost as interesting as the fact that he'd already heard the same rumor Hunt had. "—but I was wondering, since Redus worked for you—"

"Now, there're things I can't tell you because it could hurt our case against Burrell in court, and I won't jeopardize that no matter how hard you try to worm it out of me."

"I understand, but I was interested in any cases that Foster Redus—"

"No, Tom Burrell's not in the clear by a long shot. Not by a long shot. This department won't show favoritism, no matter what some people might think."

Frustrated, I went for the blunt instrument. "Sheriff, what about Foster Redus? Could you tell us anything about Foster Redus?"

"Well, sure. Sure I could. He was one of my deputies. Like family, we are. We take care of our own. You have to, this line of work. But . . ." The grin grew bland. ". . . I thought you said you weren't doing a story. You were just here to see Mike's aunt."

"We are here to see her, but, you know, I think you might have convinced me there *is* a story. Now, if I decide to do a background piece on Redus, could I come to you for an interview?"

"Sure, sure." He shoved his right hand in his pants pocket and noisily jiggled his change. "But I don't want to keep you from seeing our Gee. Scares the devil out of me, that woman does." He winked. "She'd have my hide if she knew I was keeping you this long out here. So you have a nice visit now."

"About an interview—"

"Just give my office a call."

He headed out with an airy wave and without looking back.

Mike bent a significant look on me as he opened a door into an interior hallway. I refused to meet his gaze.

Halfway down the hallway, double doors on the right led to a large room with desks gathered on one side and a squared off horseshoe of electronic equipment at the other. Richard Alvaro smiled at us from one of the desks. On one side of the horseshoe, a man with weathered skin and a complacent paunch nodded to Mike as he continued to speak into a headset mouthpiece.

The remaining person in the room turned slowly on the high-backed, wheeled chair that commanded the center of the electronic horseshoe. She was a large woman, bulky, rather than flabby. She moved with absolute assurance. She had dark auburn hair smoothly turned under and creamily pale skin set off by a turquoise tunic over matching slacks.

As I acknowledged Mike's introduction to his Aunt Gee, a phrase ran through my head: *A woman of substance.*

"Elizabeth wants to know about the Burrell case."

As I turned to glare at Mike at that indiscretion, my gaze caught on the young deputy's head coming up fast. He saw me looking and made his expression blank, but I'd seen the surprise, and something else. Relief? Expectation?

Mike might have seen the reaction, too—or my glare—because he added, "Not anything from your official capacity, of course. She wants the *unofficial* background from the person who knows this county better than any other living soul."

Not only was it only so-so as a recovery, but his tone held an undercurrent I couldn't identify.

"Of course she does," Mike's Aunt Gee said, rising deliberately. "But we can't have a proper talk in all this hurly-burly. Donald, I'm taking my break. You know where to reach me if you need me." She hoisted a handbag so large its leather could have upholstered my car, and proceeded regally to the door, with Mike and me in her train. "You and Richard behave."

Having reduced her assistant and the deputy to the status of boys awarded the honor of being left alone, however briefly, she led us out. Alvaro moved ahead of us, apparently seeking the water cooler, but as I passed, he said quietly, "Ask about Rog Johnson and Foster Redus."

I looked at him, but he was bent over, filling a paper cup, and I couldn't see his face.

We followed Aunt Gee's sedan—the QE II on wheels—two blocks south and one and a half blocks east to an excruciatingly neat wooden rectangle painted dull brown. No plants softened the cement block foundation, which looked as if it had been recently scrubbed. Possibly with a toothbrush.

She'd already disappeared inside when Mike escorted me around the geometrically precise walk to the back door and into the kitchen. Stainless steel and spotless white bounced enough sunlight around the room to tempt me to ask when the next surgery started.

"Sit. Lunch will be ready soon." Without any evidence of hurry, Gee moved surprisingly quickly, as much in command of this space as of the dispatcher's office.

"Thank you, but I'm not really hungry . . ."

Mike's slashing hand motion came too late. Gee spared me a basilisk glare. "You'll sit. You'll eat. You'll listen." Apparently satisfied that she had me cowed—which she had—she resumed slicing a potato into a skillet, and started talking.

As she served up a huge lunch of potatoes, fried chicken, string beans, applesauce and raw carrots, I did exactly what she'd said—I sat, I ate and I listened. I also took notes. She was precise, detailed and orderly.

Foster Redus had been hired as a deputy two and a half years ago. At the start he was tolerated, though not well liked by his co-workers. His arrogance and self-satisfaction had eroded the tolerance, especially when he took up with the wife of another deputy, who resigned and left the area, wife in tow.

He made a lot of arrests, though his conviction rate was low considering the volume. However, his paperwork was prompt and seldom criticized by the court. Perhaps for that reason, Sheriff Widcuff had assigned Redus as courthouse liaison a year ago, as general investigator for Ames Hunt's office and a local judge.

That assignment meant Redus, though officially assigned to the O'Hara Hill station, operated independently.

"No supervision at all," Aunt Gee said with stern disapproval.

"And unless he was investigating the bedrooms of half the women in this county, he surely wasn't putting in a full week's work."

"The sheriff didn't say anything?" I asked.

"No."

"How about the people he worked for at the courthouse?"

"Judge Claustel never took to having Redus around, so I would have been real surprised to hear he objected to any cause that kept Redus out of his sight. And I expect Ames Hunt is fully capable of not knowing anything he doesn't want to know." It took me a moment to unravel her syntax. "For someone prosecuting cases of people doing their worst to other people, he likes to hold himself above such. Always has wanted to be above the rest. Doesn't surprise me that he'd choose not to know about Redus' tom-catting."

"Well, somebody must have missed Redus, because they got a search started when he disappeared, right?"

"Six days later."

"*Six days?*" That hadn't been in the official file. There'd been a gap between when Foster Redus had left Tom Burrell's house and the time of Burrell's arrest, but I thought it had been to gather evidence.

Apparently it first took a while for anyone to notice they were missing one deputy.

"Wasn't he supposed to be on duty?" I asked. Aunt Gee nodded. "Nobody noticed?"

"Some noticed. Nobody much minded. Except Mona. She pestered me with a half-dozen calls about suppertime that Monday evening he went missing. I told her he'd come and gone, but that wouldn't do. She kept calling." Aunt Gee's mouth folded in on itself. "Tying up the lines, I finally told her I'd write up a citation on her if she called one more time."

"But how about officially? I mean, after a couple days, you'd think somebody in the sheriff's department would miss him."

"Didn't miss him and didn't miss tripping over that leather satchel of his. It might have gone longer if Marty Beck and Mona Burrell hadn't started a screaming fight outside the Walmart in Sherman over which of them had tried to steal Redus from the other. Got a 911 call.

The department had to break 'em up. When Marty and Mona calmed down and realized neither of them had Foster hidden away, they demanded the sheriff find him. Eventually they got a report that Redus had been on his way to have it out with Tom Burrell before he disappeared.

"Sheriff and some others went to talk to Tom, and he freely admitted fighting with Redus. The state lab found the blood in Tom's place, and you know the rest."

✧ ✧ ✧ ✧

"MICHAEL! MICHAEL PAYCIK, I want to see you."

The thin fluting voice stopped Mike and his aunt as we left after a post-lunch scrub-down of the kitchen. It took me a moment to track the source of the voice to a figure at the screen door of the house next door.

"Michael, you and that young woman come over here. I want to talk to you. It's about time someone took action, since the law enforcement establishment hasn't seen fit to sort it out."

Aunt Gee exhaled quickly, which I read as a sign of exasperation, but that could have been wishful thinking. Maybe I wanted the dispatcher's complete command of her universe to have a chink in it.

The screen door opened, revealing its holder as a gray-haired, thin woman standing starkly upright in a vain effort to reach five-feet tall. She wore navy slacks, a white peter-pan collar blouse, a lemon cardigan and white running shoes with purple lightning bolts on the side. "You'll come in for tea."

"Thank you, Mrs. Parens, but we just finished lunch, and . . ." Michael made eye contact with the little woman, and his protest cravenly deflated.

"I'm returning to the sheriff's office," Aunt Gee pronounced, continuing to her car.

"That's quite all right, Gisella, I prefer to talk to these two young people in private." Mrs. Parens' dismissal was unmistakable.

Aunt Gee said not another word. I uttered a hasty thanks for lunch, which she acknowledged with a regal nod through the open car window as she backed out of the drive.

Mike snagged my elbow and guided me toward the door. He performed a painfully correct introduction then added, "Mrs. Parens was my fourth-grade teacher."

That explained a lot. I still quaked at the thought of Sister Mary Robert from fourth grade—and that was only for Saturday Catechism.

"I also taught Michael in seventh-grade civics and was the principal of the high school while he was in attendance there."

As we followed Mrs. Parens' straight back down a narrow hall, I gave Paycik a sympathetic look. Sister Mary Robert was a terror for one year. If she'd followed me like that I might have joined the army— or the circus. He rolled his eyes in response, then nearly ran me over as I came to an abrupt halt at the entrance to what I felt sure Mrs. Parens would call the front parlor.

Framed photographs covered every available inch of wall space. Two whole walls and part of a third were devoted to class photos, from well-scrubbed grade-schoolers of the fifties in black and white, to styles into the twenty-first century. A quick scan suggested that the remaining pictures covered the entire history of the region.

"My God—it's a museum," I muttered.

Mrs. Parens' lips pursed slightly, but her expression showed mostly satisfaction. "Although your appreciation would be more aptly expressed without profanity, Miss Danniher, the sentiment is appropriate. However, I prefer to think of it as a classroom."

She invited us to sit. Every chair in the room was uncushioned wood and straight-backed—a classroom all right.

"This really is an amazing collection. That's . . . that's Teddy Roosevelt, isn't it?"

"Yes. President Theodore Roosevelt hunted in this vicinity in 1903 in conjunction with a trip to Yellowstone National Park."

"And Buffalo Bill Cody?"

That earned me a look of approval. It also launched a résumé of the county's history, illustrated by the photographs, some of them so far above her head that Mrs. Parens had to use a pointer with a rubber tip.

I had to bite the inside of my cheek at Paycik's expression when she pulled that out.

He grimaced at me once when her back was turned, obviously not happy I'd encouraged Mrs. Parens' lecture.

Too bad. He wanted to learn about being a journalist? Well, this was part of it. Listening. He heard a boring history lesson. I heard a potential story—admittedly with a lot of editing. The woman was a goldmine on regional history and had sharp insight to people.

"However, my reason for asking you both in was not to educate you on the history of Cottonwood County, even though you are a most receptive pupil, and Michael, I am certain, would benefit from a refresher course." Mike started guiltily, and I swear I saw a glint of amusement in Mrs. Parens' faded gray eyes.

With Mike tongue-tied, I asked the obvious. "Why did you ask us in, Mrs. Parens?"

"To find out what measures you intend to take in order to clear Thomas David Burrell."

"We're not trying to clear Burrell. We're doing background on Foster Redus' disappearance. I'm new in the area, and this is the biggest active story, so . . . . In fact, I'd be interested to know what you thought of Foster Redus."

She shook her head as she removed a class picture from the wall. "I never met Mr. Redus, so I can add nothing to your information in that regard. But these people I do know." She put the frame in my hands. "I know them all."

"This is Thomas David's graduation picture." She pointed to a postage-stamp sized photo of a dark-haired, long-faced young man looking directly into the camera as if trying to see what was on the other side. "A fine mind. He should have gone on to university instead of taking over his father's construction enterprise. He started university. He had a full scholarship. But he dropped his classes and returned home to marry."

Her thin finger pointed to another likeness. "Gina Hawkins also had the potential for higher education, although she never believed in herself to the degree that would have allowed her to pursue it." I glanced at a girl with long, reddish-brown hair screening most of a small face.

"Married to Redus," Mike muttered, and I looked again, with more interest but no more result. There was little to see of Gina Hawkins Redus.

The picture next to hers caught my eye. "Ames Hunt," I read from beneath it.

"Yes," said Mrs. Parens. "He, too, was in that class. He and Thomas David were always at the head of their class—in activities as well as scholarship. Thomas David was class president, Ames was the vice president. Thomas David was captain of the basketball team, Ames was a reserve. Thomas David was valedictorian, Ames was salutatorian. Thomas David had great natural gifts, but Ames worked with dedication and meticulous planning to make the most of his skills."

If I'd been Ames, Thomas David would have been a major pain in my derriere.

"Yet," their former teacher went on, "Ames Hunt was the one who went on to university, to law school and has attained a position of political stature in our community."

Ah, like the teenage bitch queen getting wrinkles, time can even out the score.

"Mona Praver . . ." Mrs. Parens spoke with judicial neutrality, ". . . had no interest in higher education. Or in anything beyond her pleasures."

"She was very pretty." I studied the smiling face under a shimmering fall of blond hair. It looked natural then.

Mrs. Parens' lips pursed; I almost expected her to preach that pretty is as pretty does.

"She has been an adequate parent to Tamantha," she conceded.

I must have looked surprised.

"I was called out of retirement last year," Mrs. Parens said, "to teach a first-grade class because their teacher faced a long convalescence from an automobile crash. Tamantha Burrell was a member of that class." She took the class photo from my hands and returned it to its spot on the wall.

"So you see," she went on, her voice as clear with her back to us as facing us—a useful attribute for a teacher, "I am not relying solely on memories of these people as young students many years ago."

I wasn't sure that any of this advanced us, but it couldn't hurt to ask about one other name, a name I'd forgotten about until now.

"Do you know someone named Rog Johnson, Mrs. Parens?"

Her hands stilled on the frame she had adjusted. "Yes." With no further comment, she moved to a section of the wall bearing more recent photos.

I shot a questioning look at Mike. He barely got off a shrug before Mrs. Parens turned and placed another framed photograph in my hands.

"This," she pointed with a tapered finger, "is Roger Johnson Junior before he started high school."

The pictures were larger, and judging from hair and fashion styles quite recent. I saw a sandy-haired boy with a shy smile, a faintly worried look in the eyes. Even compared to the faces around him, he looked young and vulnerable. Mrs. Parens covered the first frame by placing two more on my lap, these from an earlier generation.

"But these are the people you need to talk to. Roger and Myrna Johnson." She pointed to a young man in one class photo and a girl in another. "They married two weeks after Myrna graduated from high school, and had Roger Junior, their only child, five years later."

I was mildly amused at her care in clarifying that Roger and Myrna didn't, as they say, *have* to get married.

"I need to talk to the young man directly." Since he's the one Richard Alvaro's obscure mutter had linked to Foster Redus.

"You can't."

I quickly calculated age. He could be away at college, I supposed. "Why not?"

"Roger Junior died a year ago. The day after Deputy Redus arrested him." For the first time, Mrs. Parens' voice faltered, as if she grappled with an unanswerable question. "He committed suicide."

Chapter Five

"THERE'S A PLACE here in O'Hara Hill, has the best burgers around . . ."

I gawked at Mike. "After what your aunt fed us?"

He grinned. "It's where the locals go."

I considered my options. I do legwork on my own. Not that I'd done much enterprise reporting the past few years. Making sure I'd covered the network on the stories everyone else would have and developing sources for those stories didn't leave much time to wander off the well-worn path.

But Paycik had the connections.

"Tell you what," I offered, "let's look around town first. We could kill some time by talking to that deputy friend of yours."

"Richard? Why—"

"Which reminds me. Blabbing to the sheriff's department that I'm looking into the case not only isn't accurate—" I hadn't committed yet, at least not outside of my own head. "—it's a great way to get a source fired."

He snorted. "Aunt Gee could do a primetime special exposing every last detail of every last case there's ever been in this county, and she wouldn't get fired. Our sheriff's not the brightest, but he knows Aunt Gee really runs the department. And if she hadn't wanted the department to know, she wouldn't have told me to bring you there first."

Maybe. Gee certainly wouldn't have hesitated to make her displeasure clear if she'd felt any, so that gave his take credence.

But if this was the way things worked in Cottonwood County, it left me in a reporting landscape nearly as different from what I was used to as the mountains were from skyscrapers.

"Besides, it'll save time this way," Mike added.

I gave him only a skeptical eyebrow lift.

He grinned. "People will start coming to us with information. We won't have to go searching for them. Like Richard did with whatever he told you by the drinking fountain."

My eyebrow lost altitude. His grin gained it.

"So," Mike said with the self-satisfaction of a man who thinks he's won a round, "what more do you want to find out from him?"

For starters, I wanted an explanation of Richard Alvaro's expression when Mike said I wanted to know about the Foster Redus case. And why Richard had suggested I ask about a teenager who'd committed suicide.

✧   ✧   ✧   ✧

MIKE SAID IF ALVARO was patrolling on county roads it could take a week to find him. It took eight minutes of crisscrossing the town.

During those eight minutes, Mike told me O'Hara Hill had been born as a mining town. Wyoming had a history of boom and bust cycles in natural resources—coal, oil, natural gas, even bentonite and soda ash—while cattle ranching continued with its own highs and lows. When the mining company pulled out forty years ago, O'Hara Hill shrank, but held on as a supplier to nearby ranches and outfitters.

The marked sheriff's department car sat in an otherwise empty church parking lot. Alvaro was finishing paperwork on a speeding ticket.

"So, you two—" His finger waggled from me to Mike and back. "—an item? Carol's going to want to know."

"No." I might have made it too emphatic, because Alvaro's smile immediately disappeared. "We want to talk with you."

"Off the record."

Off the record. My third-least favorite response from a source. Least favorite is *no comment*, which is even worse than runner-up *go to hell*.

"Okay. How well did you know Foster Redus?"

The smooth olive-tinted skin of Alvaro's narrow face relaxed, and he closed the metal folder that held his forms. He'd braced for a tough question. That's why I'd asked this one. It was good to know I hadn't forgotten everything.

"When I was a rookie, I rode with him a couple times."

"When was that?"

"Not long after he joined the department—almost two years ago."

"What did you think of him?"

"He'd brown-nose anybody he thought was higher than him. Anybody else, he talked to like they're stupid or dirt or both. A bully by my thinking."

"Did he treat you that way?"

"Yeah, but I expected it." I wondered if that expectation came from Redus' reaction to rookies or Hispanics. "Once, he stopped an old pickup, said it was weaving. I didn't see that, but Redus said I must be blind. He started in talking to the woman driver like she didn't have any brains or morals. She didn't say much, but I thought she was steaming. Then, he looked at her driver's license and suddenly got nice as could be. Turns out she's a lawyer in Cody driving her brother's ranch truck because her car wouldn't start. 'Course Redus didn't give her a ticket. I heard she complained to Sheriff Widcuff, but he didn't do anything."

"So, you didn't care for Redus or the way he treated people, but that isn't why you told me to ask about Rog Johnson, is it, Richard? What do you know about the boy's suicide?"

Mike shot me a quick, puzzled look.

The tautness under Alvaro's skin returned, and parallel lines over his nose tucked his dark brows in a frown. "Not much. He hung himself in a shed on his folks' place."

"What was he arrested for?"

Alvaro's lips drew back over his teeth in distaste. "Disorderly conduct, public nuisance. Sounded to me like Redus doing his bully act, this time on a kid." He looked toward the top of a lodge-pole pine standing sentinel by the church. "And when we heard about the boy, Redus laughed. Said the world wouldn't miss one more candy-ass."

"There was something else." Alvaro brought his gaze to us. "About a month after Redus disappeared, Sheriff Widcuff told me to clean out his desk. Wasn't much, except one drawer with copies of case files. The one on Rog Johnson caught my eye. I looked through it—just copies of the official reports Redus filled out, charging Rog with disorderly conduct. Except one sheet. It had faint writing, like carbon from another sheet. That happens if you start writing straight on the pad instead of flipping the divider under the form."

He demonstrated with the metal folder.

"The faint writing had the same date as the official report, and it had Rog Johnson's name, but it also mentioned another kid, Frank Claustel. So I looked to see if Claustel had a file. Nothing."

I caught a look between Richard and Mike. "What?" I demanded.

"Claustel's father is Judge Ambrose Claustel," Mike said.

"Interesting."

"Yeah." Richard sounded weary. "It got more interesting. The time of arrest on that carbon report was an hour earlier than the official one. The next week, Redus got assigned to the court house."

Redus could have dropped the judge's son at home, possibly tearing up the original report in front of the appreciative father, then arrived at the jail with one arrestee and corresponding paperwork. And *voila*, a cushy job.

It smelled like a favor for a favor; proving it would be something else.

"Do you have reason to think this might not have been an isolated case, Richard?" I asked.

He shook his head. "Only rumor and . . . nothing first-hand."

I figured the part he wasn't willing to spill was his feeling about Redus.

"Are you going to Widcuff with this?" Mike asked.

"You think I'd be talking to you people if I thought that would do any good?" He closed his mouth tight, as if he had no more to say, but his eyes said different. It took about twenty seconds. "I told him . . . I showed him the file. He brushed it off. Said the only thing to worry about was finding the evidence that would pin down Burrell as Redus' murderer.

"Two days later, when I went to look at the file, it was gone. All Redus' files were gone. Another deputy said Widcuff had ordered them burned."

✧   ✧   ✧   ✧

ERNIE'S WAS THE ORIGINAL that certain chain restaurants try to cookie-cutter emulate.

Ernie's photos, license plates, advertisements and cowboy gear had the real-thing patina of age and dust; the glasses didn't match because there'd been a lot of specials at the Five-and-Dime over the years; and beef ruled the menu because that was the local product.

The narrow, deep room had a bar along one side with every stool filled with a jeans-clad male rear end, and every head covered with a cowboy hat or baseball cap. The zigzag of tables on the opposite side of the room included couples and family groups.

When Mike and I walked in, no one said a word, but we got plenty of stares as we took a table near the front.

"We probably shouldn't discuss the case here," Paycik said in a low voice accompanied by a tilt of his head toward the other patrons.

That suited me fine. Until his next sentence.

"Do you know what job you're going to go after when you're done serving out the time on your contract? Five months, right?"

Shit. What did I expect? Of course everyone knew my business. They probably knew the dollars and cents on the divorce settlement. Along with the fact that Wes was dragging his feet on sending me my share of the proceeds from the sale of our cottage and his buyout of our house in D.C.

The house was worth a lot more than the cottage, even though only a real estate person could describe it with a straight face as being on the edge of Georgetown. But it was the thought of no longer having the cottage that dropped a weight below my collarbone.

By the bare bones of an ad, it had the same features as the rental house here. But the difference in the flesh was the difference between a mange-riddled coyote and a burnished, beloved Golden Retriever. Had I expected this house to be like the cottage? Had I hoped Sherman would be like the Northern Neck?

I didn't know.

"Look, Paycik, I want to get this straight. While I'm working at KWMT—and I don't know how long that will be—we're colleagues, strictly colleagues. I don't know what you told anyone else—your aunt or Mrs. Parens or Alvaro or—"

"I didn't tell them anything, Elizabeth. I told you about the gossip. I won't tell you I'm not attracted to you, but I know you're coming off a rough time, the divorce and the rest of it. I won't push you . . . at least not—"

He broke off as a man with a grizzle of gray-flecked beard stubble and tobacco-stained fingers greeted Mike by name before taking a bar stool vacated for him by a younger man.

"Jack's foreman at a ranch I worked summers after my dad sold off," Mike told me.

Jack's tone wasn't as guarded; we heard him identify Mike to his cronies. Maybe I just imagined that they seemed more impressed that he was Gee's nephew than that he'd played pro football. Either way, the stares boring into us dropped from a gusher to a drizzle. Most of the remaining attention came from a small, reddish-haired woman sitting with two other women and a man at a table in back, and she was most likely looking at Mike. I relaxed, and before he could return to the earlier topic, I started asking him about growing up on a Wyoming ranch.

His expression said he knew what I was doing, but he was willing to go along. His love for the life came through despite his laconic delivery. It was obvious why he'd bought his own ranch.

The abrupt scraping back of the empty chair beside me jolted me to alertness. Partly because the move was unexpected, partly because I'd had my foot propped on the bottom rung.

The chair-jerker was a woman in her late twenties, on the fading end of an early bloom. Her long, bleached hair desperately needed conditioning and a trim. From a soft mouth, her chin retreated out of sight. And since she didn't bother to sit in the chair, I suspected yanking it out from under my foot had been a deliberate move.

"I hear you're asking a lot of questions, and you're some sort of big-deal reporter. You denying it?" she demanded.

"Told you they'd come to us," Mike muttered.

I kept my attention on the woman. "Only you know what you heard."

"So, you admit it." Smugly, she propped her hands on her hips. "Well, let me tell you, Ms. Big-Time TV Reporter, you're asking the wrong questions unless you're asking how to get that murdering sonuvabitch Burrell locked into the electric chair, good and tight. That's what you should be asking. That's what you should be doing."

"Listen, M—"

She rolled over Mike's intervention like a tank over a safety cone. "He murdered Foster."

"Why would Burrell do that?" I asked.

"Maybe he wanted that leather case of Foster's. Doesn't matter. What matters is when Burrell couldn't beat him in a fight like a real man, he must've shot him. There's some—" A toss of her brittle hair took in her audience behind her. "—say Foster took off. But that's pure, green jealousy. He wouldn't have gone nowhere without me. He was going to take me outta here, to Vegas or Miami, where there're lights and action, and a woman's free to have a little fun."

I darted in when she drew breath. "Why would they be jealous?"

"Because he was real smart. Smart enough to get what he wanted. Smart enough to keep a woman satisfied in bed and out." Her eyes filled. "He told me all the things I'd have and the places we'd go, and he woulda done it, too, if that bastard Burrell hadn't murdered him. So you just get that bastard."

She drove a demanding forefinger into my collarbone, the pointed, painted nail jabbing through my bulky cotton sweater and thin turtleneck. I leaned back, she closed the gap.

Mike stood and started around the table.

"You get him!"

Before she could land another jab, Mike clasped her arm. "That's enough. If you want to talk—"

Grating laughter stopped his words. "I said what I got to say. I know about you, Paycik. You're on that murdering bastard's side. All you high-siders." She shook off his hold and darted a glare at me, along with another, "You just get him," before she walked with short, jerked strides to the door.

The attention riveted on our table drifted away.

The Wyoming air must make its females decisive; this one was about as subtle as Tamantha, although her message was the opposite. Give Tamantha credit, I thought as I rubbed my collarbone, she didn't resort to violence.

Mike put a hand on my shoulder, let it trail down my arm as he sat. "Are you okay?" Concern darkened his blue eyes.

"Yes. The bereaved widow?"

"No." He shifted his eyes to indicate the redhead I'd noticed earlier. "The woman in the back corner, that's Gina Redus."

"Oh. So, our friend was . . .?"

"Another of Redus' conquests. Marty Beck. The one Mona fought with."

"Not too discreet, was she?"

"Neither was Redus."

It couldn't have been pleasant for Gina hearing all that, even if her husband's infidelity had been well known. "So, what's a high-sider?"

"Folks from western Cottonwood County—closer to the mountains where the land's more fertile and there's more water. Marty's family had a low-side ranch. It went under seven years ago."

As we settled the bill, I noticed Gina Redus leave her spot and head toward the back.

Mike and I went out the front door, pulling in pure, chilled air with our first breath and letting it out in a puff of vapor. The sun's warmth was long forgotten. Beyond the fan of brightness from Ernie's spilling on the sidewalk, darkness rose up like a cloud. We hurried toward Paycik's car, a block away.

We'd reached the cross-street when a woman spoke Mike's name.

Out of the deeper dark of the side street, came a small figure. Mike squinted. "Gina?"

"Yes. I want to talk to you."

As she came nearer, I could see she was looking at me.

"You're that new TV reporter in Sherman. I hear you've been asking questions." Who needed network news when you had a grapevine like Cottonwood County's? "Asking questions about Tom Burrell."

I opened my mouth to protest. It wasn't my doing that most of my questions about Foster Redus got answers about Tom Burrell. But Gina Redus' next words shut my mouth.

"I'll tell you. Tell you things nobody else will, things nobody else can."

Chapter Six

GINA REDUS PLACED two mugs of coffee on the table in front of the sofa where Mike and I sat and retreated to the kitchen, again refusing our help.

Raised trim around the table's edges showed the mellow reddish glow the entire table must have had new, but in the center the finish had given way to bare wood, scarred to a dull brownish-gray. The gold corduroy couch was worn ribless on the cushions and arms.

Gina returned balancing a tray with a plate of Vienna wafers, a jug of milk, a pot of sugar and the third mug. On the tray was a doily of real lace, its delicate, intricate swirls and whorls stark white.

"You know we went to school together, don't you?"

Mike rose to help her. "You and Foster? But he was—"

"Tom and me. We went to school together from the first grade, right up until he left for college. He had his choice of scholarships—academic or basketball. He took academic because even if he broke his leg he could keep studying."

She'd dosed her coffee from both the jug and the pot. She folded her legs under her on the only chair and stared into her mug between sips.

"Mona didn't notice him until he became the big basketball hero in high school. Then she noticed him all right."

"Uh, Mrs. Redus, about your husband . . ." I started. Not brilliant, but it should have done the trick. If she'd been listening.

"Once Mona noticed, there was no stopping her. It took her a while, but she got her hooks in Tom good, and wouldn't let go. And ruined his chance. And then she blamed him for not giving her what she wanted. The bitch."

"Mrs. Redus." Nothing. "Gina!" She looked up.

"Gina, I hoped you could tell us about your husband? I understand you'd separated before he disappeared?"

"Yes, we'd separated. End of September. Started divorce proceedings."

"So you hadn't seen him for a while before he disappeared?"

She shook her head. "He came by that Monday afternoon. He was spittin' mad about something Mona'd told him Tom had said." She leaned forward. "But Tom didn't kill him. If Tom had been the one who disappeared, I'd believe it of Foster, but not Tom. Not Tom."

I didn't argue, and she relaxed back into the chair. "So you and Foster were still seeing each other even though you'd separated."

Life flickered in her eyes, lifted her mouth, and, for an instant, I could see a much younger version of the woman before me.

"No, we weren't *seeing each other.* He'd left most of his things here. He saw no sense in renting his own place when he spent most nights with Mona or Marty or someone else. He'd stop by to pick up clothes and such. It wasn't that much different from before we separated. Only he didn't bother to lie about his other women any more."

"And that afternoon?"

"He picked up clean shirts and socks. He said he'd been at Mona's. Said she'd said Tom was threatening to make trouble. When I said it was natural Tom didn't want him screwing his kid's mother in front of the kid, Foster crammed those shirts into a pocket of his precious leather case like he'd never complained about a wrinkle in his life, cussed me out, said he'd teach Tom Burrell to mind his own business and stormed out."

She flicked her eyes from me to Mike and back.

"Only when he left, he didn't drive south like he would for Tom's place, or back to Mona's. He went north. And . . ." She drew out the word. "Since his new pickup was parked in front of a certain house over on Parallel Street an hour later when I went to my girlfriend's, I'd say he stopped off to screw Marty Beck. That's why Mona didn't start

screaming about Foster being missing right off—she was sure he'd left
her for another woman."

She sipped her coffee, but the mug didn't hide her satisfied smile.

"Gina, since you're sure the official version—that Tom Burrell
killed your husband—is wrong, what do you think happened?"

"He could have just up and left," she said without interest.

"Would it be like Foster to disappear? Where would he go? And
why?"

Even less interested, she shrugged.

I tried a new angle. "How did you and Foster meet?"

"I was dealing in Reno. He worked security, but he wanted to be in
law enforcement. We got married, came here a year later when the job
opened up in the sheriff's department. I didn't want to come back, but
he wanted that job." She bit into a cookie. "And now he's gone, one
way or another. And I won't be doing any crying over Foster Redus."

"WELL? WHAT DO YOU THINK?" Mike asked as he drove through the
dark. We were taking a different return route, one that curved farther
west and crept up the bottom slopes of the mountains. "About Gina
and what she said about Tom and Mona and Foster."

Dark has a volume, a texture, in Wyoming that I don't remember
anywhere else. Maybe it's because there's so much of it, trying to fill
that eternity of sky.

I looked over at him, his eyes intent on the headlight's narrow
band of light. "Interesting that you said them in that order, isn't it?"

He frowned. "Because that was the order of her interest."

"Mmmm." Noncommittal sounds are very useful.

"You aren't saying it, so I will. It's clear Gina was—is—crazy
about Tom Burrell. God, you live in an area practically all your life, you
think you know everything there is to know, and then you find out all
this stuff under the surface. It's scary."

"Oh, I don't know. It would be boring if everything was just out
there for everybody to see. You'd know as much—or as little—about

your mailman as you did about your husband."

Come to think of it, that had a certain appeal. But I suppose that depended on your husband. And the mailman.

"Well, Gina sure didn't seem to care to know anything about her husband or his whereabouts. How could she be married to a man and just not care about his running around?"

"I can believe she doesn't care now. Whether she cared in November, who knows? Maybe she did care then—enough to kill him. Or maybe she stopped caring a long time ago." Maybe Gina's caring and loving wore out along with the furniture. Or maybe returning to Cottonwood County rekindled an obsession with Burrell. Or maybe that only flared to life in the vacuum created by Foster's infidelity. "But she didn't realize it, not until his actions showed her the man he'd become, so different from who she'd married . . ."

Mike was cutting quick, curious looks at me. I started talking again to fill the silence of his interest.

"Did you catch what she said about Mona and Tom Burrell?"

"Yeah. That's old gossip, that Mona went after Tom and got bitter when he didn't make the big splash she'd expected. But that's nearly twenty years ago."

"So Mona's been disappointed by a man before. If Redus gave her hopes for the kind of cushy future we heard about from Marty Beck, would Mona let him get away? Or maybe not being the only woman in his life would have been enough for Mona to act."

I slued around on the seat. "You know, Paycik, all this talk about caring reminds me that you haven't told me why you care what happens to Burrell."

He hitched his shoulders—either a shrug or settling back.

"When I was maybe eight, my dad took me to a high school basketball game. Tom Burrell was the star. Everybody in the gym watched him. All the cheerleaders fluttering around him, all the other big kids fawning on him, even the adults listening to him."

"And you wanted to be just like him?"

"Oh, yeah." His half smile faded. "But it's more. I wanted the things he had, sure. But I truly wanted to be just like him. He took it all in, yet none of it seemed to touch him. I sensed that as a kid, but it wasn't until I was out of Cottonwood County, and seeing how some guys reacted to all the chances to screw up your life, that I realized what Tom Burrell was."

"But he never really left, did he?" Not the way Mike had, finding success far beyond Sherman. And he would leave again, seeking out a new kind of success. As much as he loved ranching, his ambition clearly was in television. "He didn't finish college, and he's never gone anywhere else from what I hear. But you made good out there, and you're not done with that."

He opened his hands on the steering wheel, holding it with his thumbs.

"I had a reputation in college and the pros for being real level-headed. My folks sure as hell tried to make me that way. But there were times I thought, how could they possibly know what I was facing? Then I'd find myself thinking, 'What would Tom Burrell do? How would he act if the wife of an agent offered a signing bonus not written up in any contract?' Then I'd follow the advice Tom never knew he gave me." He glanced at me. "Weird, huh?"

"I've heard weirder. So you dragged me out here because you want to clear your hero's name?"

"And want to be around you—want to see you in action. To learn."

His ambition definitely extended beyond Cottonwood County. "Uh-huh."

He grinned.

That little-boy-caught-but-surely-you-can't-yell—at-him-because-he's-so-charming grin. "Okay. And because I always wanted to play Sherlock Holmes. Aren't we supposed to look for certain things in the best Sherlockian tradition?"

"The old standbys—motive, opportunity and means—could be tough this time, even presuming Redus has been murdered—which is a big presumption."

He frowned again. If it sounds as if he didn't pay much attention to the road, that's true. We'd encountered precisely one pickup since leaving O'Hara Hill. He could have aimed the hood ornament at the center line and it wouldn't have much mattered. "Because there's no body?"

"Yup. Without a body or an eye-witness, you don't know cause of death, so you don't know who had means. And you don't know the time of death, so you don't know who had opportunity."

"So we'll focus on motive."

My turn to frown—and not only at his "we." "Motive's the murkiest, least reliable of the three. Lots of people have motive but never lift a gun or serve up arsenic."

"Uh-huh," he muttered, his attention diverted to the east side of the road. "We're passing Tom Burrell's land now—the Circle B."

"So is he a high-sider or low-sider?"

"High-side. But that's no guarantee in ranching these days. That's why he built up the road plowing and grading company his father started."

Marty had labeled Mike with the high-siders. Yet he'd said his father had "sold off" their ranch while he'd continued working on a ranch during his summers. And when he'd made money in football, he'd put it back into a ranch. It struck me that there could be a lot about Cottonwood County and its people—perhaps particularly Mike Paycik—I would never understand if I stayed holed up in Sherman all the time. But did I want to learn about them?

The vehicle slowed. "That's the road to Burrell's house."

Road? I saw only deeper black. Then, from the peripheral brightening of the headlights, I saw a goalpost-shaped structure made of logs with a sign swinging from the crossbar. A dirt track led between the vertical posts then made a sharp right and headed down an embankment.

He offered hopefully, "We could see if the light's on . . ."

I shook my head, but I noted the rest of the route back to Sherman, in case I wanted to follow it in reverse.

Chapter Seven

MONDAY, I DID a "Helping Out" segment.

A local woman got a phone call that she'd won a fabulous vacation to Acapulco. All she had to do was send a check for two hundred dollars to cover taxes, licenses and fees. She was thrilled. It was just the break she and her overworked husband Dwayne needed. She obtained the first passports of their lives.

The tickets never arrived. When she contacted the company in Dallas, a young female voice said they had closed up, but she'd get her money back as soon as possible. Ten minutes later she got a call from a man at the travel company saying none of that was true. The trip would go on as planned, not to worry. Though, if she sent a check for another hundred and fifty dollars it would guarantee the best suite in the luxury hotel.

That's when Cissy Robins called "Helping Out" at KWMT.

When the Dallas reporter I'd alerted arrived at what turned out to be a room furnished with tables, chairs and telephones, the owner was loading boxes in a van with Arizona plates. The owner claimed it was a misunderstanding, and to show his good faith, he wrote a check to reimburse Cissy—from his personal account, which oddly enough had a lot more in it than the corporate account. The check cleared this morning.

So, Cissy had her money back, the Dallas station had a good local story, the police had another scam artist to process and we had film of the arrest from the Dallas station—by far "Helping Out's" best package. Monday's plan was to tape an interview with Cissy to tell our viewers all the good we'd done, then talk to a local travel agent about how consumers could spot bogus offers.

I'd gotten Les Haeburn to give me Diana Stendahl to shoot the story.

Diana was a no-nonsense forty-two-year-old mother of two. After being widowed eight years ago, she got a job as a receptionist at the station then found her niche with the camera.

Not many women work TV cameras. Physical endurance isn't as important as it was with earlier generations of cameras . . . except at KWMT, where they still use models I hadn't seen in more than a decade outside of third-world countries. But Diana said that after growing up slinging bales of hay, then toting around two kids, even the monster cameras she'd started on were no chore.

She understood all the gadgetry and technique. Better yet, when I said I wanted a certain mood or shot, she achieved it without insisting on explaining to me how she did it.

I liked her and, until Paycik's appearance over my shoulder in the library Friday, she'd been the only KWMT staffer to talk to me like a normal person.

I was heading out when I heard my name called in Haeburn's nasal tones. He was standing with Thurston Fine.

My first reaction was a stab of hope. I'd been lobbying Haeburn to do my own lead-ins live to "Helping Out." But Fine wanted me nowhere near the anchor's chair, literally or figuratively. So far he'd won.

My hope quickly bled away—they were standing by the assignment board, and Fine was erasing "Stendahl" from behind my name for this two-hour block.

"Sorry, Elizabeth. Thurston needs Diana. Something's come up."

"What?" I demanded.

"Oh, er . . ."

"It's a story I've been working on for some time," interposed Fine, smoothing a hand over his thick hair.

Jenny, the production assistant who'd had such interesting things to say in the ladies room Friday evening, had told me Fine flew to

Denver every month to have his hair cut. He maintained he had a responsibility to his viewers. I tried to imagine a ranch family sitting before the television in a weather-beaten house dwarfed by the land and sky, listening to the news of the vast world, ineffably calmed because Thurston Fine had the right haircut.

"You've been working on all your stories for some time, haven't you?" I asked sweetly. What was this one? A flash that dinosaurs had disappeared?

Color slashed at Fine's cheekbones, but he didn't crumble. "It's a political story. Not your beat." He sneered as he strode away.

"Les, I don't—"

"Sorry, Elizabeth," Haeburn said, no trace of sincerity marring his certainty. "You'll have to find someone else."

"No one else is available."

"Then reschedule. You'll have to learn to do the work in the real world now, where resources are scarce."

Not the first time he'd delivered a dig about me expecting unlimited resources. And totally inaccurate. Nobody seeing the equipment around here would expect more than the basics. Besides, I had no intention of adding a third category—*diva*—to the *queen* and *shark* contingents, so I'd been on best watch-my-tongue behavior.

But this wasn't about equipment or resources, this was about Thurston Fine scoring points.

My time, Cissy Robins' time and the travel agent's time were all sacrifices on the altar of Fine's whim. "Les, this is a good story."

"It's consumer affairs. I told you, we don't get much response to that here."

I gnashed my teeth, and somewhere my old dentist winced. KWMT didn't get much response to consumer affairs stories because they'd never done consumer affairs stories before I arrived.

"We'll get response with this story. We should promo it and do spots for 'Helping Out' to let viewers know it exists. We'll get more calls. In fact—"

"No promos. No spots. Not until the viewers show they want this thing."

Right. Don't promo something until it's already popular.

"If we don't get this today, Les, it'll be a rush job to get it—"

"It can wait a day."

"That's—"

"Elizabeth Danniher, phone call." A reporter named Walt held up the receiver from my desk. "They say it's urgent."

Trying to pin Haeburn in place with my glare, I managed to speak civilly into the phone. "Elizabeth Danniher, may I help you?"

"Yeah, you can get your butt out here."

"Di—?"

"Don't say my name." But my slip didn't matter, because Haeburn had taken advantage of my distraction to scuttle away. "Get out here now. I'm in the parking lot, ready for that assignment we should be leaving for right now."

"But—"

"Right now, understand? I got my assignments first thing this morning and haven't been in touch since. Guess the radio in the Newsmobile's broken again."

The Newsmobile, the top of the line of KWMT's fleet of news vehicles, was actually an aged four-wheel drive. Tinted windows constituted the entirety of its anti-theft devices protecting equipment stashed in it. But then few thieves went for electronics held together by baling wire and duct tape.

Okay, I wouldn't recognize baling wire from picture wire, but I do know duct tape.

"But Fine—"

"I hear he's got an assignment on some political reception, but he doesn't need anybody 'til seven, and my boy's got a program at school tonight, so it sure won't be me."

To score off me, Fine had intended to keep Diana late on a night she didn't want to be late, the jerk. But Diana had ferreted out the whole thing, well before I'd had any inkling, and had come up with a simple way to sidestep it—be unavailable.

"I'm going to that program," Diana added. "Even if this 'Helping Out' segment's not done. And it won't be, unless you get in your car so you can follow me to where Cissy Robins lives. So get your butt out here. Now."

✧ ✧ ✧ ✧

WITH MY MOOD IMMEASURABLY lightened, we got all the film we needed in far less than the two hours allotted. Cissy seemed to feel that the attention compensated for being made a fool of, though she said for the camera, with common-sense pragmatism, that it wouldn't have compensated if they'd still been out the two hundred dollars.

"You going back to the station?" I asked Diana when we finished with the travel agent shortly before three.

"No, and I'd rather you didn't either." She was loading the camera. The best do that as soon as they've shot a story, so they're ready to go if they come across something. "I'm going straight to my next assignment, then home. I don't want anything to change that, like you mentioning where I'll be the next two hours."

"They couldn't torture it out of me. But, you've got a point. Maybe I'll do some leg work on another story."

"A 'Helping Out?' " She wound a cord into a neat loop.

"Not exactly."

Her brown eyes sharpened, but she asked nothing. It was a good thing, because I don't know how I would have explained that I had looked up the address of Myrna and Roger Johnson last night after Mike dropped me off.

✧ ✧ ✧ ✧

THE JOHNSONS LIVED OUTSIDE of town, on what locals call a ranchette and Easterners would call a county. I followed the gravel track from the highway, around a pocket of trees, to the house.

The Johnsons' place reminded me of the Midwest. The house, barn and other buildings were precisely squared to the highway rather than oriented to a view, a stream or an idiosyncrasy. The barn was the bright red more often seen in Wisconsin than Wyoming. And the small white house wallowed in the shade of a quartet of cottonwoods.

Beyond a faded green pickup, a basketball hoop stood at attention at the far end of a parking area. The only jarring note was a blackened, empty rectangle—the charred remains of a structure about half the size of a single-car garage.

Following country courtesy, I honked to announce my arrival. A black and buff dog stretched out in the shade raised its head, but made no other move. He was sleek and well-tended, yet for some reason reminded me of the shadow dog at the house I rented.

And I do mean shadow dog. That was still all I'd seen of the animal. At least I hoped it was a dog, since the bowl of leftover burger and bread I'd placed on the stump had been emptied overnight.

At that moment it occurred to me that I might be feeding a coyote. Or a wolf.

Welcome to Wyoming.

Keeping an eye on the Johnsons' dog, I headed for the back door.

The screen door whined open, and a burly man in his mid-forties emerged, tucking a shirt into the waist of a pair of overalls with the bib flapping down.

"Hey," he said, hooking one strap. "Thought I heard somebody. What can I do for you?"

This morning at the station, I'd done a quick check. Roger Johnson Senior managed a company that delivered fuel and heating oils around the state. He was active in civic groups, belonged to the local Methodist Church and coached a Little League team his company sponsored.

"Mr. Johnson, my name is Elizabeth Danniher. I'm a reporter at KWMT-TV. I was wondering if I could talk to you about your son."

It stopped him in mid-stride. His fleshy face sagged as if it had lost its underpinnings.

"Rog . . ." He barely breathed the name.

"Yes, sir. Mrs. Parens said you might be willing to talk to me."

"Oh. Mrs. Parens." His eyes rested on my solitary car, then beyond as if searching for a hidden camera van. His head turned to where the dog once more had its head dropped to its paws.

"See that old feller?" His voice sounded raw. I nodded. "He spends every day watching the road, waiting for Rog. Coldest days this winter, we had to wrestle him inside. Then he'd lie by the door, crying."

I had nothing to say to that. Nothing to heal the hurt. Nothing to pretend I understood its depths.

Roger Johnson Senior hitched his left shoulder and shook his head. "Don't suppose that's the sort of thing you want to hear." He attached the other overall strap. "I got chores to do. You want to trail along, you can."

I followed, asking him questions I knew he'd want to answer— questions about his son's life—before I had to ask about his death.

Roger Johnson made a show of cleaning out a stall while he started talking. The barn was unoccupied, with four horses visible through windows that opened on an attached corral.

After one stall, he sat on a bale of hay that protruded into the aisle. I propped myself against a rough wood wall and listened to Roger Junior's successes at school, his many friends and his way with animals.

When the account reached last spring, the son's junior year in high school, the father drifted into silence. It was resigned, ready.

"What was Roger Junior arrested for?"

"Disorderly conduct." Bewilderment lingered in his voice and eyes. "That was not like Rog. Not like him at all. There were so many odd things, but that might have been the oddest of all."

"What sort of odd things?"

"He had bruises when we brought him home from . . . from jail. It hurt bad enough he didn't go to school the next day. He said he'd fallen riding, but he hadn't said anything before, and Rog never fell from a horse in his life. It would have made me laugh if he'd said it any other time. But he wouldn't tell us different no matter what his mother and me said to him. Just said he'd forgot to mention it because he was running late to meet his friend."

"His friend?"

"Frank Claustel. Frank had his daddy's car, and they were going over to Cody to see a movie. Frank picks him up here, polite as ever, they leave all smiles, and the next thing we know we're getting a call from the sheriff's office that Rog's in jail. We never could get straight how it was the boys weren't together. Rog only said they'd had a disagreement. Then he said he was real tired and wanted to go to bed. The next day . . . the next day, he left us."

"Had he had any other run-ins with the law?"

"Never. That boy had not once caused his mother and me a moment's unrest. Not a moment. That's why I'll never understand why he wrote what he did. In the note Myrna found when . . . when she found our boy in the shed. She wasn't going to show me, but the sheriff said it was evidence, and he asked me about it. Rog said this was the only way. Because he didn't want to bring shame on us. He couldn't . . . never . . ." The man's heavy shoulders heaved with the force of his sob. "My boy."

I stood across from him. Helpless. Ineffectual. Guilty.

Another sob tore from him. If Rog had known the heartbreak his decision would bring, would whatever shame he foresaw have looked so unbearable?

"Roger?" A woman's voice called from a distance.

Roger Johnson swallowed down another sob. "In the barn, Myrna."

"Roger? I saw a car—" A woman's form appeared backlit at the open barn door. She paused then hurried forward. "Roger? What's the matter? What's going on here? Who are you?"

She was half a foot shorter than me and round. I found myself thinking Roger and Myrna Johnson could have modeled for Mr. and Mrs. Claus in their middle age . . . except for the sorrow in their eyes.

"My name's Elizabeth Danniher. I'm with—"

"It's okay, Myrna. It's not her fault." He dragged the back of one meaty hand across his eyes. "She's a TV reporter. Wanted to hear about Rog."

"You doing a story on Rog?" Her glare blended fear and hope.

"No, ma'am. I'm doing background on the Foster Redus disappearance."

Both faces before me shrank, as if time-lapse photography had caught the skin tightening over the bone structure.

"Then you'd best leave—" Roger Johnson stood. "—because we

got nothing to say about that man. Nothing."

His voice was harsh. When Myrna laid a hand on his arm, I thought she meant to soothe him. Her words proved me wrong.

"Except we hope he's dead and in hell."

Chapter Eight

"C'MON IN," I hollered in answer to the doorbell, while I fiddled to get the earring's post in place. I'd left the door unlocked, Wyoming style, but I had checked the vehicle in the drive before issuing the invitation. It was Mike Paycik in a four-wheel drive.

If you dare, I was tempted to add. But Paycik hadn't even blinked at his first encounter with the interior before we left for O'Hara Hill. It could have been that the exterior prepared him.

"Where did you disappear to all afternoon? I've been trying to call. I thought you'd forgotten we're going to Mona Burrell's—" He interrupted himself with a low whistle. "That's not your usual look."

"I didn't forget." The earring finally slid into place. I grabbed my purse and said, "Let's go. You don't want to be late."

Mike looked dazed, but I'd chosen my outfit for a particular audience—Mona. Skintight jeans and seriously fluffed-up hair to show I could play that game if I wanted to. Lustrous teal silk blouse buttoned to the neck and discreet makeup to show I didn't feel I *had* to play that game. A London-tailored blazer of Irish tweed wool, Chanel perfume and hard-to-miss solid gold hoop earrings to show I knew the genuine article when I saw it. Better yet, I could afford it. And, finally, a pair of fine-grained but unadorned western boots with chunky heels to show I could, and would, kick some serious butt if needed.

The boots were the only weakness in the outfit. Having been bought only a couple hours ago at Sherman Western Wear, they didn't have the casual broke-in air I would have preferred.

Mona's house in a North Sherman neighborhood of neat frame

houses reminded me of a woman's hair that had been cut by an expert but was past-due for a trim—basically in good shape, but getting raggedy on the ends.

Tamantha answered Mike's knock and ushered us into the living room. A camel-back sofa and a matching chair were covered in rose brocade-patterned material and had rolled arms about the size of oil drums. Above the couch three still-lifes and a starburst mirror had the stilted feel of being taken directly from a store display. The room was redolent with her scent. It made me think of church—incense and funerals—with an undercurrent of bordello.

Not that I had any right to criticize considering where I was living.

The lighting was superb. Soft, glowing, incredibly flattering. I know some aging actresses, not to mention TV personalities, who would have it in their contracts that they could only be shot in that lighting if they ever saw it.

Mona was draped in a corner of the sofa in skin-snugging black leggings and a white, cropped top, a dramatic foil against the rose.

"Please, sit down," she drawled, peering at Mike from under her eyelashes and gesturing to the spot beside her.

He dropped into the chair. "Thanks."

"Hello, Mona." I took the spot on the sofa, sacrificing my sinuses for the cause. She flicked me a look, returned her attention to Mike, then, in perfect double-take, whipped her head back to me. I could practically hear her mind calculating costs and tabulating brand names.

"You want coffee, Mom?"

"What? Oh, yeah, Tamantha, bring us coffee."

The child wore the same blue sweater she'd had on at KWMT, over a blouse that had started white but now had an uneven tinge of red, and too-short jeans.

Mike and I both used "please" and "thank you" when she asked if we wanted coffee, and again when she set it before us on the coffee table's glass top. If Tamantha noticed the courtesy, she gave no sign.

"What is it you want to talk to me about?" Mona asked.

She slanted another eyelash-screened look at Mike, but she shifted her eyes to acknowledge my existence as well. So my outfit had accomplished some good. No wardrobe could perform miracles.

"We're looking for the sort of insight only someone who knew Foster Redus can give us," Mike started.

"I already told you what I know—Tom killed Foster because he couldn't stand me being happy."

And, just like at the rodeo, she said it in front of Tom Burrell's daughter.

"What?" Mona asked after a moment of silence. Her eyes followed the direction Mike and I were looking. "Tamantha, go to bed."

"It's seven thirty."

"Then go do your homework. In your room. Git."

Tamantha looked at us solemnly when we said good-night, but said nothing. She started down the hallway that presumably led to the bedrooms. Her footsteps stopped, then came a sound of soft friction, like jeans sliding along a wall as someone sank down to the floor.

"I don't believe in lying to a child," Mona was saying.

Maybe, but I suspected Mona talked in front of Tamantha because she forgot the girl was there.

"When was the last time you saw Foster Redus, Mona?" Mike asked.

"The Monday after Thanksgiving. He left in the morning, saying we'd go to Cody for dinner and dancing Friday night." Her eyes filled, but didn't overflow. "I never saw him again."

I reached over and patted her arm. "Don't give up hope. Maybe Foster just took off. He might pass through this way again, for old time's sake."

"He's dead," she snapped.

"Nobody knows for sure. It could be he ran off and—"

"He wouldn't have left without me. He's dead."

The same sentiment, the same certainty as Marty Beck. But, if Redus had ducked out on these women, I'd bet Mona was the one he should fear.

"So when Foster left that morning," Mike dove in, "everything was fine between the two of you?"

"I told you, he was taking me to dinner and dancing in Cody that

Friday. That sound like a man who doesn't love a woman?"

"Weren't you worried about Foster going to see Tom?"

"He didn't say he was going to Tom's." She took a long swallow of coffee, lifting her lashes to stare at Mike. "I didn't hear Foster had been there until it came out about the blood."

"Hmmm."

Her head turned to me. "What does that mean?"

"Just thinking. It seems odd that Foster told Gina, but he didn't tell you. Especially since it was your ex-husband he was going to see."

"He didn't like me to worry. He didn't say anything to me."

She was lying. From Mike's expression, he was as sure of it as I was—I sure hoped I hid it better than he did. Mona knew why Foster had gone to Burrell's ranch, and she wasn't going to tell us.

Mike picked up, "Some men aren't good at telling their woman what's on their mind. They hold it all inside. It can make a woman feel real lonely."

"Foster wasn't like that. He didn't shut me out, he didn't look down on me. We talked a lot. About where he was going and the kind of life we'd have. How much better it would be than the crap work in this penny-ante county."

"Foster talked to you about arrests he made?"

"Nothing he wasn't supposed to tell," she said. "But a man with all that stress and responsibility, well, sometimes he had to let off steam."

"Responsibility?" Mike asked in a neutral tone.

She nodded, her hair tipping forward. "Law enforcement officers have such a burden. Especially the ones who really want to look after the law-abiding citizens and not just coddle the dregs of society that the government's always wrapping up in cotton padding. A law enforcement officer risks his life every minute of every day, and he has better things to do than toe all those rules and regulations that twist around him so tight he can't give a good belch."

It was eerie, having never met Redus, to be so certain we were hearing his voice—perhaps from beyond the grave—through the medium of Mona.

"Mona? You said the other night that Foster was practically running the sheriff's department. What did you mean?"

"It was common knowledge. Widcuff only won the election because nobody else ran. Next election, Foster would have run. And he would have won." I restrained myself from pointing out he couldn't both run for sheriff and shake the dust of Cottonwood County from his boots. "Then he would have cleaned out all those tight-assed deputies who thought they were so much better than him."

If Redus had been murdered, the entire roster of the sheriff's department might belong on the suspect list, headed by Widcuff. "Is that why you didn't go to the sheriff's department when Foster didn't return?"

Beneath even brush-strokes of blush, a rusty red pattern showed across her cheeks. Gina Redus had to be right; Mona hadn't reported Foster missing for six days because she'd thought he was with another woman.

"I thought Foster was on a special case. Undercover, and he couldn't shake loose to call me. Or maybe he didn't want to expose me to danger. He went up against some real dangerous people."

"You could have called Sheriff Widcuff. Surely he would have known if Foster was on a case—"

She snorted. "Him? He'd be the last to know. Foster worked over his head. And Widcuff hated him for it. He was jealous, right to the bone. Foster'd made a name for himself, and Widcuff's going nowhere. So you don't think I'd go to Widcuff telling him anything, do you?"

"Do you know anything, Mona?" As she parted her lips, I hurried on, fearing hearing another refrain in her litany on Tom Burrell's guilt. "Anything concrete? Anything new?"

She drained her cup, but instead of putting it down she touched its rim to her lower lip, dragging it slightly. "No."

I thought it was a lie. Maybe.

"If you knew something about Foster's disappearance, who would you go to?" Mike asked.

A shrewdness crossed Mona's eyes. "Thurston Fine, maybe."

"Fine?"

Her chin lifted at my surprised repetition. I'd expected her to say

Ames Hunt, both because of his position and because she'd known him since high school. "Yeah. He knows a lot of important people 'round here, the most important. And he hasn't fallen for the fairy tale of the Great Tom Burrell. He sees Tom's a nobody. A hick could've-been who never went anywhere."

She cradled her cup in both hands and brought it near her lips again, apparently liking the effect.

"That's what drove Tom crazy about Foster and me, you know. We were going to go places and do things he'd forgotten how to even dream about. He gave up, but Foster was my ticket out. Tom couldn't stand that."

Not being up to any more go-arounds on Mona's favorite track, Mike and I took our leave. Mona made one attempt to detach Mike. But she didn't seem particularly disappointed when he sidestepped. Maybe after all the talk of Foster it was too painful to be with another man tonight.

Tamantha awaited us beside Mike's four-wheel drive, parked in the street because a red Mustang with a "Blondes ARE More fun" bumper-sticker was parked at the end of the drive. I hadn't heard a sound that betrayed Tamantha's departure from her listening post or her escape from the house.

"Tamantha, you shouldn't be out. It's late, and your mom'll be worried."

Paying no heed to Mike, she said to me, "You're going to help my Daddy."

I opened the passenger door and sat to bring us to eye-level. I considered crouching, but that would have seemed condescending with this old woman in a child's skin. Besides, I wasn't sure I could crouch in these jeans.

"Tamantha, I'm going to tell you the absolute truth. But I have to ask you not to tell anybody. You understand?" She nodded. "Good. When you talked to me the other day at the television station, it got me looking into this case that your father's involved in. I—we—Mr. Paycik and I—are talking to people and trying to find out things about what happened to Foster Redus."

"Oh, him." She wasn't one of his fans judging from her clenched hands. "That's who some people said my Daddy killed. They're wrong."

"Your mother agrees with the people saying that."

"Nobody listens to her," she said with brutal clarity. "Daddy didn't kill him. You prove that. That's what you promise on TV."

I shook my head. "No. That's not what I promise. I promise to look into problems. Some problems can't be fixed, and some get fixed but in a way you don't like. That might happen, Tamantha. Because I'm not talking to people to help your Daddy, I'm doing it to find the truth. If your Daddy's involved—" Being straight with the kid had its limits, I couldn't come out and say *if your Daddy's a murderer.* "—my finding out the truth could get him put in jail."

She stared at me a long moment.

"You find out the truth." She granted permission like Queen Isabella giving Columbus the okay to find the New World. "You talk to my Daddy and you'll know. He didn't kill that man."

Tamantha's words stayed with me as Paycik and I sat in a back booth at the Holiday Inn coffee shop, while I swilled coffee and he tossed questions around. He'd suggested it as a safe place since locals mostly left it to the tourists.

I held a fluted plastic saltshaker between my thumb and forefinger and tilted it to circle on its rim while he kept referring to it as an investigation and the cast of characters as suspects. I wasn't so sure.

It felt as if Foster Redus' situation and the people connected to it were as much in limbo as I was.

But I could make a decision. I could say *enough.* I could leave Sherman, pursue a talk show job and leave this chapter for good. I *could* end my limbo.

"We don't even know there was a murder," I objected at one point. "And wouldn't the local authorities pursue it harder if they thought there was?"

"Maybe Mona offered an answer to that." Paycik kept his eyes on the spinning saltshaker. "Widcuff might not be an Einstein, but he's gotten himself elected more than once. You don't do that without a strong sense of self-preservation. There was a commission last fall to look into the sheriff's department, so Widcuff was under pressure. Last thing he'd want would be a hungry young lion eager to take over."

"So Widcuff didn't go gung-ho with the investigation because he was too busy being pleased not to have Redus around?"

"Could be. Or—" He put his hand over mine, stilling the shaker. "He could have taken a more active role in getting Redus out of his hair."

"Don't get carried away, Paycik." I slid my hand free, leaving the shaker in his custody. "Proof, evidence—remember? So far, they're sorely lacking. C'mon, let's go. Not even the caffeine's going to keep me awake much longer."

We each tossed a few dollars on the table.

On the way to my house, we passed a neon sign with a bowlegged cowboy downing a drink. Below it, a wooden door swung open, and loud music spilled out. In front was a red Mustang with the bumper sticker proclaiming "Blondes ARE more fun."

So much for painful memories.

"The sheriff seems a good direction to start asking questions," Paycik said as I climbed out of his vehicle in my driveway. "And we can share the answers."

Oh, what the hell. "Okay."

So, I'd pledged to share answers. But I'd said nothing about sharing questions. And that's what kept running through my head as I flossed and brushed, washed and moisturized.

Questions that didn't intrude on my comfort zone because they were well removed from my life, yet I hadn't asked these questions at the coffee shop. Because they had to do with jealousy, a woman's heart, and a love that took terribly wrong turns on the happily-ever-after road. They had to do with the hero worship of a boy who'd gone on to fame and glory. They had to do with the softening of an old teacher's eyes and the hardening of a sheriff's.

They had to do with a suspected killer whose impact on people was so strong that the possible victim sometimes blurred toward incidental.

What kind of man inspired that reaction?

I intended to find out.

Chapter Nine

THE PHONE WOKE me Tuesday morning.

I was dreaming. Something about teaching a second-grade class in what looked like a prison from a James Cagney movie. When the sound intruded, my dream closed around it, like a tree growing around a rope. An alarm was ringing, and all the second-graders in prison uniforms were being closed up in locked cells, except an oversized one who looked like Mike Paycik and a wispy-haired girl who stared at me with stern expectation.

The fourth ring registered as the phone. I fumbled for the receiver.

"Elizabeth Margaret. It's mother."

"What's wrong? Is something wrong?"

"Nothing's wrong," she said with a sound between a chuckle and cluck. "Your father and I want to know how you are."

It was short of six a.m. in Wyoming, but in my mother's Illinois household it was prime long distance calling time. She still hasn't adjusted to having low rates any time of the day.

"I'm fine. How's everybody there?" Two brothers and two sisters and their families lived within half an hour of my parents, and they saw each other regularly. My second-to-the-oldest brother and I were the far-flung members of the family. But Steve seldom stayed one place long enough to get phone service.

"Everyone's fine. Though there's some concern Justin—that's Bill's youngest—"

"I know who Justin is, Mom." It was her way of saying I didn't come home often enough. Subtle she's not.

"—is allergic to wheat. Or maybe corn."

"That's too bad."

"It's not a tragedy, just an inconvenience. That's what I told An-na." I sent my sister-in-law a sympathetic thought. "Now, polio—that's a tragedy."

"We didn't call to talk about polio, Cat," came my father's voice.

"Hi, Dad."

"Hi, Maggie Liz." The childhood inversion of my names made me smile despite the hour. "We tried to call you Saturday. Everybody was here."

"I'm sorry I missed that. I was shopping for wallpaper."

"Wallpaper? Have you found a place to live?"

"I am living someplace, Mom. Remember? You helped me move in." Not an experience I hope to ever repeat.

"Of course, dear. I mean someplace permanent."

She hadn't taken to my temporary housing, especially after the act of plugging in the coffeemaker blew several fuses and caused a burning odor. But as for finding someplace permanent here, that edged too close to topics better not discussed at this hour. Maybe any hour.

"I've been busy, Mom."

"Oh, Elizabeth, I wish you didn't work so hard in that job of yours. It's cost you enough already. Can't you slow down now?"

I had just committed the conversational equivalent of jumping from the frying pan into the fire. Dannihers are supposed to achieve, excel . . . but not at the expense of family. Clearly my marriage broke down because I didn't keep the right balance. Though, my ex, of course, was the real villain.

It's not logic, but it is Catherine Danniher.

It's also hair-pulling, stop-me-before-I-scream-at-my-sainted-mother crazy-making.

I went for the biggest diversion I could think of. "It's not exactly the job that's keeping me busy. I've—"

"You've met someone."

Another landmine. "I've met lots of people but not the way you mean. It's something I'm investigating. A missing person's case.

Possibly a murder."

"A murder?" My father's baritone disapproved. "What are you doing investigating a murder? You told us you're doing consumer affairs stories."

"I know you're surprised," I started, soothing as I went.

"I'm not the least surprised," my mother said firmly. It is one of Catherine Danniher's tenets that nothing her children does ever surprises her because she knows us better than we know ourselves.

"Our girl's out in Wyoming, cut off from family, living in a shack, working in some tin box of a TV station, all alone in life, and now she's investigating a murder, and you're not surprised!"

"Now, Jimmy, don't get excited. Elizabeth is perfectly capable of taking care of herself," said my mother, not believing it for an instant, but believing that she believed it.

Dad couldn't very well argue I wasn't capable, at least not in front of me, leaving the floor to Mom. "Elizabeth has always had an overdeveloped sense of justice," she proclaimed.

"Justice is justice. There's no such thing as an overdeveloped sense of justice," Dad retorted.

Oh, Lord, they could wrangle about a point like that for days, enjoying it thoroughly and making all around them miserable. I fell on the hand grenade. "I don't have an overdeveloped sense of justice, Mom."

"Of course you do. Remember the first time you saw the movie *A Wonderful Life*? You were four or five. I remember it perfectly. Jimmy Stewart's uncle mislays the money for the savings and loan, and the old miser picks it up and hides it. Then Jimmy Stewart gets so desperate that the angel Clarence has to help him see how much his life has meant. Remember?"

"Sure." I've seen the movie so many times I can recite passages.

"At the end, when we were all crying because his friends are helping Jimmy Stewart make up the money, you stood there demanding somebody take the miser to jail. 'He shouldn't get away with it.' That's what you said."

Well, he shouldn't. It's heart-warming and tear-jerking that Jimmy

Stewart's friends help him, but Mr. Potter steals eight thousand dollars and doesn't get punished. Is that justice?

"You were just a little thing, but so sure about what was right."

A certainty long gone from my life.

"Uh, I have to go. I'll be late for work." There was a backyard ghost to feed, along with a consumer affairs reporter.

"You be careful," came my father's gruff order.

"I will. Give my love to everybody."

I SPENT THAT MORNING on Cissy's story. Writing, editing, and doing the voice-over.

Diana's footage was great. She'd framed shots of Cissy and the travel agent just right during the set-up—it's really frustrating when the shots are so tight you end up planting the ID over someone's chin. Then Diana brought the shot in close, and Cissy's face filled the frame.

It was honest and touching, and it alerted listeners to a scam that could be tried on any consumer with a phone and some hope. With that and the video of the arrest from Dallas, it was a good piece. I treated myself to lunch at the Haber House Hotel, where I saw Ames Hunt and Sheriff Widcuff seated with four other suits I didn't recognize. The county prosecuting attorney smiled at me, the county sheriff did not.

I also worked in some calls on a story I'd spotted on the wire.

Nomad scam artists would show up, saying they'd noticed your roof needed work. Since they were in the area, they'd be happy to inspect it, no charge.

In no time they'd come down, shaking their heads. It's in bad shape, very bad shape. You need a new roof. Tell you what, since they've got work not far away, they can give you a real good deal. But you've got to decide now, because they'll finish the other job tomorrow. When you say yes, they whip out a contract. There's a stipulation that half is paid on delivery of materials.

The next evening, a truck shows up with roofing material. You give them a check, thinking you never could have gotten the work done this fast by getting estimates from established roofers. That's the last you see of your roofers. And most likely you discover the material was stolen from another job. You're out the half payment, and the crooks have moved on.

I was about to call consumer affairs sources back East when Les came to my desk. "Have you got something going for next week?"

"Yes. These so-called roofers—"

"Something local? More than a toaster."

That was a low blow. "Folks are watching how things are handled before they volunteer problems. It takes time. Especially without a high profile. With promos and ads in the *Independence*—"

"Whoa. We've got a budget, and that's not in it."

"Why did you hire me to start 'Helping Out' if you don't believe in it?"

"It's not that I don't believe in it. This whole 'Helping Out' shtick was added way after we'd set our budget and . . . . But consumer affairs—I mean every station ought to be reporting that, right? I mean, who are consumers? Our viewers, right? But you need to key into our audience. Cottonwood County. This isn't the network, you know. This is where real people live. That's who our viewers are—real people." *And if they watch network news, what? They turn into pumpkins?* "They want to hear a story that affects them. Something in their own back yard."

A devious thought struck me. Tamantha *had* come to me as a result of a 'Helping Out' segment. And what was more important to consumer safety than resolving a possible murder? In their own back yard, no less.

"I have a lead on a local story, but it could take longer to develop . . ."

"If we skip segments of 'Helping Out' to achieve the end goal, that's okay." Especially since I figured his goal was getting rid of 'Helping Out' reporter E.M. Danniher. Or, more accurately, Haeburn's goal was to keep Fine happy, and *his* goal was getting rid of E.M. Danniher.

"No need. I can keep up—" After seventy-hour work weeks,

'Helping Out's' schedule was a breeze. "—and work the story. But I'll be out of the office more."

His lips pulled back from so many teeth that his grin looked wider than his forehead. "I'm behind you a hundred percent. Keep up the good work."

He thumped his knuckles on my desk twice and departed.

With Haeburn behind me a hundred percent, I better not get close to a cliff.

I decided to visit the heart of Cottonwood County. The local audience, you know.

Chapter Ten

DRIVING INTO THE hinterlands of Wyoming to interview an alleged murderer alone, in a car that came no closer to four-wheel drive than having four tires, wouldn't qualify as one of the smarter things I've done. Unfortunately, it doesn't qualify as the stupidest, either.

I pride myself on giving that *alleged* full weight unless a jury's guilty verdict tells me to delete it. That's not to say I don't carry a healthy respect for the *murderer* part. So I was not particularly at ease driving the roughly graveled lane that led to Thomas David Burrell's house.

I'd found the entrance road Mike had pointed out without much trouble. After passing over a cattle guard and under a swinging sign that I saw had a capitalized B within a circle, the road made the sharp right and dipped.

It wound along a creek bed, following the erratic course of water cutting through hard land. I could see cattle on two distant hills and three horses in a pasture closer to the road. But mostly, I could see space.

After a few minutes a branch of the road went east, but it was even less traveled than the one I was on, so I wasn't tempted. No signs of buildings. I was beginning to wonder if these ruts were truly a road or just a path made by a wide moose, when the road curved around a low hill, dipped down and crossed the creek on a clattering wooden bridge.

The road branched to the right toward a Quonset hut, a big old white barn and a scattering of smaller buildings. Two brown horses regarded me from behind a fence that formed a corral beyond the barn. The reddish horse at the far side couldn't be bothered. A formerly white pickup, which might have been new when Carter left office, displayed fans of reddish mud along its side. The truck bed held coils of wire fencing, metal stakes and long metal tubing.

Straight ahead, a newer pickup of dust-hazed marine blue sat before a log house that was either fairly new or remarkably preserved. A chimney rose from the middle of a steep-pitched roof. Three broad steps led to a central door with a window at each side. Scrubby grass came up to the base of the house, with no sign of landscaping. It was as simple and symmetrical as the boxes children draw to represent houses.

With the car engine off, I heard a rhythmic sound, too widely spaced for hammering and not the right tone. Wood-chopping.

I saw no dog, so I didn't toot the horn. Besides, crossing that bridge was as good an announcement as a trumpet fanfare. I got out and followed the sound toward a bare-dirt path around the house. As I skirted the blue truck, I looked inside. Pine needles and dead leaves were the only things loose in the bed. A built-in box behind the cab was closed and padlocked, some long-handled tools including several varieties of shovel were lashed to the side and covered with a tarp. Yes, I peeked under the tarp.

The passenger compartment was equally neat. A shotgun was in a rack behind the seat. It looked well-cared for. Not a wrapper, not an empty can, not a crumpled newspaper marred the seat or floor.

The side of the house was as spare as the front. But the back was something totally different. This—I thought with a glance that took in double glass doors to a wood-slatted patio, picnic table, grill and a sort of log jungle gym—is where somebody lived.

My second glance took in the man who lived there.

He was about fifty yards from the house, where the creek curved back around, forming a rear limit to the civilized area. A dead cottonwood tree had fallen from the far creek bank, bringing down a fence on the near side. Someone had sectioned the trunk, and he was chopping the sections into logs. He didn't pause with his chopping, though I was certain he knew I was there.

This man could be Abe Lincoln's cousin—from the good-looking side of the family.

Growing up in Illinois, I knew Abraham Lincoln's face as well as my grandfather's.

Burrell had the hollowed cheeks, deep-set eyes, prominent brow of Lincoln. His skin was better, well tanned and not as lined. Beneath a baseball cap, his hair was dark, though he clearly had a more skilled barber than Abe. Even at this distance, I could tell Thomas David Burrell's dark eyes were not filled with the same sad, but kindly interest that Abe's always were. More like the rock-solid determination of Burrell's daughter Tamantha.

There was another difference. I've heard stories about Honest Abe splitting logs, but never saw any evidence of it in his physique. This guy qualified as lanky, but he showed the evidence.

A navy plaid shirt hung from a protruding log. Burrell wore a white short-sleeved T-shirt, faded jeans and hefty boots. Each time he raised his arms, the thin cotton went taut over ridges of muscle. Under other circumstances, I might have appreciated that. In an alleged murderer hefting an ax it was not a particularly reassuring attribute.

"Mr. Burrell? I'd like to speak to you."

"I'm busy."

Against the crisp smell of the living vegetation fed by the creek, the pungent scent of cut logs pricked my nostrils. The chainsaw he'd apparently used to section the trunk to fireplace-sized lengths was off to a side with safety glasses beside it. Sawdust covered the ground and stirred with each motion. Even a spider's web laced between two saplings at the edge of the creek held grains of it like a doily dotted with tarnished glitter. Around the stump he used as a splitting platform, chips littered the ground. On the other side grew a stack of fresh-split logs with not a stick out of place.

A man who didn't mind making a mess, if the result was orderly.

He cleaved a quarter-round of log into a pair of perfect wedges, laid both on the pile, snagged his shirt and started toward me.

I sure wished he'd left the ax behind.

I swallowed as he neared. If Tamantha was wrong about her father, it was going to be very sad for her, but it could be damned tragic for me.

Those kinds of thoughts can slow your mind. So it had almost happened before I realized he intended to walk right past me and into the house. Rushing to stop him, I used what had been my best weapon for most of my life—words. "I'm E.M. Danniher, Mr. Burrell, with—"

"I know who you are." He stopped just beyond me, turning his head.

"Oh. Well, you might not know that Tamantha—"

"You stay away from my daughter."

I would if I could. I was tempted to say it, but the straight, narrow line of his mouth didn't encourage that bit of honesty. "Tamantha came to me and—"

"I don't care. Stay away from her."

He turned, rested the ax against the railing and went up the two steps to the deck. Just as I was sure he was about to slam the door on me, he turned back.

"And quit nosing into my life. Quit asking questions about me."

Of all the unfair accusations—

"I haven't asked questions about you. I've asked about Foster Redus, but I can't shut people up about you." I moved to the bottom of the steps, looking up at him. "For some reason they seem to connect you and Redus."

That one hit. I was glad, until I saw that it made him all the more dangerous. "So, you came to see the scene of the crime?"

"No."

"Wanted to see a murderer for yourself, then?"

I was fed up. "No, I came to see the person Tamantha believes in. But all I see is someone who doesn't care what this might be doing to his daughter."

Silence. The sort of silence where your own words echo at you like a taunt. He narrowed his eyes. "That little speech supposed to make me break down and say I'll tell you anything you want to know for my daughter's sake?"

I stared right back at him. Me and Admiral Farragut damning those torpedoes and steaming full-speed ahead.

"Of course it was supposed to do that. Would anybody say something that sappy if it wasn't supposed to break you down?"

His knees didn't buckle. His damned mouth didn't even twitch. But he did step back enough to let me in his house.

Chapter Eleven

"**WHAT DID TAMANTHA** ask you to do?" he demanded before my eyes had fully adjusted to the dimmer light inside. The house was like his truck. Organized, neat, but with enough dust to show he wasn't obsessive.

In addition to a couch, a recliner covered by a quilt, and an open cabinet that held books, DVDs and a TV, there were several distinctly Western touches. A wrought iron tree just inside the door held hats; I counted eight cowboy hats and three baseball caps. A ceiling fan descended from an old wagon wheel. A coiled rope and old spurs were mounted over the fireplace.

What I saw of the room was around his shoulder because he stood in front of me, arms crossed over his chest. But a good reporter knows getting in the door's the toughest part. After that, it's a matter of degrees. "Ask? You don't know your daughter if you think she asked anything. She ordered."

"She's always known her own mind."

"I don't mind that. It's the effort to take over mine that I find irksome."

His eyes lightened, as if he'd stepped out of a cave. "What's she ordering you to do, besides pester me?" That almost sounded human.

"Prove you're innocent."

Back to the cave. "Of what?"

"Killing Sheriff's Deputy Foster Redus." My diplomacy in saying "killing" instead of "murdering" was lost on Burrell.

"How do you know he's dead?"

"I don't know. I made that assumption for the sake of—"

"You know what happens when you assume—makes an ass of you and me."

It was journalism teachers' favorite saying, along with the three most important rules of reporting being accuracy, accuracy, accuracy. Having it drawled back at me by him was downright irritating.

"It would be redundant in your case."

For a moment I thought what my mother called my Irish tongue—fast and sharp—had gotten me in real trouble. It caught me off guard, because I thought I'd put a permanent curb on it years ago when Wes and I moved into TV news. Now a lurid image popped into my head of Burrell's strong arms swinging the ax toward the block.

"Be careful, E.M. Danniher." His soft words sent atavistic shivers along the fine hairs on my arms and up the back of my neck.

He then turned away. I let out the breath I'd been holding.

"What does E.M. stand for?" He moved into the L of a kitchen off to the left, probably figuring he had me cowed enough to ease up on guard duty.

"Elizabeth Margaret."

"Elizabeth Margaret Danniher. That's a mouthful. What do they call you at the television station?"

"Mostly *her.*"

A sound came from him that might have been a chuckle. "What will they be calling you after you've been here a while?"

I pushed back my uncertainties about whether I would—or should—be here a while, and said, "Some will stick with Elizabeth. Mostly it'll be Danny. That's what it's been other places."

"You've been a lot of other places?" he asked as he poured a cup of coffee the color of sin. With his back to me, his voice sounded almost casual. Maybe it was the eyes that gave him such intensity.

"A few."

"I haven't been any other places. Only here." He imbued it with neither pleasure nor regret, simply recognition of a fact. "You think you'll get accepted by doing this story? A scoop?"

Letting him see that Job had nothing on me in the patience department, I sighed.

"In case you didn't notice, no camera. That means no story. And in case you haven't watched KWMT, this isn't my story. My beat's consumer affairs."

"Not your story, but you came out here to ask questions? Why?" He drank down a good mouthful of coffee, though heat curled steam above the mug.

"Don't think I haven't wondered that. I keep getting sucked into it—by your daughter, by Mike Paycik and his aunt and a deputy who doesn't look old enough to shave and—I admit it—curiosity about things that just don't fit."

He looked at me for forty seconds with those Tamantha eyes. Abruptly he poured another mug of coffee, handed it to me and gestured that I was to sit at the built-in booth to the left of the door. I sat.

"Sugar? Don't have cream, but there's milk."

Milk for Tamantha, I guessed. When I declined both, he sat opposite me. We shifted around to sort out knees in the confined space.

I didn't wait for an invitation. "What happened the Monday after Thanksgiving?"

"Redus came here. A few minutes before five. We started shouting—" I tried to imagine this man shouting. "—he threw a punch. I landed one. Few more punches. A little blood spilled, and we didn't do that table any good."

He jerked his head toward an end table beside the muted green plaid couch. One of its front legs was a lighter color than the other three, as if recently replaced.

"When Redus had enough, he stumbled out the front door, shouting."

"What about?"

"When he left? My parentage."

"What was he shouting about at the start? Why did he come?"

"Mona and I had words. Redus stuck his oar in. I preferred it out."

"What were the words about between you and Mona?"

"None of your business."

Did he think that would stop me? Very little of what I asked about was strictly my business. "Give me some idea."

"You know anything about the way things get twisted around and confused when a man and a woman who once were married go their separate ways? Sex and loyalty and rusted-out old arguments?"

"Some."

He raised his head slightly, as if adjusting his angle on me. I had the feeling that, for the first time, he was looking at me as more than an annoyance. "Maybe you do."

"Who started it?" I saw the glint of dark humor in his eye, and before he could say something about Adam and Eve, I added, "Your fight with Redus."

He hitched one shoulder. "Not much of a fight. He took a swing at my gut. I blocked most of it. He'd left himself open. I landed a right to his eye and a left to his nose. Maybe broke it."

Those hands engulfed a coffee mug now, the knuckles like knobs of rock. Certainly capable of breaking a nose and splitting the skin above an eye. But wouldn't his knuckles have bled as well?

I looked up to meet the bleak, unrevealing eyes of Thomas David Burrell, and knew he had no trouble reading my thoughts.

"You missed your chance to see the bruises, but Sheriff Widcuff took pictures. The skin didn't break, not from a couple punches. That's all it took. Redus hollered about assaulting a sheriff's deputy. I told him I'd start hollering about a sheriff's deputy using his position to add to his income, along with messing with other men's wives, especially when he still had one of his own."

"Did he?"

"You're not much of a reporter if you haven't heard about Redus' womanizing."

"I meant did he use his position to add to his income."

He returned my look, giving nothing away, including words.

"You have no proof, but you have suspicions, is that it?" I asked. Maybe the fact that I'd heard that line too often came through in my voice, because his expression grew even blanker. "Okay. So, he hit you, you hit him back. He's bleeding, and you're shouting at each other.

Then what?"

"He left."

"He just turned around and left?"

Burrell spoke with studied patience. "He shouted some more—backing up all the way—got in his truck, ran over a bush and high-tailed it."

I didn't try to hide my frown. "That's it?"

"That's it."

Maybe I could have gotten more out of him if I'd had the equipment and leisure for torture. I started to rearrange my legs under the table in preparation for standing.

"Now, I have a question, Ms. E.M. Danniher."

Warily, I settled back.

"What are the things that don't fit that made you curious about this?"

I went with the obvious. "The limited investigation into Foster Redus' disappearance. Why didn't they have a full-scale search? Why didn't they call in the state crime lab and state investigators to handle the inquiry? When one of its own is involved, law enforcement pulls out all the stops and never gives up. At least that's the way it's been everywhere I've been before."

"You're not anywhere you've been before," he pointed out.

"That's for sure."

Driving away, I knew I hadn't answered any of the questions I'd gone there to resolve. But I knew with absolute certainty that Tamantha was her father's daughter.

Chapter Twelve

JUDGE AMBROSE CLAUSTEL wasn't hard to find. He had a corner office on the third floor in the old section of the Cottonwood County Courthouse.

The Sherman Chamber of Commerce brochure makes a point that the four-story courthouse, complete with stone turrets, was nineteenth century—the dawn of "civilization" in these parts. It was built in 1899.

Eighty-five years later, when they needed more space, they left the original building, tore down a 1950s wing and put in a two-level addition on the back half of the courthouse square shaped like a staple, with the two open ends inserting into either side of the old structure. It created a central courtyard, furnished with benches and plants. The sheriff's office, Sherman police department and jail occupied most of the long side of the addition, farthest from the broad front steps of the old building and facing Basin Street, like the service entrance of a grand old hotel.

I'd been waiting ten minutes in the anteroom crowded by his assistant and a clerk, when Judge Claustel arrived, a bulky man with a lumpy nose and cratered skin under a hat identical to a Stetson I'd seen marked at three thousand dollars at a store in Cody.

He'd been one of the suits I'd seen lunching yesterday with Ames Hunt and the sheriff.

"Judge, this woman says she's from KWMT," started the assistant, who made it sound as if the identification were extremely suspect.

"Come in," he said heartily to me, ignoring the woman. He swept me before him into his office.

None of the addition was visible from this third-story office. The side window, which might have offered some view of that area, was covered by drawn blinds. So the view was strictly to the front of the building, looking down on small figures walking up the wide path across the stubble of grass valiantly greening after a hard winter.

He hooked his nearly shapeless sports jacket and his well-tended hat on a coat rack made of a fence post and antlers. His robe already hung there. The big wooden desk, matching leather desk chair, couch against the side wall and two guest chairs were standard judicial trappings. Book cases, filing cabinets, a side door that probably allowed a side exit completed the setup. But the hoof ashtray, Remington and Russell prints on the walls, and horn frame around a school photo of a good-looking teenage boy blared his geographic loyalty.

"Judge Claustel, I'm—"

"I know, I know. You're the new reporter for the TV station, and you made an appointment to get background on the Wyoming political situation. You came to the right place, even if it is blowing my own horn."

I'd simply said "background."

"That shows initiative, young lady. I wouldn't ordinarily take the time for this sort of thing, but I believe in rewarding initiative, making sure that worm goes to the early bird. So let me get right down to brass tacks. We got a state senator retiring, so his seat's up for election come fall."

I reminded myself not to underestimate him, just because he was condescending to me. Sure I'd dealt with Washington politicians for years, while he was a minor player in the least populated state in the country. That didn't mean he wasn't smart or sneaky or both.

"This area has quite a little reputation for sending its men on to bigger and better things—a couple U.S. senators, three governors and more than our share of U.S. representatives. So whoever wins this state senator election could be setting his feet on the path to the governor's mansion in Cheyenne or the Capitol in Washington, or both. It's been done, it's been done."

He leaned back until his chair groaned.

"That's why in choosing the candidate you got to look beyond the trees to the forest. We owe it to ourselves, we owe it to our county, and we owe it to our state to look for the right man."

"Or woman."

He didn't blink, didn't pause and didn't respond.

"And that means we can't be tied to our first impressions. When circumstances change, we must change with them. Choosing a candidate is like buying a truck, you might have to test-drive a few before you settle on the one you're ready to put down cash for."

Mixing talk of candidates and cash didn't strike me as particularly tactful, but I had other objectives to pursue—or fish to fry, as Judge Claustel would probably say.

"So you backed someone else before you endorsed Ames Hunt?"

His eyes nearly disappeared as his heavy lids lowered and his full cheeks drew up in concentration.

I'd goofed. He'd thought I already knew who he'd backed. I shouldn't have let on I didn't. I should have faked it until I could find out, until—

Then it clicked. Of course. Mike had said something about it.

The silence had gone extra beats, but I went on as if there'd been no pause. "But when Thomas Burrell got arrested, that changed everything."

"I hadn't committed to Burrell," Judge Claustel said instantly. "When others mentioned his name, I felt I owed it to his standing in the community to consider him. His people had been in this area a long time. Tom's done well, until . . . . Not that he was a shoo-in. No, sir. He'd raised some hackles with that commission of his on the sheriff's department. There were some who didn't take kindly to a youngster like Burrell sticking his nose in. Not by a far sight. Bob Widcuff has friends. Influential friends. I tried to drop a hint to Burrell that he'd do better to build bridges than enemies. A word to the wise, you know."

He shifted his weight to one side, smiled and went on in the hearty tone he'd started with. "Well, I don't suppose you came to talk about Tom Burrell."

"No, sir." Though it hardly made any difference. Whatever I intended to talk about, it always came back to Burrell.

"What you're wanting is background on how Ames Hunt is likely to stack up in the election come fall. Ames Hunt has been a fine—"

"Actually, Judge Claustel—"

"—county attorney here, a fine attorney, and—"

"—what I wanted to ask you about was your son. I understand Frank was with Roger Johnson Junior the night he was arrested by Deputy Foster Redus, the night before Roger committed suicide."

Claustel retreated far beneath the surface. "Frank wasn't arrested."

"No, but he and Roger Junior were together that evening, weren't they?"

His chair came forward. "Just what are you nosing into, Miss Danniher?"

"The disappearance of Foster Redus. I'm looking into some of his cases."

"But those files . . ."

"Have been burned," I finished smoothly. And he'd known it. "I hope your son can clarify what happened when Roger Junior was arrested."

"He wasn't there. And he's away at college."

"But he and Roger Junior were good friends, perhaps Frank talked to him. Or he might know if Roger had had other run-ins with Redus. Or maybe Frank had trouble with Redus himself. Or—"

Claustel was on the move, heading to the door. "My son cannot help you. That boy's death was hard on my son. I won't have that wound re-opened. We're out of time, Miss Danniher."

"But—"

"Good afternoon, Miss Danniher." He was holding the door open. That sort of hint even a reporter found hard to ignore.

✦ ✦ ✦ ✦

A GLIMPSE OF WHAT MIGHT have been a slightly less skinny dog disappearing around the garage as I emerged from the back door with refilled bowls was the high point of my night. There wasn't much competition for that honor since the rest of it was spent chipping off green paint from the bathroom light fixture, then falling across the bed in my work clothes only to be awakened by sunrise and a lingering scent of old paint—who says I don't have fun?

I was back at the Courthouse the next morning for two hours of light reading. I had searched through ordinances to answer a viewer's question about whether her neighbor had to keep the goats she raised off a shared access road. I considered the viewer's contention that the neighbor was selling the goats to a satanic group a side issue.

Coming down the hall toward me were Thurston Fine and Sheriff Widcuff. My lucky day.

Fine set himself in my path. "We want to talk to you."

"Good morning," I said with a big smile, just to annoy him. It worked.

"What are you doing talking to people all around the county?" Fine demanded, while Widcuff leaned against the wall, arms crossed over his chest.

It figured that word would filter back. And I wasn't particularly surprised at his attitude. Even bad journalists can be extremely territorial. Maybe especially bad journalists.

"That's what reporters do, Thurston."

"You're not going to find out anything."

"Not if I don't ask."

"You're trying to dig up dirt, but Haeburn won't use it. You won't get around him like you have with the lead-ins."

The lead-ins? What about the lead-ins? I sure wasn't going to ask Fine.

"You can't go bothering important men like Judge Claustel," Fine added.

Ah. "A friend of yours?"

"Yes, I'm proud to say he is. Around here we treat men like Ambrose Claustel with respect. Maybe where you've been before they don't, but—"

"I'm not anywhere I've been before," I supplied, quoting Tom Burrell.

"What?"

"Never mind." I flipped a hand. "If that's all you have to say, I have more dirt-digging to do, so I'll say goodbye."

But Widcuff pushed away from the wall and took Fine's place. If these men insisted on having hash browns for breakfast, I wish they'd skip the onions.

"You shouldn't mess in things that don't concern you."

"That's the definition of journalism, Sheriff. If we mess with things that do concern us it's conflict of interest. You're familiar with that concept, aren't you?" I stepped around him. "Good morning, gentlemen."

First Burrell and now these two. The curb on my tongue apparently had rusted.

Rounding the corner under a head of steam of undispelled anger, I spotted a charcoal gray suit straightening from the water fountain, but too late to avoid impact.

"Ooof," protested the suit as I connected with his ribs. A mist of water sprayed from his mouth.

"Sorry! I didn't—oh, hello Mr. Hunt. I'm sorry, I didn't see you."

"That's quite all right, Ms. Danniher." From the chill in the air, the water should be turning to icicles.

I brushed dew from the shoulder of my jacket. "Boy, I'm glad you'd swallowed most of the water, or I'd look like I'd run through a sprinkler."

Ames Hunt was not amused. He used a snowy handkerchief to wipe at the lapel of his jacket. His finely cut lips disappeared into a compressed line as he then used the handkerchief to wipe his wire-rimmed glasses.

"I really am sorry." I stopped brushing at my jacket, which needed it, and gave a placating swipe at his, which didn't. "I guess I forgot hallways aren't like the highways around here. I've gotten lulled by Wyoming traffic, where I'm practically the only car on the road. No, make that I *am* the only car on the road, because everybody else drives a pickup."

His lips unfolded. "Not everybody. I'm partial to sedans, myself.

And please, call me Ames."

"Thank you. And I was hoping to talk to you for a few minutes." I hadn't really intended to talk to him, but I figured it would be worth my time to smooth any remaining ruffled feathers, and there was nothing a politician liked better than to be sought-after. "That is, if you have time?"

"A few minutes, perhaps," he allowed, then smiled. "As long as we don't tell my assistant you didn't have an appointment."

We went up three flights of side stairs to the top floor of the old building.

Without introducing the busily typing fifty-something woman whose nameplate said Mrs. Martin, he ushered me to his inner office. Like Claustel, Hunt had a corner office, but his was in the back of the old building. It had a view of the courtyard and, over the roof of the addition, to Basin Street.

His office was more modern and less aggressively Western than Judge Claustel's. A computer occupied a wing extended from the desk. The in and out trays on the main desk were filled but not overflowing, apparently the sign of a man who had finely balanced what he could handle in a day.

He removed his suit coat, hung it on a wooden hanger and hooked that on a peg of the standard coat tree beside the door. He waved me to a chair with tweed upholstery and wooden arms while he settled into the ruby red leather chair behind his desk with a satisfied sigh.

"I understand you went to Tom Burrell's ranch," he said. "Do you think that was wise?"

Not knowing which to react to first, I covered my hesitation by rearranging myself in the chair, then ignored both how he knew I'd been there and his cautioning me, and went straight for the hot-button issue.

"Do you think Burrell killed Deputy Redus?"

He tipped his head then shook it—a more-in-sorrow-than-in-anger reaction. It was marginally better than Sister Mary Robert's wagging finger in fourth grade catechism. "You know better, Elizabeth. As county attorney I cannot comment."

"But you've known him since you were kids."

He started to shake his head again, then stopped. His eyes fixed over my right shoulder with a wide, unfocused stare.

"In high school it would have been unthinkable." He spoke slowly. "Tom Burrell had unlimited potential—athletic, academic, professional. He's the one everyone expected to have it all. I suppose that looking at what he'd once hoped for and what he actually had could push a man to an extreme. The years of frustration could build up until they formed a burden too heavy for any man to bear." He looked at me. "That was off the record, Elizabeth."

I raised my hands to remind him they were empty of notebook or recorder. "All on background. Tell me about Redus. I'm having a hard time getting a feel for him. But you're observant . . ." There's something in the Bible about flattery being a trap, but only if the mouse is greedy for that cheese. "So tell me what he is like."

"He seemed to be attractive to a number of women," he answered with more dryness than I would have expected from him. There might even have been a twinkle of amusement in his eyes.

"So I understand. Did he, uh, cultivate the women's interest?"

"With the thickest layer of manure you've ever seen."

We both laughed.

"What kind of deputy was he?"

Caution settled over him like dust. "A zealous officer."

"A lot of his arrests didn't result in convictions. So, I have to wonder why you went along with his being liaison to the courthouse."

His caution thickened. "That was not my decision to make or oppose."

I tried again. "Was it to keep an eye on him?"

"I can't confirm or deny—"

"Oh, c'mon, Ames. This is on background. The courthouse obviously isn't in dire need of a liaison with the sheriff's department—you haven't replaced Redus. So there must have been another reason. Was Redus a loose cannon?"

"Let's say he made decisions that raised concerns about his judgment." Lord, this guy was in full Washington form, and he hadn't been elected to the state level yet. "It was decided moving him to the courthouse would be best."

"Who decided? You?"

"That wouldn't be my decision."

"So whose was it? Widcuff's? Somebody else's?"

He wasn't going to answer, and I'd instigated this conversation to smooth over his dented dignity. I raised my hands in surrender.

"Okay, Ames. No more questions." I stood. "For now."

"You're welcome any time." He could afford to be gracious, he hadn't told me squat. "Elizabeth . . ." I turned to see the corners of his mouth lift in a tight smile. "I'll tell you this, Foster Redus wouldn't ever die of low self-esteem."

Chapter Thirteen

INSTEAD OF HEADING east toward the station across land so flat they call it the Jelicho Table, I went west, straight toward the Rockies.

It was hard to recognize that the ground was rising here, because the mountains ahead gave the impression of jutting straight up from the level ground. Then I'd glance in the rearview mirror, and it was as if the world fell away behind me.

The rodeo grounds sat where the highway to O'Hara Hill intersects with U.S. 27. Three miles beyond that, and the only sign of human habitation was a wire-fenced compound with road construction behemoths sitting behind a trailer. A white sign with red lettering said Burrell Roads.

It was the sort of trailer you couldn't imagine ever being mobile. Three concrete steps led to the door marked Office.

The wind playfully tried to wrench the car door out of my hand and plastered the fabric of my slacks to my legs. The wind always seemed a presence in Wyoming, like languid humidity in New Orleans or heat in Phoenix or mist in San Francisco. Out here, unfettered by the manmade buffers of Sherman or the natural barriers of the mountains, it reigned.

I knocked and waited.

The equipment had a settled-in air. That and the fact mine was the only vehicle out front gave the place an even more forlorn air than nature and heavy-machinery designers had intended. I knocked again. No answer.

But the handle turned. The door wasn't locked. I hesitated then pushed in. Way out here in the middle of nowhere, and they didn't bother to lock—

"Oh! I didn't think anybody was here. I didn't hear you answer my knock."

Tom Burrell sat on the corner of a desk straight ahead of me, one long jeans-clad leg hooked over the edge. One hand rested on a pile of dusty-looking folders sitting beside him on the desk. A battered straw cowboy hat rested on the far corner, and a dent rimming his head attested that it had been in use recently.

"I didn't answer."

"The door wasn't locked and—"

"Not answering a knock's enough around here for most people to stay out."

I shrugged. "As you've pointed out, I'm not from around here."

He stood and circled around behind the desk. "What are you doing here?"

"I saw this building as I was passing—" That was a fib. I'd looked up the address for his road construction business. "—and I wondered why it was way out here alone on the highway, nowhere near the rest of your property, so I just—"

"This is part of the Circle B."

"It must be *huge,*" popped out. "How many acres—"

"Not considered polite to ask a man about the size of his holdings out here, E.M. Danniher." He gave *holdings* just enough emphasis to layer in a second meaning. The glint in his eyes was half humor, half point-scoring. And he picked up smoothly, "And being by the highway makes sense for a road construction operation. But I meant Wyoming. What are you doing in Wyoming?"

We'd shifted to more familiar ground. Not necessarily comfortable ground, but familiar. I pulled the door closed behind me. "I thought everybody had heard the details of my exile to Sherman by now."

"You could have said no," he said, proving he had heard. "You could have done another sort of job."

My heart accelerated. It took my brain another half minute to recognize why. A temptation to pour out right here and now the pitfalls and snakepits that stretched out in every direction from this crossroads I'd been dumped at. In the middle of Wyoming, for God's sake. My career, my life, my priorities, maybe my sanity. All trying to peer down faint tracks in the hard ground that surrounded me. Trying to figure out which one of these paths shimmering under the hard sky might lead to an Eden. Or was Eden behind me? Maybe I was fighting to hold on to something that had crumbled to dust in my hand.

Yeah, pour all that out to him. This stranger suspected of murder. Right.

"Maybe I like doing this job," I said.

"Digging into other people's lives?" *And deaths.* That potential addition to his statement hung in the dust-mote plagued air between us.

"Finding out the truth."

"And you expect to find it in the offices of Burrell Roads?" His tone cut a fine line between polite disbelief and sneering.

"I thought it might give insight to what's been happening," I said mildly.

"See for yourself. Nothing's been happening here." The tip of his head encompassed the trailer.

Along the back wall were another desk, a glass-fronted cabinet with a rifle and a pair of shotguns, and a squat, iron gray safe. On the opposite wall were shelves topped by a window, and a closet-sized enclosure with an open door showing a toilet and sink. Across the narrow end was the boss's desk. It had to be the boss's desk because it was nearly as wide as the trailer and as neat as Burrell's truck and house.

Through the angled glass of the cranked-open back window I saw the roof of a white pickup, and, beyond it, the corralled equipment.

"People aren't hiring because you've been a suspect in a possible murder?"

The lines at the corners of his eyes flickered deeper like he'd fought a flinch. He sat on the desk again, on the back corner, resting one forearm along his thigh and twisting his torso to face me. He moved without hurry, yet there was power in the deliberateness. And when he was still, he gave the impression of being both at rest and prepared for motion.

I hadn't advanced from beside the door.

"It's not a total washout, but I wasn't going to hold people to a contract they were itching to get out of, and some left. With less work for my people, some hooked up with other outfits."

"Some? But not all."

"No. Not all." I remembered what Mike had said about Burrell being liked and respected in the county.

"So you have enough people to do the work that's left?"

"Slowly."

"Can you recover? I mean the business."

Under those would-be sleepy eyelids, his eyes had flashed to me at the question, their sharpness easing at my clarification.

His shrug was fluid fatalism. But the lines in his face told another story.

"Why do you even have this business? You've got a big ranch—a high-side ranch, right?—and that's—"

"High-side, huh? Somebody'd think you were planning on staying 'round here, with you learning the lingo and all." His eyes got that out-of-the-cave look again. It made his whole face lighter. I wondered what he'd look like if he actually smiled. "Yeah, the Circle B's a high-side ranch."

"And the Circle B is doing fine—so why have this other business?"

"It's a hard life. Even for a high-sider. You want a hedge against drought and low cattle prices. And then you want a hedge against dips in your hedge, like happens if the bottom drops out of oil prices or tourists stay home, so nobody needs roads fixed. Or if people go elsewhere to have their roads fixed."

He stood. I backed up. And he was back in the cave before I could blink.

"Tom—"

"Don't mean to be rude, Ms. Danniher, but I've got a lot of work to do here." His level gaze was smooth as marble.

As I left, I realized that neither of us had once mentioned Foster

Redus.

I was falling into the same trap as everyone else, making this the Burrell case. If it was a case at all.

✧ ✧ ✧ ✧

I PULLED OPEN ONE of the station's glass double doors at lunchtime Friday, as Mike pushed out the other. He snagged my arm and spun me around the opposite direction.

"Let's go to lunch," he said. "I'll drive."

We ended up at the Dairy Queen. It wasn't the food I minded (a chef's salad for me and a quarter of a cow plus French fries for Paycik) it was the ambiance—Paycik insisted on eating in his four-wheel drive. Eating in bed can be cozy, even romantic, but eating in a car is never anything but undignified. Yes, I dribbled salad dressing down the front of my blouse.

"All right, Paycik, why'd you hijack me?"

"I thought you'd like to come along to the high school. I'm going to talk to a jumper." I must have looked blank. "Track and field," he supplied. "Rog Johnson ran track. These kids knew him. They know Frank Claustel, too. You could ask questions while I'm doing the interview."

"Paycik, don't ever consider a career change to espionage. You're transparent." Especially after Tom Burrell. "You know something about what these kids might say about Rog and Frank, so why not just tell me?"

"I can hide things." His voice had an edge to it I hadn't heard before. I'd definitely stepped on some psychological toes. "There're a lot of things about me you don't have a clue about."

And he wasn't telling me—not what he knew or suspected the high school kids might tell me and not whatever he believed I didn't know about him. I was just going to have to find out for myself.

Chapter Fourteen

TRACK IS ONE of those disorganized sports, like gymnastics or horse shows, where there's lots going on at the same time. The few times I've attended those events, I always seem to be watching someone warm up or adjusting equipment or arguing with a coach, while someone else is setting a world record.

"That's the varsity," Mike said with a gesture to youngsters contorting their thin, young bodies in hideous ways I suppose were meant to stretch muscles.

Paycik took off diagonally across the football field toward a grassy area near the school building where a cameraman named Jenks stood with two adult men and a skinny boy. I waited until a trio of runners loping around the track passed before venturing across it. About a dozen boys were doing basically the same contortions without any discernible leader or direction.

"Hey, guys! Can I talk to you for a minute? Yes, you. All of you." With little visible enthusiasm or curiosity, they gathered around me. "My name's Elizabeth Danniher, I'm consumer affairs reporter with KWMT-TV."

"Fletcher lodge a complaint about his rubber breaking again?" asked a voice from the back.

Laughter came from every direction. A couple faces turned red. I ignored the hormone humor.

"So, I understand you guys knew Rog Johnson?" A few nods. "I've talked to his parents. It must've been hard on all of you when he died."

I got the standard teenaged male response of mutters and shuffling feet.

"He was on the track team, right? What event?"

"Relay mostly," offered a voice from the second row, a boy with the ropy muscles and gaunt look of a distance runner.

"Was he good?"

The boy shrugged. "He was okay. He'd fill in if the team needed him."

A new voice spoke up. "Rog didn't have a big head. With him, the team came first."

The new speaker was a hefty boy standing to my left. His words had an edge. I wondered if he meant to score points off the first speaker, whose face tightened, or to protect Rog Johnson's memory.

"How about Frank Claustel? Do any of you know him?"

All eyes shifted to the burly boy to my left. "He's older'n us. He's graduated," he said.

"I know, but I thought you might know him—"

"He didn't hang around with us."

I scanned the other faces and got a few head shakes. They weren't talking. Not about Rog Johnson, and not about Frank Claustel.

"How about Deputy Redus? Any of you had contact with him?"

"Asshole," came as a mutter from two directions.

I shook my head. "There's no generation gap on that opinion."

The tension eased, and a freckled towhead grinned. Again, the distance runner in the second row spoke. "Most of the deputies, well, if you're not hurtin' anybody they won't hassle you, you know, if you and a girl are parkin' or something. But Redus, it was like he was watchin' and waitin' 'til you got the most, uh, involved, then he'd show up, makin' you get out, and the girl, even if her clothes—"

"Shut up, Terrant." It was Hefty Guy. "We're not answering any more questions. She's poking her nose in all over. Been to the Circle B and—"

"Don't tell me to shut up, Hanley," shot back the distance runner. "Just because—"

"All right you guys, get a move on! We're not going to beat Central by standing here talkin'."

The coach's roar cut off Terrant. When I looked up, Mike gestured from the other end of the field to meet him at the car.

First, I snagged the beefy boy's arm. The others had taken off.

"Hanley?" The face he turned to me was not friendly. Was his reaction about Rog? Or was the fact he knew I'd been to Burrell's ranch significant? Was he another of Burrell's loyalists? "You were a friend of Rog's, weren't you. Wouldn't you like to know what happened to him?"

"I know what happened. He hung himself. And I'm not giving you tabloid journalists a story."

"*Tabloid?*"

But he'd insulted and run.

I hadn't found out much, except that perhaps there was something to find out. I considered that as I headed across scrubby grass toward the parking lot.

"Look out!"

The shout from behind me didn't mask another sound, a rushing, like a localized windstorm. Instinctively, I ducked to the right. My ankle went sideways, and the duck became an all-out tumble, as a sixteen-pound ball whizzed past where my left ear had been a moment before.

The earth seemed to shudder under the feet that ran toward me. Odd, I thought, lying there, I wouldn't have expected them to be heavy enough to have that kind of impact, except maybe Hanley.

I sat up as the first youngsters reached me.

"Did it hit you?" one asked with an eagerness that sounded ghoulish.

"No. I'm okay." I brushed dust and grass off my jacket and pants, while more arrivals joined the circle.

"Are you all right, Miss?" A hand took my elbow, hoisting me to my feet. A wrinkled, weathered face frowned from under a gray buzz cut. "You walked right across the shot put area." Before I could answer that indictment, he glared over his shoulder. "How many times've I told you to be sure the area's clear, Hanley? How many times? Now, you apologize."

The coach's hold on my arm spun me around to face Hanley, his face blood-red from his chin to the roots of his hair.

"Sorry." His eyes came up from the toes of his shoes, and met mine for an instant. "You gotta watch where you're going around here."

Chapter Fifteen

HAVING NEARLY GOTTEN shot-putted in the head, I was in just the mood to be greeted the minute we walked into the station with word that Les Haeburn wanted to see me.

He smiled when I stepped into his office after a perfunctory knock.

"Elizabeth, come in. I know you haven't felt that Thurston's lead-ins to your pieces were precisely what you were looking for." If I bit any harder on my tongue I'd taste blood. "And he's been so busy this week . . ." I coughed, relieving the pressure on my tongue, but drawing a frown from Haeburn. With an effort, I smoothed my expression to bland interest. "So it seemed an ideal solution to have you do your lead-ins live."

That explained both Thurston's mood and his comment about the lead-ins.

Actually, it was a good idea. Such a good idea, I wondered who'd thought of it. The only drawback was I had only twenty-three minutes to airtime.

The segment was all set, and I'd written the lead-in, so I knew it. But I'd written it as fool-proof as possible for Thurston to read. Now I could play with it.

Also, there was the matter of getting camera-ready. On screen, the black and beige houndstooth check blouse I'd worn would look as if the camera had the DTs. Not to mention the salad dressing on it. There wasn't time to go home, and KWMT only had a couple men's jackets and white shirts for such emergencies. I borrowed a blue blazer from Diana, clip earrings from the receptionist and used one of the men's white shirts.

By the time I'd untangled my hair from its afternoon at the track and applied makeup, the news was starting. My segment came fifteen minutes into the half-hour broadcast, just before the weather, so I had time. I slipped onto the set during the first commercial to look over the set-up.

Thurston Fine sat in the exact center of the anchor desk.

Well off to the left, in front of a montage of sports stills, was Paycik's empty chair; he didn't come on until twenty-three minutes into the show. The only other chair, at the far right of the curved anchor desk, was a clunky plastic model built on a continuous aluminum frame.

I should have thought of this. Warren Fisk, the weatherman, stood throughout his segment, never joining Fine at the anchor desk as most did to close the forecast with chatter. On KWMT, Fine did all the chattering.

"This chair won't turn," I objected.

"No need for it to turn," Fine snapped. Not a happy camper, our Thurston.

"It has to turn so Jerry can get the right angle."

Even years ago, the other stations I'd worked on had at least three automated cameras, operated electronically from the control room, with no need for a cameraman. KWMT had two old cameras and one operator. He would set up the shot on one camera and leave it running while he moved to the other. The director remained with the first camera until Jerry reached the second one. It was like tap dancing on spring ice.

"He'll just have to move to the other camera." It would be a tricky and quick change from the time Fine introduced me until I started my live intro, and chances were excellent that my first seconds would be heard with the camera still on Fine.

"Then he won't get the background."

"He won't get *my* background." The lighting wouldn't be as good and Jerry would have to work twice as hard, because Fine didn't want anyone else associated with the KWMT logo behind his anchor desk.

The director and producer, along with other technical people in the control room, could hear all this. No one said a word. I sat in the chair, hard. It protested. "This chair squeaks."

"Then don't move," Fine said with a smirk.

"Coming back," Jerry said. He also doubled as floor director.

I got up and moved off set, catching a sympathetic look from Jerry.

It was only standing behind the cameras that the full extent of Fine's deviousness hit me. The weather was shot against a special blue wall that is transparent to the camera and lets the maps and satellite shots show up behind the announcer on the TV screen. In the studio, all you see is the weatherman gesturing to a blank, blue wall. He gauges his motions by checking monitors at either end, which show the maps as they're seen at home.

My problem was that not only does the wall become transparent, so does anything blue in front of it.

Like the blazer I wore. My white shirt would look like a disembodied dickey and the rest of me would look like Casper the ghost.

"You're up," Jerry said as we went to commercial again.

As I stepped on the set, debating between moving the chair, squeaks be-damned, after Fine started his spiel and standing, which would make it tougher on Jerry, but had the benefit of making Fine look up to me, the studio door opened, and Paycik wandered in. Squinting against the lights, I saw Jerry say something to him, then Mike strode to his side of the anchor desk.

He grabbed his chair and rolled it behind Fine.

"What are you doing?" Thurston demanded, his head whipping around. "Are you nuts? We're back on any second."

"No time to waste, then," said Paycik. "Have a seat, Elizabeth."

I grinned at him, Galahad with a desk chair. I slid six inches closer to Fine, positioned the chair, got a nod from Jerry and a glower from KWMT's anchor, an expression caught on camera, I was happy to see later.

Perhaps feeling off balance, he stuck to the script. When my piece ended, he said only, "Interesting," in a tone that meant the opposite.

By then I didn't care. I knew it had gone well.

At the next commercial break, I returned the chair to Mike.

After the close, Fine stalked out without a word. I insisted on taking Jerry and Mike to dinner. Mike was a little distant, apparently still miffed that I didn't consider him a man of mystery, or at least hidden depths. Having Jerry there filled in any gaps.

At Hamburger Heaven—their choice, honest, I said anywhere they wanted—I had the adrenaline of deadline mixing with the camaraderie of a small operation that I'd missed in recent years. I'd done a good story, and done it under less than ideal conditions. Mike and Jerry treated me with hilarious stories of how Fine ran roughshod over Les Haeburn.

That resurrected my question about why, then, Haeburn had allowed me do my own intros, when Fine so obviously disapproved, but they had no answers. Back at the station, I fielded calls from Cissy, her cousin, her sister-in-law and the travel agent, all thrilled with the segment. I suggested they encourage their friends to send more stories to "Helping Out."

After reworking my second intro from its original Fine-proofing, it was time to go on again. An appropriate chair had magically appeared, with a hint of its origins coming from the wink I got from Jerry, and everything went smoothly right through my piece and my segue to return to Thurston Fine.

"Elizabeth, you said these trips are often to foreign destinations, making it more difficult for local consumers to check up on their reservations."

"Yes," I said as confidently as I could. This wasn't scripted.

"Don't you think the U.S. government should be looking out more for our residents when they're abroad?"

He had jumped the tracks. Completely. But that didn't matter. I had to answer. I had to fill the dead air. I had to hand the show back to him in one piece—or I would look like the incompetent.

If I said *Yes*, I was making a political statement, practically a damn editorial. *No*, and I could sound as if I were all for leaving Americans to the nefarious wiles of ferriners.

"As Jean Chalmers of Chalmers Travel said so well, Thurston, it's not so much the destination, as the means you use to get you there that you have to be careful of. If you would like a sheet of travel tips, please send a self-addressed envelope to 'Helping Out' here at KWMT-TV. And if you have any consumer problems, contact 'Helping Out.' Thank you, and good night."

Not even Fine dared battle the finality of that closing.

❖ ❖ ❖ ❖

STILL STEAMING, I PULLED into my driveway faster than usual, barreling along to where it curved behind the house. If the brakes hadn't been good I would have plowed into the back end of a pickup truck parked to one side of the garage.

In the seconds my headlights strafed across the dusty blue of tailgate and side panel, they also flashed across a tall figure in jeans and dark T-shirt.

I had the lights and engine off and had exited the car with a temper-venting slam in seconds. Another handful of breaths marched me up to where Thomas David Burrell hadn't budged from resting his rear end against the front door of his truck.

"That's a damn stupid place to park that thing, Burrell. What are you doing back here?"

Out of sight of the street and witnesses? And if so, for nefarious reasons?

On the other hand, if he'd been looking for a place out of sight and with no witnesses, the encounter at Burrell Construction would have been a whole lot better.

"If I'd known you used your drive as a Formula One course, I wouldn't have parked here while I waited for you." My eyes had adjusted enough to the moonlight now to see the white of his teeth in a faint smile. "You should be more careful. You could've hit your dog, too."

"He's not my dog. And why didn't you wait out front?"

The white grin evaporated. It was the reverse of the Cheshire Cat, the body remaining and the smile disappearing.

"You know what they say about the company you keep," was all he said.

He was trying to say that staying out of sight was some gallant gesture to avoid sullying me by association? Talk about barn doors after the horse has departed.

"The word already seems to have gotten around about the company I kept—and the places I've been. I didn't tell anyone, yet I had someone mention it earlier today. So, who did you tell?"

His Lincoln eyes considered me a moment. "I had a talk with Tamantha."

Somehow I didn't see Tamantha chatting with the high school shot-putter about such matters.

"The kid who tried to bean me was considerably older than Tamantha's pals. You sure it wasn't some of your troops in the Burrell Guard spreading the word?"

He shook his head once. It had the feel of a commentary more than an answer to my question, an impression backed by his next words.

"It didn't need telling from Tamantha for the whole county to know. And any who didn't know about you coming to the ranch, do know about today by now. You park in front of Burrell Construction in full view of the highway, and you don't think everybody in the county's going to hear about it?"

So he'd parked out of sight tonight—to avoid word getting out that I was talking to him, or that he was talking to me?

No time to ask, because he was giving more orders. "Leave those kids alone, E.M. Danniher. Leave it all alone. You already know it can be dangerous."

"What can be dangerous?"

"Asking all sorts of people all sorts of questions."

"If I got answers, I wouldn't have to keep asking so many people so many questions." His skeptical brow rose, but I took his silence as permission. "Foster Redus is the one missing, presumed dead. But Tom Burrell is the one everybody talks about. Why is that?"

He looked at me from under his brows. "A fall from grace is always interesting."

"What about Redus' fall from grace? I have leads that he was abusing his position, bullying some people, letting up on the ones from well-connected families."

"Any hard proof?"

"If there's something there, I'll find it."

"Maybe it's better left unfound."

"I'd think you'd want that dug up. It would open a whole range of motives for other people to have killed him."

"You don't know that he's dead."

It was chilling, that subtle reminder that the man in front of me, the man I was talking to alone in the dark, the man with the log-splitter forearms just might be the only person who knew for certain if Redus was alive or dead.

"Neither does the rest of the county, and I'd think they'd be more interested in knowing. Being missed so little—isn't that a fall from grace? Shouldn't that be interesting?"

"He didn't have far to fall."

"He was a deputy," I argued.

He gave a snort. "You met our sheriff?"

"So you don't think much of Sheriff Widcuff and his deputies."

"This county had more arrests and fewer convictions than any other in the state last year, by far. We were—" He stopped, then restarted in his usual calm monotone. "I don't think much of Widcuff and some of his deputies."

The commission looking into the sheriff's department that Paycik had mentioned. Judge Claustel had said Burrell ran it and was finding fault with Widcuff. A situation Redus might have hoped to take advantage of to squeeze out Widcuff and take over. Now both of Widcuff's headaches were gone.

"But nothing came of that commission, did it? Not with you so occupied with accusations that you killed Redus. Now, that's interesting . . ."

He stepped toward me, close enough to cut off the wind. The absence of that buffeting felt like heat. And into my mind popped the most incongruous of thoughts. He'd seen the dog. *You could've hit your dog, too,* he'd said, so he had to have been close to the animal when I drove in. Maybe he'd been close enough to tell if it was starving or sick or . . .

"Leave it alone, E.M. Danniher."

I looked down to his big, raw-boned hand, dark on my arm, up to his eyes. They'd gone nearly black.

"Or what?"

He jerked his hand back and strode away.

"CALL FOR YOU. LINE FOUR," Jenny said as I reached my desk Wednesday morning.

Good. I needed to stockpile more "Helping Out" segments.

After a quiet weekend of paint-scraping, family phone calls, and two possible sightings of the phantom dog, I'd spent Monday with the goat lady and her neighbor. An older cameraman named Jenks had been out with me. He didn't say much, but what he'd shot and I'd started editing would make a nice story about two long-time neighbors finding a workable compromise.

The quiet weekend had reached downright silent on the Paycik front. Only when he returned on Tuesday did I learn from Jenny that he'd been in Chicago, combining a charity event with reports for future use. I suppose that was one of the things I didn't know about him.

I'd been so busy Tuesday with preparing last night's report on the nomad roofers, we still hadn't said more than hello.

"'Helping Out,' Elizabeth Danniher, may I help you?"

"This is Gisella Decker." The name didn't click. "Mike's Aunt Gee. They said Mike's in a meeting, and I have news. Foster Redus' body has been found."

Chapter Sixteen

MIKE WAS RIGHT. There were spots in these mountains you could hide a body until some future explorer came across the dust and bones and wondered at an ancient civilization that left individuals to die so alone.

Diana and Mike knew where I meant when I said Aunt Gee told me a road crew laying gravel to fill winter washouts found Redus off Three-Day Pass Road. We drove past the Burrell Roads trailer, then north on the more western of the roads to O'Hara Hill. About a half mile past the entrance to Tom Burrell's ranch, Diana turned the van west on a gravel road that ran shortly through rising pastures then started climbing between walls of pine green.

"Anybody else at the station know?" Diana asked as she steered expertly through a switchback.

"No. The scanner was turned off."

"Fine," Mike mumbled.

Right again.

After finding Mike in an editing booth, and telling him to snag Diana and meet me in the van, I'd checked the police scanner in its door-less closet outside Thurston Fine's office. The scanner was off, and a rumble of snores came from beyond Fine's office door.

For forty seconds, I debated notifying someone that Redus' body had been found. Then I decided to let sleeping Fines lie.

When we arrived, the bitten away shoulder where a work crew member had fallen earlier today was raw and ragged. The man saved himself by holding on to a tree branch, while dirt and gravel landed below with a distinctly metallic ring. After rescuing their coworker, two men clambered down and found Redus' Ford truck lying on its side, with him inside, very dead.

Nobody would have spotted the green truck from the road unless they stopped on the banked curve and looked directly down. Not an exercise I would have considered conducive to health.

Still, that's what about ten men were doing—toes to the raw edge and peering down, down, down—when Diana parked the van behind a line of construction trucks, a sheriff's department four-wheel and two private vehicles.

"So much for preserving the crime scene," I muttered as we reached the outskirts of the group.

"Good thing for us, isn't it?" said a white-haired man to my left. "I'm Needham Bender, editor of the *Independence*."

I shook his hand. I liked his sharp gray eyes. I liked his easy smile. I liked the three pens in his checked shirt's breast pocket. And I liked his newspaper. "Nice to meet you. I read the *Independence* every Tuesday and Friday. I'm—"

"Oh, I know you," he interrupted. "Kinda surprised to see you here, though. Thought Fine'd bust a gut before he let you cover a story like this."

"Let's just say I caught him napping." The deep lines at the corners of his eyes crinkled deeper. Chalk up another member in the Thurston non-fan club. "How come the *Independence* sent its editor and publisher—" I was showing off a bit, proving I read the masthead, "—out on this story?"

"I'm an old fire horse. Cagen's got the assignment, but you couldn't keep me away. Heard it on the scanner. You might want to grab those guys—" He tipped his head toward three men in dusty orange coveralls. "—they found him."

Mike and Diana nodded and headed toward the three men.

"That was very generous of you," I told Bender.

He laughed. "No need for suspicion. You'll be on the air several times over before the next edition of the *Independence* is out, so we're not really competitors. But you can't do more than skim the surface—

and that makes folks all the readier to read all about it."

My hackles smoothed, I admitted glumly, "I know."

He laughed again. "Shall we take a look?"

Even knowing what was there, it took a moment to find it. The truck rested on its passenger side, nose slightly downgrade, about a hundred feet below the road. From this distance, a couple major dents showed, especially in the front, but it looked pretty much intact.

The driver's door was open, revealing what looked to be a bundle of tan cloth.

Foster Redus.

I traced the truck's path backward to the top, following signposts of a sapling snapped in half, a brown and uprooted bush, a broken tree limb. They could have been the normal ravages of nature, and enough had grown back to make it clear the truck's descent wasn't recent.

To our right, I scanned beyond the newly missing chunk of shoulder.

"Notice anything?" Needham Bender asked.

"No skid marks." He tipped his head in acknowledgment. "But would they be here this long after?"

"Good question. We'd had a snow that melted a couple days before Redus disappeared, left things muddy. Two days after Redus disappeared, it froze up hard. Stayed that way 'til spring. So if there'd been marks last November, they should be here now, especially since this road was closed—in theory, anyway—in mid-October and won't open regular until repairs are done."

The road climbed here, laboring toward the pass Mike had said was a couple miles ahead. Before the curve ahead, the otherwise narrow shoulder widened enough for a vehicle to pull over.

"If I accidentally lost control up here," I said, "I'd have my foot on the brake so hard it would go right through the floorboard, and I'd end up like Fred Flintstone, leaving lots of signs of skidding, braking, something."

"How much strength you think it would take to push a truck that size?"

"I would say that depended on whether you did it with brawn or brains." Bender raised an interested eyebrow, so I continued. "Say you're parked behind Redus, wouldn't take much to use your vehicle to bump his over the edge. Especially, if you're driving something about the same size, which as far as I can tell everybody in this county does except me and a couple other oddballs."

"Good point." He squinted at the edge Redus' pickup had tumbled over. "If the pickup was in neutral, it wouldn't take much of a push."

I looked back at the hard-packed surface our hypothetical pushing vehicle would have occupied. Surface now covered by a layer of material the crew had laid down. If there had been tire prints, they were gone now. The throaty drone of more vehicular beasts coming up the road announced a sheriff's department four-wheel drive.

Deputy Richard Alvaro emerged from one side, clamping his hat on his head and his jaw around a mouthful of mad. "What the hell are you doing, Lloyd? Where's Sheriff Widcuff? Did he tell you to let everybody and his sister tromp around the scene?"

A tall, thin blond separated from four other guys. It wasn't that he stepped forward, more like the others melted away. "Uh . . . no."

Alvaro turned to the assembled representatives of Sherman's media, all five of us. "All of you, get back over there." He jabbed a finger to the far side of the roadway, against the face of the mountain. "Lloyd, get everybody's name, address, phone number, who they work for, when they got here and an account of what they did after they got here—precisely. Then, see these media people on their way. No, not you," he interrupted himself to point at one of the three highway construction workers who'd shown signs of wandering off. "You're here for the duration."

Alvaro glanced toward his vehicle where a gray-haired man who'd gotten out of the passenger side was unloading cameras and other equipment, then at the ledge, crisscrossed by footprints, then back to Lloyd.

"And get the kind of shoes everyone's wearing and their damn shoe size."

It was nearly twenty minutes before Mike, Diana and I were processed—Needham Bender graciously suggested we go first.

I made a stab at getting a statement from Alvaro with no luck—he was back in the fold of silent law enforcement types—but Diana got some video.

"Back to the station?" she asked as we reached the van.

"Let's go by Burrell's, see if we can get a comment."

Mike cut me a sharp look, but Diana handed him the keys and said, "You drive, Mike, while I set up."

"Why not me?" I asked, mostly to keep Mike from expressing the reservation about our destination that I saw in his eyes.

"You kidding?" Diana asked, settling into the back seat and hooking her seat belt. "I don't want a flatlander piloting me on these roads."

✦ ✦ ✦ ✦

THREE SHERIFF'S DEPARTMENT CARS, including Widcuff's, were parked in Burrell's drive. Widcuff stood in the open door of his car, talking to Tom Burrell, about four feet away. The two deputies stood by their cars, one to each flank, pretending they weren't listening for all they were worth.

Mike slowed the van as we crossed the creek, and Widcuff looked around.

His face turned red, and he started shouting to the deputy closest to us. The deputy headed toward the van, waving his arms, emphatically indicating we were not welcomed.

"Circle to the left, Mike," Diana ordered from the seat behind me.

"Okay." He rolled down the window and shouted to the deputy, "We're going, we're going. But I gotta turn around."

Diana lowered her window and shot as the van swung around.

"Hey! You can't do that!"

The deputy's shout didn't deter Diana, but it brought Burrell's head around.

He still looked like Abraham Lincoln's good-looking cousin. But the bones seemed higher, the lines deeper. Like Abraham Lincoln's good-looking cousin after the Battle of Gettysburg.

No one said a word on the drive to the station.

✧ ✧ ✧ ✧

IN THE CLOSEST LES HAEBURN probably ever got to a moral dilemma, he had to decide whether to infuriate his anchorman or skip the biggest story of the year.

Haeburn did what was best for him. He ran our video the way Mike, Diana and I edited it. And he gave Thurston Fine free rein for a long-winded, sideways voice-over recap. Since we'd incorporated enough facts—including that Burrell now was being questioned at the sheriff's department—in the body of the segment, Fine's narration didn't bother me much more than a football stadium's worth of fingernails on a blackboard.

Diana went home to her kids, Mike did his stint on the early news, and I punished myself by watching Fine on a newsroom monitor while I checked messages and planned out the next few steps.

It felt good. Not that a man was dead. But to know what to do. Instinct and training and experience kicked in. No questions. No wondering what to do or where to go. It fell into place in my head, crisp and clear and prioritized. No limbo.

Mike pulled up a chair as he loosened his tie. His on-air suit jacket was back on its hanger awaiting the late news.

"You want to get something to eat?"

Apparently we were back to normal, with the lost weekend past and forgotten. Suited me.

"On the way." I stood and slung my purse over my shoulder.

"On the way where?"

"To Mona's house."

Chapter Seventeen

"I TOLD YOU he was dead."

I'd guessed Mona didn't devote much of her day to keeping up on world events, so I thought we stood a fair chance of being the first to tell her Foster Redus' body had been found.

I was right.

She answered the door in a flowing caftan of polyester chiffon. It was like a pink arrow to the sallowness of her skin and puffiness of her eyes. I caught a whiff of stale beer, stale smoke and stale perfume when she led us into the living room, where she clashed mightily with her sofa. She had the flu, she told us.

Flu? More like the day-after-a-night-at-the-Kicking-Cowboy, but maybe I'm getting cynical.

"They were all laughing behind my back, thinking I'd been dumped. Well, now they know. I wasn't dumped. Foster was going to take me away. He adored me. Couldn't do enough for me. And that's why he's dead."

Better dead than gone was Mona's motto, judging by her triumphant tone.

"You still think your ex-husband killed Redus?"

"Of course," she snapped at me. "This proves it. Now maybe Widcuff will get his head out of his ass and do something. Arrest Tom, get him convicted. Nobody knows those mountains better than Tom. He was always going off to moon around somewhere up there when we were married."

"If he knows the mountains so well," I said, "he was damn unlucky to pick a spot that somebody found, wasn't he?"

"If the man'd been lucky he'd've made something of himself."

"This must be a shock, Mona. I mean," Mike said, taking a seat, "even though you were certain Foster was dead, the reality . . ."

I sat in the chair opposite Mike, out of Mona's line of sight as long as she focused on Mike, which she did.

"You have no idea, Mike. It's a tragedy. We had our whole lives to look forward to. We had so many plans, so many dreams. Now, they're all gone."

She sniffled. Reaching to a brocade-covered box on the end table, she pulled several tissues free and dabbed at her eyes. She leaned farther over the arm of the sofa, reaching to the lower shelf of the end table, and Mike's gaze drifted to the deepening V of her caftan before jerking away.

"I have pictures of Foster and me. Want to see them?"

Mona flipped past several pages in the album she'd retrieved before she held it out to Mike.

He looked at the photos with grave interest, while I itched with impatience. All I'd seen of Foster Redus so far had been a grainy official photo in the clips from the *Independence*.

"You look very happy," he said at last.

"We were. So happy." Mona sniffled again. When she brought the tissues to her eyes, Mike passed the album to me.

While Mona talked of happy times with Redus, I considered the images of the late deputy.

He was about Mona's height, with a compact build. When he smiled all out, as he did in several photos, his top lip curled, forming a rectangle, pushing his cheeks up and squeezing his eyes closed. It sounds repulsive, but it wasn't. I shouldn't have been surprised that he was appealing, since he had enthralled, at one time or another, Gina, Mona, Marty Beck and reportedly many others.

I flipped to the photos Mona had passed over. Three formed a sequence, with Foster and Mona on the front steps of this house. In the first two Redus' smile was in full force. In the third, he was looking partly over his shoulder, and the smile had become a sneer. Behind him, shadowed by the screen door stood Tamantha.

"But I can't dwell on all that," Mona said. "I can't live in the past. I'm too young to let this ruin my life. My future's ahead of me."

I'd be surprised to find it anywhere else.

No, I didn't say it. Antagonizing the person you're interviewing isn't necessarily a good tactic.

Then her phrase echoed in my head like it had been shouted in a distant cavern. *My future's ahead of me.*

Did I believe mine was ahead of me? Or was this limbo of mine a towel I'd tossed in, saying I figured my future was long-gone? Accepting what divorce and demotion had said about me—that I no longer offered any appeal, personally or professionally. I might not be in a position to assess that first part—I might never be as long as my image was reflected back to me daily amidst that sickly green bath-room—but the second part, that was something I needed to face.

Was my reluctance to do a final sign off on news and consider a talk show professional pride? Or refusing to face the facts? Because there were two levels of sign offs—the anchor signed off a newscast, sure, like Cronkite's iconic "And that's the way it is." I'd already done my version of that.

But stations also signed off. Ending broadcasting for the entire day—or forever—and going to static. Was some childish part of me dreaming that the network would come crawling back, begging me to return to my former position and saving me from my personal static?

Wasn't going to happen.

The acceptance that came with that certainty was almost a relief. Had I been holding myself in limbo by refusing to let go of that hope? Maybe I should—

"What's with you?"

Mona's demand snapped me out of my trance.

Apparently, she'd been keeping an eye on me and having me stare unblinking at nothing had disturbed her concentration on herself.

And she was right. This was not the time for me to sort out my past, present and future. There was a story to follow. I felt my mind click fully into reporting mode, and I could have sung hallelujahs.

"Never mind her." Mike recaptured her complete attention with three words. "What about your future, Mona? You're a young woman, attractive and unattached. What're you going to do?"

I savored those words. There could come a time when I could exact great pleasure from reminding Paycik of them.

Mona savored every word, too.

"I'll go on. I'll cry inside, but I have to go on. I'll try to find a little happiness in this life. And security." I noticed she didn't mention going on for her daughter. "I was just wondering, was anything said about Foster's leather case? I mean, was it found? He had a little bitty key to it, kept it on the chain with all his other keys."

"No," said Mike. "Why?"

"Oh . . . I'd sure like to have it. To remember him by. It had . . . uh, real personal things in it, you know, mementos from our being together." Had Redus gone in for risqué photos of his conquests? It would fit. "I'd like to have those."

"It's a credit to you that you are thinking about the good times and memories when you must have so many practical concerns weighing on you."

"Like what?"

Mike faltered at her blank reaction. "Well . . . the funeral."

"The funeral? I'm not doing that. Why should I?"

"You lived together, you and Foster."

"Gina's his widow. That's for her to do, not me." If she'd dusted off her hands, it couldn't have been clearer. No funeral duty for Mona. Maybe Tamantha's single-mindedness hadn't all come from her paternal gene pool.

"How about financial matters, Mona?" I asked. "How are you going to support yourself and Tamantha without Foster's help?"

She stifled a mild snort; apparently Foster hadn't been all that helpful in that regard. "Going to do it the same way I've been doing it. I've got alimony, don't I, and child support. Tom's doing good enough that he shouldn't leave his wife and kid to scrimp along."

"That could change if his business keeps suffering," I pointed out. "And what if he's convicted of murder? How will he pay alimony and child support then?"

"He's got things he can sell. The ranch. That business."

"Legal fees eat up a lot of money. Especially for a murder defense."

Her eyes narrowed as she chewed on her top lip. At first I thought it was irritation, possibly divided between me for bringing it up and Tom for considering using her money on such frivolity. But I changed my mind when she spoke.

"Maybe I'll have to be looking into other sources of income."

"Like what?"

She blinked her eyes wide and smoothed over her lip with her tongue. "Oh, I don't know. Something might occur to me."

RATHER THAN RETURN to the station and watch another round of Fine, I went home. I had an early date the next morning with the telephone to catch people on the East Coast.

It felt good, thinking about who to call to find out what. Less than the standard six degrees of separation got me a "tell him I said to call" for someone who worked in the Wyoming state crime lab. Alas, my friend's neighbor's former college roommate was off yanking innocent fish out of an idyllic existence in some lake and unreachable.

I declined to leave a message with my next target. I might be out of the mainstream, perhaps for good, but I still didn't want anyone at the FBI lab to know Dex did E.M. Danniher a favor now and then. That was how the nickname Danny started, quickly picked by most of my old friends.

I had better luck calling the newsroom of the *Philadelphia Inquirer*.

"Hey, Danny, you scared any rattlesnakes out there in the Wild West?" Matt Lester greeted me.

We'd started fresh out of journalism school together, Matt and me. He never shied away from accusing me of going over to the dark side with the move to TV, but we remained friends. I'd stayed with Matt and his wife Bonnie for a few of the last, worst days of my marriage.

"After a snake like you, what's another rattler?"

He made a sound that I supposed he thought was a rattlesnake. Not that I knew if he was right or not. After an exchange of "how are you's" and quick but honest answers—"Dead tired. This kid will never sleep through the night" from him about their third and "I'm not sure yet" from me—he cut to my chase.

"Whaddya need, Danny?"

"There's a kid from this area named Frank Claustel." I spelled it. "He's a freshman at Temple. I want anything you can find out."

I told Matt about Frank and Rog Johnson and Foster Redus. I didn't tell him about Tamantha Burrell and her daddy. Or Mike Paycik and his ambitions.

After we hung up, I listened to the radio while I thought about old times and dead marriages, until the local news came on, dominated by the finding of Redus' body. The solitary bit of new information was that Burrell had been released after some eight hours of questioning.

The second time I called, Dex was back.

I described what I'd seen of the truck and where it went over. "So, tell me this, Dex, if you wanted to kill somebody, how sure could you be that they'd die when you pushed the truck off the side of a mountain?"

"It depends."

Everything *depends* to Dex. That's why prosecutors so seldom ask him to testify, even though he's tops in the lab.

"It sounds consistent with a truck being pushed over the edge. But I wouldn't go any stronger without a lot more facts."

"Wouldn't the truck have been likely to burn, maybe explode?" I asked as I looked out the window over the sink. A shadow detached itself from the garage and ventured toward the tree stump and the newly re-filled bowls. I found myself grinning.

"You've watched too many chase movies, Danny. Not many vehicles burn and fewer explode in crashes. Fireball scenes are special effects."

He explained why, with an amount of detail I found reassuring as a driver of our nation's highways, but not particularly helpful.

"So," I interrupted, "if someone pushed that truck off the mountain with Foster Redus in it, they were just lucky he died?"

"It all—"

"Depends," we finished together.

"Get me more, and maybe I can tell you more," he said in closing.

Some time later, Mike's knock on the back door startled me out of a directionless reverie and into the realization that I'd tumbled directly from bed into a pair of sweats without benefit of shower.

As I opened the door and looked past him—bowls were empty and no shadow in sight—he held up a paper bag exuding the distinctive aroma of donuts. I stepped back and let him in.

Chilly air streamed in with him. He wore a denim jacket partly zipped. Summer apparently had taken a detour.

"I come bearing news and gifts," he said. "But first, do you have coffee?"

I pulled a mug from the row at the back of the counter. "Help yourself. Now what news and gifts?"

He looked around as he poured from the half-full pot while I helped myself to a donut.

"You know, this is a really ugly house."

"I know."

"And it's like a wind tunnel. It's a good thing you weren't here during the winter." What did he call what Warren the weatherman had reported all through April? "I would have thought somebody from the network could afford—"

"I know, I know. Now tell me the news."

"They took Redus' body out last night. The state guys would have preferred to examine it where it was, but the truck's not stable. They're hauling the truck up about noon. After they get the right equipment."

"Want to go?"

"Yeah."

He nodded toward the telephone and a fan of notes on the table. "Progress?"

"Not really. Waiting for answers to some calls. For others I need more grist to feed the mill before any flour comes out."

"That's where I come in." Mike dug a hand into the donut bag and came up with a golden brown specimen. Smug, he definitely sounded smug. It's not fair that the man could look that attractive this early and with his mouth full of donut. If the networks knew about this, he'd be co-hosting a morning show in nothing flat. "I've got prime grist. What I don't have is a good mill. Not the kind you've got. So I propose a cooperative effort. Your mill, my grist. Share and share alike on the flour."

"I haven't been holding out on you, Paycik," I hedged.

"How about your trip to the Circle B and the construction trailer?"

Good grief, Burrell was right—everyone in Cottonwood County did know about everything. "Just trying to catch up with you, since you know Burrell."

"Share and share alike from now on?" he insisted.

You'd think he didn't trust me. "Deal."

"Good." He drew down his jacket zipper and pulled out a manila folder. He dropped it on the table. "Preliminary report on Sheriff's Deputy Redus."

"Where'd you get that?"

Mike shrugged and chewed. "There was a plain envelope with my name on it by my door this morning. I was taught not to question gifts. However, the envelope met a terrible accident and burned to a small pile of ashes."

In other words, he at least guessed his aunt was responsible, and he was covering her considerable derrière.

Firmly wiping my mind of any considerations of Paycik's family loyalty, his looks and his broadcast future, I opened the file and skimmed the contents. It listed the victim's clothing as a regulation deputy's uniform. His wallet (with three-hundred and sixty-two dollars) was in the usual pocket. His handgun was holstered and showed no sign of being fired since its last cleaning.

Then, hedged around by qualifiers, it described the state of the body. I needed a second reading to bring the legalese and medicalese into focus.

Redus had been bashed on the head with a blunt object. An image clicked into place of Tom Burrell's arms, muscles taut, tendons straining as he swung the head of an ax through a log.

"Are you cold, Elizabeth? Want me to heat up the coffee?"

"What?" Reminding myself an ax didn't qualify as blunt, I focused on Mike, who had a hand out for my coffee cup.

"You cold? I'll put your mug in the microwave."

I felt goose bumps on my arms. "No, it's fine, thanks." I took another swig to prove it. "Hold on a minute." I picked up the phone and hit redial. "I got more information, Dex."

"That was fast. Thought you were out where the living is easy."

"That's South Carolina from *Porgy and Bess*, not Wyoming. Now, listen." I read the information about the truck and injuries. He asked me to repeat one bit, but that was probably my pronunciation.

"Well," Dex said, "it's what I would have told you if you'd asked how I'd make sure someone in a truck I pushed off a mountain would die, instead of asking how likely it was that pushing him off would kill him."

I had a lot of sympathy for any lawyers who'd encountered Dex as a witness. "Okay, Dex. How would you make sure someone would die in a truck you pushed off a mountain?"

"Kill the guy first. In this case, your basic blow to the head. Left rear quadrant."

I tried to picture it. "So, for someone sitting in the driver's side of a truck . . ."

"The blow would come from the side and a little behind. Somebody standing outside the open truck door, swinging a baseball bat or—no, the wound was narrower."

"How much strength would it take?"

"Nothing out of the ordinary with the right weapon and a good swing. Any adult of sound body, male or female. Any teenager who wasn't a weakling."

As I thanked him, then repeated the information for Mike, I realized the only person Dex had eliminated was Tamantha.

Chapter Eighteen

THE GREEN TAILGATE of Foster Redus' pickup appeared over the edge of the broken-off ground like an action scene in slow-motion reverse. It even had sound effects—the grinding and whirring of the monster-sized tow truck that inched Redus' pickup upward with the help of stabilizing side-wires.

Alvaro had herded Cagen and Needham Bender from the *Independence*, KWMT's cameraman Jenks, Mike and me behind crime scene tape that kept us backed up against the mountain. But the road was narrow, so we could see almost everything, right down to the chrome wheels, broken spotlight on the cab roof and scratches in the stylized flame racing stripes. As long as the state crime lab guys didn't whisper to Alvaro, who was taking notes, we could hear, too.

The bed of the pickup, they described as empty. In my notebook I itemized the contents of the cab as they read them off:

—A handgun in a special holder under the driver's seat.
—A second handgun in the glove compartment.
—Handgun and rifle ammunition, shotgun shells.
—Various maps, an owners' manual and maintenance schedule.
—Four boxes of super-ribbed condoms.
—A scattering of keys broken loose from their ring.
—One interior gun rack, partially detached, apparently during the trip down the mountain.

No one said it, but for all the looks exchanged, it might as well have been shouted: There was a gun rack and ammunition, but no rifle or shotgun.

—The hinged, metal box used for forms, citations and reports.

—One carbon copy of a Cottonwood County Sheriff's Department arrest report.

The state guy put that in a plastic sleeve, which Alvaro picked up. The paper looked as if it had been previously crumpled in a fist. He kept his back to us, but his shoulders seemed to tense, and the back of his neck reddened. I had a hunch whose arrest report it was.

Something else nibbled at the edge of my mind, but I couldn't entice it to the forefront.

When the lab guys started buckling down to the painstaking jobs of checking for fingerprints, fibers and other trace evidence, I said, "Let's go" to Mike.

"How about if we talk to each of the suspects," he suggested when we were in his four-wheel drive. "See how they're reacting."

I agreed, because I figured it wouldn't pay to irk the driver on these roads. Besides, it would be interesting to see whom he considered suspects.

"I THOUGHT WE'D START with the official version," Mike said as he pulled his four-wheel drive into a spot behind the courthouse after a quick stop at the Dairy Queen. We ate inside this time, and I didn't spill.

"No one's going to get away with the murder of one of my deputies," the sheriff declared as soon as we were ushered in. "No, sir. Not going to happen. Bob Widcuff personally guarantees it."

"So, it was officially murder? Redus' truck didn't go off the cliff by accident?" Mike asked. That was a nice touch, since we weren't supposed to know about Redus' head.

Widcuff's cheeks puffed out. "Well, now, let's not get hasty. That's not an official statement. No, this is just between us, some honest, caring folks talking about the tragic death of one of our fine law enforcement officers."

"But you didn't call in the state guys right off. Why not?" Mike said.

Oh, yeah, I could see who was No. 1 on Paycik's suspect list.

"Redus always talked about getting out, going someplace bigger. Maybe he'd finally backed his words with action. We had to consider that," Widcuff said defensively. "But I pushed for a fuller investigation earlier. Thing is, there're a lot of factors that go into a decision like that and a lot of people who get involved. Sometimes my hands are tied."

I took that to mean someone else had been giving him orders. That was in keeping with the general opinion of the sheriff. The question remained, if Widcuff was a puppet, who was pulling the strings?

"In the end it didn't matter," he said with heavy self-satisfaction, "because we had the right man, right from the get-go. You know who worked Three-Day Pass Road last season?"

"Who?" I obliged.

"Tom Burrell's company." He nodded for emphasis. "Another company took over this year, but he probably thought he'd be back supervising this year, and he could make sure the body wasn't ever found."

I didn't see how without inexplicably dropping several tons of material over the edge of the highway to cover up the truck permanently.

"That's another thing," Widcuff went on. "The crime scene was six miles from Burrell's house as the crow flies. Could have tailed him easy."

Only a crow could follow that six-mile route. For the rest of us it was slow-going, twisting, climbing roads. It seemed more reasonable that Redus' killer was someone he'd arranged to meet. Someone who'd driven up separately, and then used his or her vehicle to push Redus' over the edge.

That didn't rule out Burrell, since he had no one to confirm he'd been home all night.

"Yup, finding the body will make this a piece of cake, but we were building a case against Burrell all along. Methodical investigating, that's what it takes. Putting each piece of evidence together. Not missing a thing."

"So the files Redus kept didn't have anything that pointed to Tom Burrell?" I asked.

"Nah. There wasn't anything about him in—wait a minute, what do you know about those files?"

"Just that they must not have helped your case against Burrell. Otherwise you wouldn't have burned them, would you?"

"Of course not," he reassured me. Then he saw the cliff at the end of the road I'd led him down and stood on the brakes. "I didn't burn no files. Don't know what you're talking about."

"No? The man you had do the burning probably remembers. Probably kept the memo, too."

"I didn't write a memo. I just told him to . . ." His triumph evaporated as he felt the ground start to give under his foot—the foot he didn't have in his mouth. "You don't know anything, Ms. Bigshot Reporter." His smirk was downright nasty. "I don't know what you think you're doing here—"

"Why, Sheriff Widcuff, I don't know what you mean." I stopped just short of batting my eyelashes. "I just thought we were talking about this tragedy."

He didn't thaw completely.

He was vain, and I suspected that his vanity chafed at the restrictions placed on him. Whether those restrictions were simply the vagaries of politics and political alliances or something even less benign, he wasn't going to tell us. He was vain, but not entirely stupid.

"Yes, it is a tragedy, A terrible tragedy," he said. Then, in case we didn't get his drift, he added, "A terrible, terrible tragedy."

"It is," I agreed. "And it's tragically ironic that the one file Deputy Redus apparently had loose in his truck at the time of his death was the one on that poor young boy—now, what was his name?"

"Rog Johnson," the sheriff supplied. He shook his head wisely. "Situation like that boy's suicide—that cuts up a law enforcement officer something fierce."

Mike tried a couple more questions, but the sheriff had settled firmly behind his "tragic" bunker and was not going to be lured out again.

"So you got confirmation of what Richard said about Widcuff ordering Redus' files burned," Mike said as we walked out.

"We still couldn't use it in a story. The sheriff would deny it, and we don't have him on tape. But we got an indication that the loose file found in Redus' truck was the one on Rog Johnson—though not whether it's the official one or the one Alvaro saw. We also got interesting hints that our sheriff is not the captain of his own fate."

"Yeah, I caught that." Mike looked at me over the roof of his four-wheel drive. "You did that very well." It didn't sound entirely complimentary.

✦ ✦ ✦ ✦

MIKE'S NEXT STOP was the county high school.

When I raised my eyebrows, he turned off the engine, unhooked his seat belt and stretched in a thoroughly satisfied way. "Since you got Widcuff to admit that loose file in Redus' truck was a copy of the one on Rog Johnson's arrest, this seemed the next logical stop."

"Your logic escapes me, Paycik."

He grinned, but it wasn't nearly as attractive as usual. Smugness is not a charming expression. "I found out something interesting yesterday."

"What's that?"

"That shot-putter, Brent Hanley, is Myrna Johnson's nephew. So Rog was his cousin. Rog was older, but Brent was bigger and tougher. The way I hear it, he was protective of his cousin."

"The last time I talked with young Brent he tried to bean me with a shot put, remember? I'd just as soon keep my brain matter, if it's all the same to you."

He opened his door. "I'll talk to him alone, then."

I got out of the car.

He didn't grin, but he sure wanted to. "Don't worry. They're in classes, and he won't be carrying a put. Probably."

"How reassuring."

As we crossed the threshold of the angular brick and glass building erected when oil was a hot commodity, a bell went off. In an instant we were caught in a maelstrom of rushing young bodies.

"Here, Elizabeth!" I caught sight of Mike, standing taller than the students, on the far side of the hall and fought my way through the currents to him.

He had Brent Hanley by the arm. Even Mike's good-sized hand didn't close around that stalwart limb.

"We have a few questions, Brent," Mike said as I came up.

"I don't have nothing to say."

"You can't know that until you hear what we ask," Mike said with unimpaired reasonableness. "Brent, did you hear about Deputy Redus' body being found yesterday?"

"Everybody heard. Nobody gives a shit."

"But you have a special reason to give a shit, don't you, Brent? Because you consider Redus responsible for your cousin Rog's suicide, don't you? So maybe you're happy about his being dead."

"So what. Redus was a prick."

"And you feel Rog is avenged now?"

His eyes slashed to Mike, then away. "I didn't say that."

"Maybe you helped that vengeance along some last fall, huh?"

Without a shot put in his hand, Brent Hanley looked a lot more like a scared sixteen-year-old. Big, but scared.

"I didn't say that. I didn't say nothing. And I got a class now."

"Okay. But this isn't over, you know." Mike took my arm—in a decidedly more gentle grasp than he'd used on Hanley—and started down the clearing-out hall.

I looked over my shoulder as we reached the door, and changed my assessment of Brent once more. Big, scared, and furious.

✧   ✧   ✧   ✧

FOR THE NEXT STOP on our tour of Paycik's suspects, we pulled in at the Johnson place on our way out of town.

Myrna wasn't there, but Roger Senior was washing his hands at an outdoor spigot under a rapidly leafing-out cottonwood tree. He looked about a decade younger than he had the first time I saw him.

He smiled at me and raised a hand in casual greeting. Then he looked at my companion.

"Hey, you're Mike Paycik. I followed you from the time you played for Sherman High. Knew even back then you'd be great."

"Thank you, but—"

"Right through UW and into the pros. Why, we even got a satellite dish so me and my boy could keep up with you in the NFL. Shame about your knees. Glad to have you back in Cottonwood County, though." Mike took Roger Johnson's outstretched hand. "Real glad."

"Mr. Johnson." I waited until he'd dropped Mike's hand and looked at me. "You've heard that Foster Redus was found dead, haven't you?"

"Yep. Heard on the radio yesterday, then saw it on the news last night." He smiled broadly. "Heard that truck he was so proud of got smashed, too."

"Yes, uh, the truck was in pretty bad shape. That was quite a drop."

He faced me, shading his eyes with a hand to his forehead. "You saying it was an accident?"

"I don't know." I thought of Redus' head. "It seems unlikely."

"Good. I don't want Redus to have gotten off that easy."

Mike and I looked at each other. If he had anything to ask, it didn't show in his face. And in the face of this man's unabashed satisfaction at Redus' death, my mind was as empty of questions as the sky was empty of clouds. Not a puff.

As we turned to go, Roger Johnson lowered himself into an aluminum-framed chair with green and white webbing with a satisfied grunt. His right arm trailed over the side and he stroked the dog, who lay facing the road. Waiting. "I suppose this old dog and me'll both die looking down the road waiting for Rog Junior to come home. Difference is, I'll spend the years 'til then resting easier now I know that bastard Redus is dead for sure."

It should have been chilling, to have one human find such comfort in the violent death of another.

I wondered what it said about me that it didn't chill me.

GINA OPENED THE DOOR. She was pale, her hair flat on one side as if she'd slept on it strangely and hadn't bothered to comb it. Her T-shirt and jeans were wrinkled and carried the faint stale scent of having been worn too long.

Gina stared at us from red-rimmed eyes for an uninterested moment, then stepped back, leaving us to come or go, to close the door or leave it open.

She went into the living room and sat on the chair. Newspapers spread around the chair and across the worn coffee table like oversized confetti. Papers from Denver, Cheyenne, Billings, Butte, Bozeman and Cody, plus a couple others whose mastheads were obscured. Mike and I took the same spots on the couch we'd occupied last Saturday.

All the papers were opened to accounts of the discovery of Foster Redus' body. Some were briefs, some were multi-column headlines.

"We're sorry, Gina," Mike said quietly. "If you'd rather not talk . . ."

She lifted her shoulders. "It doesn't matter. It's not exactly a shock."

Yet she looked like someone dealing with a shock.

"Have you had a lot of officials asking you questions?"

"No. They know Foster and me were getting a divorce. Probably figure I don't count for much in this." Gina's attention never wavered from the gap between my right shoulder and Mike's left. "You know how Mona got Tom to marry her?"

"Gina, we're hoping you can tell us something about Foster that might help—"

She gave no sign of hearing. "You know how Mona got Tom to marry her?" she repeated, then didn't wait for an answer. "She told him she was pregnant. So Tom dropped out of college and married her right away."

"But Tamantha . . ." I knew I was being detoured, but inconsistencies grab me, and this was a decade's worth of inconsistency. Tom Burrell had graduated from high school eighteen years ago, and his daughter was eight.

Gina nodded. "She lied, pure and simple. Mona Praver got Tom Burrell by the oldest trick in the book. After they were married she told Tom she miscarried. Got more sympathy that way. But she never was pregnant. She outright lied because she couldn't stand Tom getting away, going off to college, off to this world where she wasn't important. She couldn't stand it."

"How could you know she wasn't ever pregnant? Were you friends?"

Gina looked at me. "No, we've never been friends. But the silly bitch told someone she did think was a friend—bragged about it. And, of course, it was too good a story not to pass on. Pretty soon everybody'd heard, everybody knew how that bitch cheated Tom.

"It could've been just a story. Only, you see, I was working as a summer replacement for Doc Drescott's secretary that next summer, and I looked up Mona's records. She'd never been pregnant, she'd never had any miscarriage. I didn't tell anybody, not ever until this moment. But I had to know. I had to know for sure.

"She tricked Tom out of his future, and then she let Foster turn her head." Her contempt soured her disbelief. "God, she had her choice, and the stupid, silly bitch chose the wrong man."

Chapter Nineteen

MIKE WANTED TO COME to my place after he did his late sportscast to hash over what we'd learned. He said he'd be gone all the next day doing a report on fishing, so we wouldn't have a chance to talk things through until Saturday.

I begged off, saying I was beat and was going to make it an early night.

I *was* beat, but I discovered after watching the early news, then trying to pass restless hours by starting to peel wallpaper from the wall behind the bathroom mirror, that I also wasn't sleepy.

After the ten o'clock show added not one iota of information to my store, I got in my car and drove through a steady rain to sample Sherman's work-week nightlife. Not in the center of town—they weren't kidding about rolling up the sidewalks—and not at any of the bars on the outskirts of town.

Sherman Supermarket, open 'til midnight every other Thursday. Nothing like a little recreational grocery shopping to soothe the soul. My soul needed soothing after Gina Redus. After that initial burst, she'd seemed to sink inside herself. Finally, Mike had called his Aunt Gee, who shooed us out, saying Gina needed a hot toddy and a good night's sleep.

I joined some half dozen other shoppers and Penny. The place echoed with the drumming of rain on the roof. Shopping wasn't really holding my interest, but I still loaded a jumble of the items that keep body and soul together into a cart around the dripping umbrella I'd propped in one corner of the basket. I had added a twenty-pound bag of dog food to the shelf just above the cart's wheels, and was turning to head up the second-to-last aisle when I caught sight of a lanky figure topped by a damp cowboy hat.

Tom Burrell.

He gave no sign of seeing me, but doggedly steered his cart, pausing only long enough to snag an economy-sized carton of oatmeal from an end cap before disappearing behind the row of shelves.

That's when I became aware of five other sets of eyes trained on the same spot—the four remaining customers and Penny. In those faces I saw avid interest, and deep discomfort.

I pushed hard to make up time, hoping to meet Burrell as he started coming down this row. But I was only halfway up when he crossed my line of vision and kept going, skipping my aisle.

"Tom, can I talk to you?"

He ignored me.

I kept going and turned to follow him. He was almost out of sight. Those long legs could really move a grocery cart.

He had his cart partly unloaded and his selections passing under Penny's expert hands by the time I cleared the last aisle. Worse, a man I didn't recognize stood in line behind him.

I stepped in behind the stranger. Burrell never looked up.

The stranger made determined conversation about the weather, addressing his comments evenly between Burrell and Penny. The fact that Penny allowed anyone else to talk had to indicate how rattled she was. The three other customers stood nearby, making no pretense of shopping while they listened.

Burrell contributed a few grunts of agreement, enough to not be outright rude, not enough to be encouraging.

After Penny handed over change and Burrell started out, the man said loudly, "Good to see you again, Tom."

Burrell waved without turning around.

I stepped out of line with my cart.

"Burrell, can I talk to you?" I kept it short of a shout, but he had to have heard me.

He kept going.

I abandoned my cart, not bothering to grab the umbrella. The rain fell as if it wanted to punish the earth, hard and fast. He was a dim figure, moving steadily away. I ran. When rain penetrated to my scalp, I yanked up the hood of my slicker, but moisture dripped down the left side of my face as I reached him. He was loading bags on the passenger-side floor of his truck cab.

"Burrell!" He stopped only when I grabbed his arm. He looked down at my hand, then slowly up to my eyes. I removed my hand.

"You should have stayed inside."

"I would have if you'd stayed inside. I want to talk to you."

"You got your pictures, didn't you?"

If he was trying to make me cringe, I refused. "Pictures, yes, but no words. I want to talk to you."

"I thought this wasn't your story."

"It *is* a story, and you'll have to talk to somebody sometime. Might as well be to me."

"I'm not giving television interviews." If I hadn't already removed my hand, I certainly would have at that tone.

"Did you ever think that I might find something that'll help you?"

Before I finished, he was shaking his head, creating a slow-motion spray of water off the back of his hat.

"You don't understand, do you? I told you before, this isn't any place you've been before. Now that they found Redus, there's no more pretending it might not have happened. It's black and white now. Each time they see me, folks have to make up their minds—am I a murderer or aren't I? Anybody who's with me gets painted with the same brush. Including you."

I'd never had anyone refuse an interview before with the argument that it was for my good. It boggled me enough that I didn't think to protest that I was hardly *with* him before he went on.

"They got to make a decision now and stick to it. Every turned head's a verdict. It won't matter if a court says not guilty in six months or a year. They won't believe it. And not just the ones that think I murdered Redus. The ones that side with me, too, they won't ever believe, not if they saw film of me doing the deed. Because none of them—either side—will want to think they've been fooled. Only ones who can stay neutral are the ones who stay away from me."

"So what are you going to do? Sit on your ranch by yourself like a hermit?" The hood was slipping back, letting rain plaster hair to my forehead.

"Pretty much," he said calmly. "Maybe there's a few around here who don't care—who think if I did kill him it was no great loss, but I'm not sure I want to be around them." The lines around his mouth had eased momentarily, but now they returned. "It's best if I stay away from folks 'til this blows over."

"'Til this blows over? *'Til this blows over?* You're the primary suspect in the murder of a sheriff's deputy. That doesn't just blow over."

"It will." He tugged the hood back over my head, the way he would for Tamantha. "One way or another."

"And what about your daughter? What if when this blows over, you're in prison, convicted of murder? You think she's going to be satisfied?"

His hands dropped from my hood. "Leave my daughter out of it. And you stay out of it, too." He leaned in, a deliberate encroachment. "You hear me, E.M Danniher, you stay out of it. Quit asking questions."

"Asking questions is how I get to the truth. Are you afraid of the truth, Burrell?"

"Sometimes you learn as much about the truth from the questions that don't get asked."

With that cryptic comment, he slammed the passenger door, went around to the other side, climbed in and drove off without another look at me.

Learn the truth from questions that don't get asked? What the heck did that mean?

I went back in the supermarket, mostly to retrieve my umbrella and the dog food. I had no interest in the food for myself. I felt weary, deflated.

But my cart, still filled, had been neatly parked to one side of the register lane and no one else was in line. What the hell. I pushed the cart into place and started unloading.

Penny put down her nail file, drew in a breath, and was off.

"Well, that was something, wasn't it? Hard on a body to know how to act in a situation like that. Hard on him, too, I suppose. What with people acting so strange."

I wondered if she included herself.

"Comes to that, all sorts of folks are acting strange these days. It's not like it used to be around here. Word's all over about Gina buying things."

"You told me that, Grey Poup—"

"Not just the food," she said. "The fancy mustard and breads an' all. That's what I'm saying. That's all I saw, but when it came out about them finding Foster dead, and it looks like he was murdered, well, then some of us started putting our heads together.

"Lou, that does Gina's hair, says last fall Gina started having highlights put in, not just rinse for her gray, but a special process. Costs double. And Wendy, whose mother-in-law lives kitty-corner from Gina, says the UPS driver's been leaving packages regular the past six months. Some of 'em from Victoria's Secret." Wendy's mother-in-law must have very good eyesight. "Nobody knows where Gina's getting the money. Used to be she stayed home all the time, hardly spent a dime. But she eats supper out at Ernie's right regular since November."

Penny nodded wisely. Any fool could see a regular diet of Ernie's cooking clearly indicated guilt of something. High cholesterol at the very least.

"Not exactly a widow in mourning, that's for sure. 'Course that Marty Beck what was taking on with Foster isn't qualified for being a saint, either. And Mona, for all her wailing, hasn't stayed home night after night.

"She's getting her ducks in a row, that one. Went to see a lawyer, that Ames Hunt that's going to run for state senator, and she found out all about her legal rights and all that. That's what she said, standing right here in this line."

I would have found it difficult to believe anyone said anything while standing in Penny's line except Penny, if I hadn't seen it happen, not ten minutes ago. On the other hand, maybe Mona had said those things in the farthest reaches of the store, and Penny's radar picked it up.

"She's looking what rights she's got to take Tamantha away." I focused fully on Penny. She nodded, emphasizing her statement. "That's right. Mona's talking from here to tomorrow about leaving Sherman and taking Tamantha."

On that dramatic finale, she sent me on my way.

Momentum carried me to the automatic door. But there I stood, the curtain of rain in front of me, the chatter of Penny's voice and register behind me, staring in the direction Tom Burrell's taillights had disappeared.

Did he know of Mona's talk about leaving and taking his daughter?

Chapter Twenty

WHEN I GOT HOME, there was a message on my machine from Matt Lester in Philadelphia.

"Give me a call, Danny. I'll be in the office 'til eleven your time."

It was almost an hour later than that, but I tried the number. I got his voice mail, and told him he was now "it" in telephone tag.

AFTER EDITING THE GOAT STORY for "Helping Out" in the morning, I waited for Myrna Johnson to leave the storefront office her husband used for managing delivery of fuel and heating oils.

"I'd like to talk to you, Mrs. Johnson. May I take you to lunch?"

She glanced back as if to check if we were visible from inside her husband's office. We weren't.

"I don't know what I could tell you."

"Let's have lunch and see."

Several people said hello to Myrna as we ordered at the Sandwich Shop. I suggested we eat in the park since it was a nice day.

We found a bench across from the courthouse. A fluttering wind licked at the paper wrappings of our sandwiches and swirled her curly hair into a froth.

"How did your son and Frank Claustel get to be friends?"

"Through the track team, I think." She chewed slowly, methodically, a woman eating for sustenance, not pleasure. We sat slightly skewed toward each other. We could have made eye contact if we'd both wanted to. She didn't.

"When was that?"

"His sophomore year. He was flattered a junior like Frank would be friendly with him. Frank was real popular. With girls, I mean. He's very good-looking."

"Yes, he is, judging from the picture I saw in Judge Claustel's office."

Her mouth tightened, but that was all. Was she scared? Angry? Bitter? Or simply wary. I kept on. "Did Rog Junior date?"

"He was too young. He had a lot of friends, though."

"How about Frank? You said he was popular with girls—did he date?"

"I suppose."

"Any girl in particular?"

"I don't know. And I don't know why you're asking me these things."

"I think you do, Mrs. Johnson."

"No." She started to shake her head, then stopped in mid-motion. I followed the direction of her stare and saw a flash of red turn the corner. It could have been Mona Burrell's red Mustang. Or it could have been a fire truck for all I saw of it. "No," Myrna Johnson repeated more firmly, "I don't."

"How about any reason your nephew Brent might not want people asking questions about Rog?"

"I don't know what you're talking about. And I don't know what any of this has to do with this story on Foster Redus. Now that you know he's dead, shouldn't you be looking for his killer?"

"I am."

No doubt this time. She was scared.

She stood, wadding the sandwich wrapping in her fist. "I have nothing more to say to you, Ms. Danniher. And neither does my husband. Or my nephew. Leave us alone. All of us."

I stood, too. "Mrs. Johnson, Myrna—I don't want to hurt anybody." I didn't want to get hurt myself, either. Particularly by a shot put to the head. "But I'm going to keep trying to find the truth. I would think you'd want the truth, too. It's the only way to reach justice." Lord, that sounded pompous, even though I meant it. "Now that we know Redus was murdered, it's more important than ever to know what kind of man he was. I think what happened the night Rog Junior was arrested can tell me a lot about that."

She shook her head, two sharp jerks. Her eyes focused over my shoulder. She was so much shorter than me it looked as if she were studying a treetop.

"I told you, I have nothing more to say."

She walked away.

I turned around to see what she might have been looking at over my shoulder. In the window of the third-floor corner office of the courthouse, where Judge Ambrose Claustel hung his hat on an antler rack, a shadow shifted, then retreated out of sight.

✧ ✧ ✧ ✧

"IS JUDGE CLAUSTEL IN?"

His assistant looked at me oddly, perhaps because I was huffing enough after taking three flights of stairs at top speed to lift the papers on her desk. But it was other muscles that I could feel stretching and flexing—mental muscles.

"Judge Claustel and Mr. Hunt just left."

"Do you know where they went?"

"Mr. Hunt had something for the judge, so most likely to his office."

I thanked her and headed to the back of the building.

Hunt's assistant was stowing away her purse in a bottom drawer.

"Hello, Mrs. Martin, is he in?" I asked breezily as I moved toward the door to Hunt's office. Before she could object, I knocked once and opened the door.

Ames Hunt, seated behind his desk, looked up in surprise. He was alone.

"Hello, Ames. I was hoping to catch Judge Claustel."

"He just left."

"Where?"

"He has court." A frown tucked his even brows. "Did we have an appointment?"

Chasing Claustel into open court was not an option, so I made use of the bird in hand. I smiled. "No. I'm presuming on your saying to stop by any time."

"I suppose I have a few minutes."

I closed the door and took the same chair as before. "I'm interested in your take on the Redus case, now that his body's been found."

"I'm not sure finding a body changes the outlook much, unfortunately."

"But there'll be physical evidence."

He shook his head. "Not much good from a crime scene horribly compromised. Including—" He compressed his lips. "—by the media, from what I am told."

"Only following in the footsteps of others—literally."

He rested his elbows on the chair arms and steepled his fingers in front of his chest. It resembled the pose of an ancient Asian deity.

"Be that as it may, I'm afraid the physical evidence is not going to be tremendously helpful in our investigation. Although it might help as circumstantial evidence in trying the case eventually."

"You thought you had enough evidence several months ago to arrest Burrell—what do you mean, no?" I demanded of his shaking head.

"That was not my decision. You might not be aware, but I was out of town at the time Sheriff Widcuff made that arrest."

I was aware, of course. I'd hoped by this round-about route to find out what Hunt really thought of the case against Burrell. "You didn't think there was sufficient evidence to arrest Burrell?"

"Not at that time."

So he was simply being a cautious prosecutor. One with political ambitions, who would want to look as good as possible in this high-profile case. He would take no risks.

"Do you now?"

"Is Tom Burrell under arrest?" he parried.

"But you're working on it."

"We are pursuing the investigation with vigor. Especially now that we have confirmation that Deputy Foster Redus was murdered."

He was in full interview mode, even without a camera. "Are you investigating any other suspects?"

"Yes."

I hadn't expected such an unequivocal answer. "You are?"

He allowed the tiniest of smiles. "Yes. Deputy Redus was not, unfortunately, the best-liked man in the county, nor the best-liked law enforcement officer."

"So you're investigating Redus' activities as a deputy?"

"I cannot comment on an ongoing investigation."

"Aw, c'mon, Ames." I help up my empty hands. "No camera, no notebook, no tape recorder. Tell me on background."

"Not even on background." The tips of his fingers tapped against each other. "But I will tell you, we are not ignoring the obvious."

I frowned and rubbed at my neck. "You mean Burrell?"

He shrugged, but I knew I'd missed the answer somehow. *The obvious* . . . "You mean his nearest and dearest?"

"The perpetrators of most murders do fall into that category," he said.

"Okay, I can see Mona and Marty killing one another, but killing him? They both wanted him around too much. It wasn't like he'd chosen one over the other."

"How do you know?"

Sure that I was on firm ground, I shook my head. My neck tightened, and I rubbed at it again. "First, he wasn't the type. Second, he wouldn't have done it voluntarily, so the winner would have had to nag him into it. Which means that woman would have known he was going to give the other one the heave-ho, and there's no way she would have kept quiet about that."

"I'll defer to your greater knowledge of females. But jealousy isn't the number one reason people murder within their, shall we say, family circle."

"Money. Did Redus leave Mona a bundle in his will?"

"He was not the type of man to consider his own mortality. He did not have a will."

"So that knocks the stuffing out your nearest-and-dearest possibilities."

He adjusted one earpiece of his glasses. "Not completely."

"Gina? But they were getting divorced. She certainly showed no sign of wanting to hold onto him, and she would have gotten a decent settlement."

"And now, she'll get it all, the insurance, widow benefits, the house."

My hand stopped in mid-rub. "She still gets the insurance and benefits even though they were getting divorced?"

"They weren't divorced yet."

"Gina said she'd filed the papers."

"She did. But the divorce wasn't final when Foster disappeared, and she stopped proceedings. Separated or not, she was officially Redus' wife when he died, so she'll get his insurance and survivor benefits."

"Are you sure?"

Hunt gave me a superior smile. "I do know the laws of Wyoming."

"Of course. I'm just . . . surprised, I guess."

"That a hick Wyoming gal would see those angles and play them? Don't let Gina fool you. She's clever enough to trick a fox. She just doesn't show it a lot. We went to school together, and she could have been top of our class, only she always had such an itch for Tom, she let him finish ahead of her." His tolerant amusement acquired an edge that lifted his upper lip. "Because Tom couldn't ever be anything but the best."

"But I thought you were second behind Tom?"

Hunt blinked at my question. Then he laughed, starting with a rather rusty sound, but ending in a genuine chuckle. "So I was, so maybe Gina wasn't quite as good at figuring the numbers as I always gave her credit for, because there's no way she would have let me finish ahead of her on purpose. You might have just given me a different view on this whole matter."

I was certain he didn't mean the issue of rank from his high school graduating class, but instead, the matter of whether Gina thought herself clever enough to try to get away with murder.

Chapter Twenty-One

MATT HAD LEFT another message on my home machine.

"What are you doing there so late?" I asked when I got through to him. Dinnertime in Wyoming was way past his usual working hours in Philadelphia.

"Our night cops reporter broke her leg sky-diving—can you believe it? And I lost the pool to fill in this week. It's not so bad, as long as the mean streets don't get any meaner than usual. It's kind of interesting, actually. Like when we first started?"

"Yeah, I remember." And I understood.

I heard nostalgia in his voice. Matt had been doing project pieces for the *Inquirer* for several years. Just the kind of in-depth work we'd dreamed of when we were starting and reporting by the seat of our pants, writing stories in our heads as we dictated by phone from notes while we stood in the rain.

What we didn't realize then was that when we got out of the rain, we would miss some of that messy, adrenaline-pumping, elemental reporting.

"So how can you think about giving it up and doing a damned talk show?"

So much for nostalgia. "I have to do something, Matt. I've been stuck in neutral since fall. Longer, really, because I knew something was wrong with Wes, with us, and I just wouldn't look at it. I'm sick of neutral, sick of this limbo. If the network . . . but it's not going to happen. I can't go back, not to how things were. So I have to go forward. My future's ahead of me."

"Whose isn't?" he muttered, and despite the stinging in my eyes, I grinned. I'd tossed Mona's phrase out there knowing he'd jump on it. And he did. The world was still spinning on its axis. "Fine, go forward. Just don't do a talk show. You're too good a journalist, even if you did get seduced by damned TV. I know you, Danny. You'll hate it if you give up doing stories completely."

"Hey, talk shows do stories in a way, so—"

"Bullshit."

I laughed. "Tell me what you really think. Listen, Mel's just looking into possibilities. I promise I'll talk to you before I make a decision. And in the meantime, I am working a story. Want to hear about it?"

He wanted to keep arguing, but even more he wanted to hear what I was working on—as always with Matt, curiosity won out.

"Tell me."

So I did. When I finished, he whistled. "Interesting doings out there in the Wild West. And I've got my little bit to add to it. I got something on Claustel."

Which was a lot better than I'd done with his father, who'd left the courthouse for the weekend when I'd left Ames' office to try to track him down. Maybe that was for the best. It gave me time to do more digging before I tackled him again. Including whatever Matt had found.

"My God, already? What is he, famous back there?"

"Guess you could say he's famous in a very small way in a very small world. One of our copy aides is a junior at Temple. Smart kid. I asked if he'd heard of this Frank Claustel, figuring that might be a start. Bingo! Claustel has made a name by being very active in gay causes. He was named editor of a gay newsletter in January when the previous one quit—first freshman to be editor."

Was that the sort of achievement Judge Ambrose Claustel was likely to brag to his friends about?

"Other than that, nothing too remarkable. He's solid academically, but not genius level. No discipline stuff. Nothing to make him stand out."

Not in Philadelphia, but would he stand out in Cottonwood County, Wyoming?

"So, is this what you were looking for?" Matt asked.

"I told you, I didn't know what I was looking for."

"But you're not surprised, are you, Danny?"

"No, I'm not."

Saturday morning was predictably quiet at KWMT. A few reporters and cameramen wandered in on the way to or from assignments, but the skeleton crew that would produce the evening news didn't come in until they had to. Especially on a crisp day with a sky so blue it looked as if it might vibrate.

So I figured I would have solitude to look through KWMT's back copies of the Sherman *Independence*. No one else would be stupid enough to be inside on a day like this, especially inside the windowless library that would beat out a bomb shelter on any least-cheerful-places to spend a sunny day list.

I was almost right. About twenty minutes into my dusty duty, Thurston Fine wandered into the tape library.

"Oh," he said with a studied start. At the same time he tried to read what I'd written on the legal pad I'd covered with my forearms. "I didn't think anyone was in here."

I didn't believe him. For one thing, my car was easily identifiable as a rarity among a society of pickups and four-wheel drives.

"Working on a story?" he asked.

"Getting familiar with the area. I don't have the background since I haven't been here as long as you."

Blotches of color marked his cheeks. "I haven't been here that long," he snapped. "And I was the youngest anchor in the region."

"I just meant you know the area well," I said mildly. "I'm still trying to get names and faces straight."

"Yes. Well." He stretched his neck, like a goose smoothing down its feathers. "It will come, eventually."

I ground my teeth at that condescension, but didn't retaliate.

"What are you doing here on a weekend, Thurston?"

"I need a file to prepare for an important meeting of county leaders this afternoon in O'Hara Hill." He opened a drawer and took out the first file in it, which I identified as he headed to the door. He called a breezy goodbye and was gone.

He should have signed out the file, but I didn't suppose anyone would be too upset that he'd taken the file on Dwight D. Eisenhower's inauguration. That should be some meeting this afternoon.

Without further interruption, I worked through four years of semi-weekly "Police Beat" reports in the *Independence*, which listed arrests, charges and arresting officer. The progress and final disposition of each arrest was also accounted for in the paper. I was grateful for, but not particularly surprised by, Needham Bender's thoroughness.

The first year after Redus joined the sheriff's department, he made a high percentage of the arrests. But a good number of times the charges were quickly dropped, and almost every one of those dropped cases involved someone I had heard of, even in my short time here. A drunk driving charge against the owner of the county's biggest insurance agency, a speeding ticket and resisting arrest against the president of the Chamber of Commerce, and others. All dropped.

Then, the number of arrests Redus made fell significantly, even before he was moved to the courthouse. For nearly the entire year before he was murdered, I didn't recognize a single name as I copied the list of his arrests onto my legal pad.

Most interesting.

The hum of the overhead lights resurfaced. I straightened, stretched, then froze. I rubbed the stiff muscles connecting my neck and shoulders. For the first few years of our marriage, Wes gave me the greatest shoulder and neck rubs. They faded away like our promises and dreams and future.

Early on, I'd teased him about being a control freak. It turned out to be no joke. What had started off as massages of my career and image had turned into manipulation. Not that I saw that until long after everyone else did.

Wes carried a leather notebook-sized portfolio with phone numbers, addresses, names, connections, reminders, notes of relationships, lists of to-dos. Even as others switched to electronic equivalents, it never left his side. The past few years, when we sat on the couch side by side the few evenings we were both home, that portfolio sat between us.

I once mentioned the symbolism of that. He gave me a blank stare. I asked him to humor me by moving it. He did—to his other side.

I sipped from a can of soda that had been warming on the table.

Of course. I felt like slapping my forehead—Foster Redus had had his own version of my ex's portfolio. That's what had been nibbling at the edges of my mind when they hauled up his truck. That's what was missing. The leather case that several people had mentioned Redus never let out of his sight. The only thing Mona had asked about.

That case had last been seen the same time as Redus . . . and the same time Gina started buying Grey Poupon mustard, designer bread and Victoria's Secret frou-frous.

I folded the legal pad sheets I'd torn off and slipped them into my purse. Maybe I'm a cynic, but I was betting on a connection linking my list, Redus' leather case and Gina's buying habits.

The opening door squeaked, but before I could get my creaky neck around to see who had come in, all the lights went out. Probably with one sweep of the hand on the switch by the door.

"Hey! Turn the lights back on."

No answer. Only the sound of someone breathing.

"Who's there?" I didn't expect an answer, but there are some questions you just have to ask.

The breathing advanced. I slung the shoulder strap of my purse crosswise over my body, then groped across the library table. The empty soda can clanked.

The noise seemed to make the breather bolder. It—the quality of breathing had no gender—came faster. I got up as quietly as I could, leaving the chair in the aisle and headed for the back of the room, arms extended to trail my fingertips along the front of the cabinets as a guide. It was the long way around to the door, but the lump in my stomach suspected the door was locked anyway.

I crept, holding my breath so I could hear the breathing and gauge its position. Almost there. Almost . . . *Clang! Crash!*

The crack of shin against chair, then the metallic rattle of chair against cabinet was a jolt of electricity to my heart. I sprinted for the door, shouting as I went. My hand slipped on the handle, then closed around it and jerked. It was locked. I pounded on the door and hollered as loud as I could, but not for long.

I couldn't count on there being anyone to hear. And if I remained in one spot, the breather would surely come to me.

In the renewed quiet, the breathing, now with an added wheeze, coming closer, retraced its steps from where it had encountered the chair.

I groped for the light switch, couldn't find it. Jammed my fingers painfully against the side of a cabinet.

The breathing was almost here. No time for another swipe at the wall.

I guessed the distance to the far aisle. A sharp graze against my left arm told me I'd found the corner of the first filing cabinet. I kept my hands on it to guide me to the next one. With as little noise as possible, I slid my hands down the cool metallic surface, curled my fingers around the handle and drew out the drawer at shin level. I backed up several paces and drew out another. Then one from the opposite side.

Just then, the breather let out a wail of shin-cracking agony.

From the sound, the breather ricocheted into the filing cabinets on the outside wall and into the open drawer on that side, sending the entire cabinet thudding against the wall like a huge door knocker.

Maybe I became careless as I moved on. Because, as I opened yet another drawer on the outside wall, about chest level, I was nearly wrenched off my feet when a hand wrapped in my hair and tugged.

Swinging wide as I fought for footing, my fist connected with something solid enough to earn a grunt from my foe. I jerked my head back, prepared to sacrifice a hunk of hair for my freedom. But my hair didn't give.

They identified the killer from skin found under the victim's fingernails.

I'd reported it often enough. I reached to scratch my attacker. If I didn't get away, I wanted justice.

The move left me off balance. The hold on my hair dragged my head around like Michael Jordan palming a basketball. I knew what was going to happen. With each fraction of an inch like a stop-action photograph in my mind, the cool, rounded metal of a drawer handle connected with my temple. Then the depthless dark that exists behind our eyelids rose up and swallowed the lightless room, the breather and me.

Chapter Twenty-Two

"DO YOU HAVE any idea who could have wanted to scare you?"

The one time in my life I'd fainted I remember coming to in the middle of Maple Avenue during the Fourth of July parade surrounding by the avidly curious faces of my fellow Brownies, and feeling as if a trick had been played on me. How the heck had I gotten there?

That was how I felt finding myself blinking into the faces of co-workers hovering around the couch in Haeburn's office where I was stretched out. Except my Brownie-sized head hadn't sported an ostrich-egg bump as my adult head did.

And my concerned cohorts hadn't included a serious-eyed deputy whose tone implied I could clear all this up if I tried. I used to like Richard Alvaro.

"Scare her?" Jenny shrilled. "Somebody was trying to kill her. Just look at her head."

My hand started toward the throbbing.

Jenny forestalled me by placing a cold, wet towel on my forehead. A drop plopped into my eye and I jolted.

"See!" Jenny said. "I think she should go to the emergency room."

"No." I started to push myself up. Stopping abruptly, I groaned.

"Oh, God! What is it, Elizabeth?"

"It's a stiff neck. I must have slept funny." I succeeded in sitting up, but left my legs on the couch. "I'm okay." I looked around. "What happened?"

"That's what we'd like to know," said Audrey Adams, an assignment editor who doubles as weekend producer/director.

"We were editing a package on the Yellowstone Street Sidewalk Sale," said Jenks, "when we heard a ruckus from the library. Sounded like somebody trying to break through the wall." That must have been the file cabinet my attacker had set rocking. The library and the editing rooms back into each other, sharing a wall, but they open to opposite sides of the building. "When we got around, the library door was open, and the lights were out. It was lights out for you, too." He chuckled.

"You didn't see anyone?" Deputy Alvaro asked. "Anybody else in the building?"

My fellow employees exchanged looks, then shrugs. "People come and go, nobody pays much attention," Audrey said.

"Okay. If you think of anything, give me a call."

After everyone heeded that dismissal, Alvaro pulled a chair up beside the couch. "You feel up to answering questions?"

I started to nod. Mistake. Both my neck and head lodged complaints. I told him my tale, saying I had been doing research, but not what research.

"Was anything taken?" Alvaro asked.

"I . . . I don't know. My purse, my other stuff?"

He handed over the purse. "You had this with you. There's an empty can, two pens and newspaper files scattered around the table."

No legal pad.

I unzipped my purse. My fingers found the folded sheets of notes immediately. Aiming for nonchalance, I drew out my wallet. A quick check there and some pawing around amid keys, phone, mini-brush, makeup kit, notebook, a half-dozen pens, a corkscrew and two mini-Snickers bars, and I could assure him nothing of value was missing.

"So you didn't see this guy—this person," he corrected himself. "Can you tell me anything about the person?"

"Only that he or she breathes and has a real strong grip."

He stood, walked to the window, turned the wand that adjusts the blind slats to block the glare. Until he did that I hadn't realized I was squinting. He came back, but didn't sit. "Do you have any idea who could have wanted to scare you? Or harm you?"

I looked up into the serious, earnest face of Deputy Alvaro and decided against telling him the truth. Whoever killed Foster Redus.

There were too many candidates.

If I was right about Redus' omnipresent leather case, Gina could have killed him for the money. Mona could have had the same motive. Marty Beck, too, in this strange love quadrangle. Especially if one found out or suspected Foster was going away alone or with one of the others.

Even without the money motive, I could see Mona killing Redus if he intended to leave her. Gina's version of Mona's history with Tom certainly indicated a woman prepared to take extreme measures.

Widcuff could have killed Redus to eliminate a threat to his ambition, Judge Claustel to shield his son and the Johnsons as revenge. And that last group included Brent Hanley, who had displayed the physique and temperament for a physical attack on the media in the person of E.M. Danniher.

And then there was Burrell, who definitely wanted me off this story.

Of course, there was also Thurston Fine, who wanted me not only off this story, but out of what he surely considered his state. If only I could imagine Thurston being that strong—or magically bulking up his body in the space of a few hours—I'd have served him up to Deputy Alvaro with pleasure.

I couldn't very well demand a lineup of Sherman County citizens and check their shins for bruises. Besides, the only thing missing was my legal pad.

But I sure would like to know whom Fine talked to after he left me.

I met Richard Alvaro's dark eyes. "Not a clue."

MIKE'S FOUR-WHEEL DRIVE was parked in my driveway, and Mike's buns were parked on my front step when I pulled in nearly two hours later. You'd think the delay was because no one wanted me to move too soon. Nope. Paperwork. For Alvaro. And for the station. Audrey had called Haeburn, who insisted I sign releases to cover the station's ass, as well as his.

The bill of Mike's baseball cap with the Chicago Bears logo on it shadowed his face, masking his expression.

He picked up a combination phone and answering machine from beside him on the concrete and stood as I approached, adding the step's height to his advantage so he towered over me.

"Where have you been?" he demanded.

I stretched my five-feet-nine and glared up, hands on hips. My headache had downgraded, but it didn't improve my mood any. The sun seemed unnecessarily bright, even behind sunglasses and the straw hat Jenny donated to mask the burgeoning bruise. "Let's break that habit right now, Paycik."

"What habit?"

"Showing up on my doorstep and demanding where I've—"

"Habit? It's no habit. I—"

"The first night we went to Mona Burrell's house you grilled me about my afternoon. I'm a free agent. You should understand that term."

His open, handsome face shifted and shuttered. "Understood. I just meant that I'd been waiting for you and—"

"Well, don't. You go about your business, and I'll go about mine, and we'll forget this working together crap."

"Okay," he said slowly. Even before he swung it, I could feel a punch line coming. "I guess that means you don't want to come with me to meet Mona."

I held my breath for a balancing second, then let it out in a whoosh. I had overreacted, taking out on Paycik a bad headache and a flashback to a bad marriage. "Damn. You win." I went for all-out contrite. "Yes, please, may I come with you to meet Mona."

I let him have his grin, even let myself enjoy—just a little—the picture of good-looking Mike Paycik grinning at me that way, then got down to business.

"Mona asked to meet us?"

He extracted another ounce of humble pie. "Me, actually. The phone was ringing when I walked in, and the machine picked up, so it recorded everything, you want to hear?"

"You bet."

He followed me into the house and through to the kitchen. He put the recorder on the counter and plugged it in while I poured us each a soft drink and made myself a sandwich.

He rewound. "Ready?"

"Ready."

He hit the play button.

"Mike? Mike Paycik?" It was clearly Mona's voice, but had a distracted quality to it.

"Yes. Hello? Who's this?"

"Mona Burrell. I want to talk to you. You're still doing this reporting stuff on Foster being murdered, aren't you?"

"Elizabeth Danniher and I are looking into the story, yes."

"Yeah, you and her. Well, I might have something to tell you before I go. There's something—well, I didn't get it right off. Not 'til they found Foster, but then it made sense. I thought I could . . . but Foster thought that, too. Maybe this is better. I can still get something. It doesn't mean I can't. But this'll be my cushion. Like some insurance, you know?"

"What are you talking about, Mona? If you want to tell me something—"

"I'll tell you." Significance dripped from her syllables. It was the voice of someone with the power of a secret. *"I'll tell you, but not on the phone. Not now. Meet me at Tom's office. I gotta get something. It's the trailer, you know? You know where it is?"*

"Sure. I know it."

"Okay. Meet me there. One hour."

"Okay. But, Mona, tell me what—"

The click of Mona hanging up and Mike's curse were the final sounds.

"That was forty-eight minutes ago," Mike said.

Chapter Twenty-Three

MIKE OPENED THE trailer's unlocked door.

"Mona?" There was no answer. He called again as he took a step inside, with me on his heels. "That's her car out front. She's got to be here."

"Maybe she's in the bathroom," I suggested. The door in the southwest corner labeled restroom was closed. The desk Burrell had sat on during my first visit was now as neat as the large desk in back.

"Mona," he called louder. No answer.

"Maybe she left," I offered.

"Without her car and leaving the safe open?"

He was right. The safe along the back wall had its door hanging wide open. Papers spilled from its bottom shelf to the floor. Two small, navy blue folders with gold lettering rested atop the white papers.

After a glance that way, I started after Mike, who was skirting around the desk closest to the door, which blocked a direct path to the safe.

I sniffed. "What's that smell? Like something's burning."

"More like a—" Mike stopped so abruptly, my nose connected with his back.

"What—?"

But, beyond the corner of the second desk, I saw what.

Blood. Glinting wet where it puddled on the floor and just starting to dry stiffly in the pale hair like some grisly hairspray. Blood that meant Mona Burrell had gone from "who" to "what."

"She's dead." Mike's voice sounded like someone had a grip on his throat. His body blocked part of the scene from my view, but from where he stood there would be no screen. He would see much more than a sweep of blue, a pale patch of flesh.

My future's ahead of me.

Now she had no future.

I stepped a quarter turn away. A spider had been busy, building a web from the door pulls of the deep gun cabinet to the windowsill. Droplets of red clung to it, outlining the intricacies that man so idly pushed aside without thought when they got in his way. A fine spray of blood traced the web, brought it to light like dyes that doctors use to trace veins.

My head throbbed, the pain so piercing it brought tears to my left eye. My vision all seemed tinged red, even the slanted glass of the open back window was stained with the color. Smells clashed and clawed at each other, the mustiness of the carpet, the slight sweetness of blood, the sourness of the emptied body, and mingled in with all of them, the strong, oily scent of Mona's perfume. My stomach dipped, rose toward my throat, then plunged.

"Let's get out of here, Mike."

He hadn't moved. "Should we . . . should we check the body?"

"You said she's dead," I said sharply. If there was a chance, and we'd just been standing here . . .

"I meant for clues."

"No." But I found myself looking around, taking in details. Identifying the navy folders as passports, the papers as business contracts. The stretch of blue as the sleeve of the sleek jumpsuit Mona Burrell wore. The patch of flesh as the back of her clenched fist. Had Mona gotten close enough to her killer to grab hair, scrape skin? "We don't want to interfere with the crime scene. This isn't like Three-Day Pass Road six months later. The experts will get a second chance at this murderer. Let's get out of here. We'll call it in from the car."

Out in air that seemed so pure and sharp after the cloying, acrid mix of death, my mind started working again. Experts could tell a lot more from the body and crime scene than we could, but if there was one area I prided myself on it was reading people.

"You call, I'll drive," I ordered, and Mike, ashen and with a faint tremble in his hands, silently handed over the keys to his four-wheel drive. He called 911 on his cellular phone and told the dispatcher what we'd found and where. After a second of listening, he looked at me while he repeated, "Who am I?"

I shook my head. We'd tell the sheriff's department we'd found the body, but I wanted some time first.

"I'm—" Mike scraped the ring he wore across the mouthpiece. "What? Can you hear me? I think the line—"

He pressed the "end" button. Not bad.

If my head would shrink to normal size so my neck didn't have so much to hold up and if my stomach would stay in place instead of threatening to take permanent residence in my throat, we might pull this off.

Closing the phone, he looked around. "This is the way to the Circle B."

"Yup. Now, make another call. Get Diana up here."

His eyebrows rose, but in short order he was telling Diana to meet us without letting anybody know where she was going.

Mike listened, then said to me, "Diana's just about to leave some event in O'Hara Hill, and she's assigned to hit a political fund-raiser barbecue for Thurston at six, she wants to know if she'll make it."

"No."

He repeated that. More listening, then Mike said, "She wants to know if she'll be in trouble for more than stiffing Thurston."

"Yes."

He listened about a sentence's worth, said, "Okay, 'bye," and hung up.

"She said she has one short chore to do then she's on her way. She'll meet us at Burrell's." His voice dropped. "I hope to hell you know what you're doing."

"Diana said that?"

"No. I did."

Chapter Twenty-Four

BURRELL'S BLUE TRUCK was parked in front of the house. I pulled up to the right and behind it.

As I passed the truck a sound caught my attention. The pinging of an engine cooling came from beneath the pickup's hood. A palm to the hood confirmed more heat than the filtered sunshine would have produced.

"Mike." I stopped him with a hand on his forearm. "At the trailer, when I said it smelled like something burning, you started to say something but stopped when . . . when you saw Mona. What were you going to say?"

He frowned in an effort to remember, then grimaced and laid his hand over mine. "It smelled like a gun had been fired. That's the burning you smelled. The powder and gasses."

"How long?"

My eyes went to the shotgun in the rack behind the blue pickup's seat. I debated getting in for a close-up smell of the gun, but the lab guys would do a hell of a lot better job of that, and we didn't have much time.

"Not long. The office was closed up, but the smell was strong. And the blood . . ." He cleared his throat over the *was still wet* that might have ended that sentence. "A few minutes, maybe ten—but I'm guessing."

As we started forward again, Mike put a hand at the small of my back. The contact was reassuring. Though I still needed to focus a lot of energy on not getting sick.

That's why it took me an extra half step after Mike stopped to do the same. Burrell stood on the top step, with the half-closed door at his back, arms crossed over his chest. He was looking at Mike, his face as granite-like as the Lincoln Memorial and considerably less expressive.

As if aware of my attention, he glanced at me, then back to Paycik. "Mike."

Paycik nodded and murmured, "Tom."

Burrell looked at me again. "What do you want?"

Mike stepped next to me. "Tom, we have—"

I cut him off with a hand to his arm. "Burrell, where were you just now in your truck?"

His eyes had followed the movement of my hand to stop Mike's words, but now they came to my face. "Why do you want to know?"

"It's part of our investigation into—"

"I told you to leave it alone."

"I can't!" That was strident enough to raise a protest from two neighboring birds, crease Burrell's forehead and surprise myself. I took a deep, calming breath. "We have to ask where you were in your truck."

He never took his eyes from mine, not as if he wanted to convince me of the truth of his words, but as if he wanted to read what was in my head. "Up the mountain."

"Anyone with you?"

"No."

"You have no one to corroborate your whereabouts, no one who could testify you weren't at your office this afternoon?"

"My office? What were you doing . . . ? What the hell is going on?" His arms dropped to his sides, and he shifted his glare to Paycik. "What's going on, Mike? Were you two at my office?"

"Yeah."

"Why?"

Mike mounted the first step and put one foot up on the second. "I had a call from Mona. She asked us to meet her there. She—"

"Mona . . ."

"She's dead, Tom. Murdered, looks like. In your office."

"Tamantha?" It was barely a whisper through lips almost blue against skin gone gray under his tan.

"She wasn't there," I said.

He pulled in an audible breath, then closed his eyes.

When he moved, it was so sudden, both Mike and I stayed rooted as he grabbed a ring of keys off a hook inside the door and plunged down the steps toward his truck.

"Tom!" Mike shouted. "What are you doing? You can't run."

With less ground to cover, I beat Burrell to the truck and stood in front of the door.

"Burrell, listen." He shoved me out of the way and opened the door. "They'll be on you before you're halfway to town."

With one hand on the top of the door frame and the other on the roof of the truck, he stopped, staring straight ahead.

I kept talking. "It'll only make you look more guilty. That won't help Tamantha."

His head dropped forward, hanging between his spread arms like a figure on the cross. I reached to touch him, almost afraid of what I'd feel.

The skin of his forearm was very warm, very human.

"Shit." The single, explosive curse ripped any image of saintliness, and almost startled a nervous laugh out of me.

Burrell didn't notice. He was on the move again. Slamming the truck door, striding past me, then Mike, up the stairs and inside.

Exchanging a look, Mike and I followed.

Burrell let the dial of an old rotary phone pivot back in place after dialing a final number, then waited, staring out the back window, giving no sign of awareness of Mike or me.

Tires rattled across the wooden bridge, and I thought Burrell's hand would crush the sturdy black plastic of the old-fashioned receiver.

Mike squinted outside. "It's the van," he said. "Diana."

"Our camerawoman," I added.

Burrell flicked a look at me that might have raised blisters if it had lasted more than a second, but his voice was absolutely calm as he spoke into the phone, asking for James Longbaugh. His lawyer, I knew from the clips.

Diana parked beside Mike's vehicle.

"James? Tom Burrell. Listen, Mona's been killed. Listen, dammit, I don't have much time. Some people found her and they came and told me. The sheriff's on his way . . . Yeah, I expect so . . . No. That doesn't matter. I want you to get Tamantha. Right now. Get her to my sister in Red Lodge. Do it yourself. Tell Jean-Marie what happened. Will you do that?"

Red lights strobed through the trees as more vehicles turned to cross the bridge. Burrell blinked at them, and the tension in his face eased.

Diana came out of the van, already shooting video of the cars, then shifted to the house's open doorway.

"Thanks, James . . . . Yeah, I expect I'll be there waiting."

He hung up as the first vehicle pulled in crossways to block the truck and Mike's four-wheel drive. Burrell passed us in the doorway and started down the steps. A deputy I didn't recognize crouched behind his car, with a rifle aimed across the hood. Richard Alvaro, followed by Widcuff, stepped into the open.

"Stop that damn camera," Widcuff shouted at Diana.

She ignored him.

Widcuff shot a glare toward Mike and me before addressing Burrell. "Since you've already got the news, there's no use trying to ask you questions here, so I'm placing you under arrest—" his voice resonated with officialdom, "—Thomas David Burrell for the murder of your ex-wife, Mona Burrell. Put the cuffs on him, Alvaro."

Burrell placed his hands behind his back and turned to make the job easier. Impassively, he stared straight ahead until the locks clicked home and Alvaro put a hand on his arm to lead him away. Then Burrell looked up and said with something near a smile, "Thanks for the warning."

Widcuff glared at us as he followed Burrell and Alvaro.

"Sheriff! One question. How'd you know Tom Burrell and Foster

Redus had a fight here?"

"Anonymous tip." He'd answered automatically, snapping his mouth closed too late. "That's all I'm saying."

All the while, Diana and her camera followed the action.

"Was he going to run or was he just trying to get to Tamantha?" Mike asked as the sheriff's department vehicles headed out.

"The hell if I know."

"YOU'RE SUSPENDED. All three of you. One week, no pay." Like many weak men, Les Haeburn stated every position with absolute certainty.

"Don't you want to see the video of Tom Burrell being arrested?"

"No. It might be interesting footage—"

"*Interesting?*"

"—but you got it by interfering with an investigation. This station will not stoop to such levels."

Especially not when it would irk Thurston Fine's good ol' boy network.

"Unless you want the suspension to become permanent, you will go directly to the sheriff's department office from here and answer all questions you are asked. You'll be lucky if Sheriff Widcuff is too busy to lock you up."

I felt the instinctive journalist's aversion to answering *all* questions shudder through my bones. Or perhaps it was journalists who'd gone to the great news conference in the sky rolling over in their grave.

"One week. Without pay." Haeburn appeared to be running out of steam. "While I take up this matter with the general manager and owners."

The smirk that had stretched Fine's mouth since Mike, Diana and I stepped into Haeburn's office dipped.

It was a measure of the magnitude of this story that both Haeburn and Fine had come into the office on a Saturday night, especially since both had been at the barbecue with the political movers and shakers.

No doubt Fine had wanted us fired, perhaps tarred and feathered, without consulting the higher-ups who might be swayed by such issues as the incredibly hot stuff still in Diana's camera.

Or maybe not still in Diana's camera. With luck, the technician Diana trusted had retrieved it and started copying it as she'd instructed during our slight detour on the way to Haeburn's office.

There'd been no doubt Widcuff would call Fine to complain about us, and that Fine would go to Haeburn. We'd hoped to get to KWMT before Haeburn. When we saw his four-wheel drive and Fine's red sedan there, the only question was protecting the footage, in case someone got, shall we say, overzealous.

I wished I could have protected Mike and Diana, too, since I'd led them to the Circle B. "Les, don't take it out on them. I'm the one who made the decision, so—"

Fine interrupted. "You've been so busy trying to prove you're hot shit—"

"I make my own decisions." Mike leaned past my shoulder, the better to fire his indignation at Fine. "And . . . . What the *hell?* What happened to your head, Elizabeth?"

"It's a long story. I'll tell you later."

Haeburn said, "She got herself attacked here in the station."

"Attacked?" Mike repeated.

"I didn't invite the attacker in, you know, Les."

"You might as well have."

"Hey, that's not fair. If you want to ask anybody about that episode in the library, ask Thurston. He *happens* to drop by and not an hour later, somebody's bashing me on the head. Quite a coinci—"

"*Me?*" Thurston recoiled with both palms to his chest. "You're accusing *me?*"

The red in Haeburn face ratcheted up another notch to neon. "You can't go making wild accusations like that. If I didn't have orders—"

My radar for secrets flared to life. "Orders? What do you mean orders?"

"Who attacked you? What the hell happened?" Paycik demanded.

"They can screw their orders," Haeburn shouted over all other voices. "I don't care. I'm saying it now. You're all suspended! Without pay!"

While I came up with no answers to who *they* might be, and what orders Haeburn was in the process of screwing, Fine, Paycik and Haeburn bellowed in a testosterone trio that, finally, Diana's mother-of-two voice cut through.

"You can't suspend me without pay."

"I most certainly can," spluttered Haeburn, his sunken cheeks mottling from neon to magenta.

"No, you can't," Diana repeated calmly. "That form you signed before we left O'Hara Hill was authorization for me to take vacation time next week."

Chapter Twenty-Five

I FELT ASHAMED.

Snagged by a formidable little girl, irked by a competitive colleague, tempted by Paycik's flattery, and yes, craving a distraction from my limbo, I had meandered into this investigation, taking individual steps seriously enough but acting as if the end result was vaguely frivolous.

Perhaps worst of all, I'd used it like a training program to get my investigating skills back in shape. A challenge to shake off the mothballs of the past months of brain fog and the past years of forty-second sound-bite reporting of political maneuvering. I'd had twinges, talking to Tom Burrell and the Johnsons, but it had taken Mona's death to slap me across the face. I was ashamed I hadn't treated it as deadly serious all along.

As a number of religions know, guilt can be a great motivator.

It can also outshout self-centered whispers about an unknown *they*, their mysterious *orders*, and other anomalies of E.M. Danniher's career at KWMT. That mystery would have to wait.

We'd spent three hours at the sheriff's office answering questions. There are only so many ways you can say you touched nothing except the door handle and you didn't tell Tom Burrell any specifics. That didn't mollify them much. They were peeved we had left the scene and even more peeved we'd gotten to Burrell first. But, after a lot of blustering, repetition and bad coffee, Widcuff cut us loose.

Mike and I set up headquarters in my small living room, trying to work through the implications of Mona's death, aided by legal pads, coffee, cola, chips and salsa—mild for me, make-your-ears-sweat hot for him.

He left close to two and was back by eight the next morning. It wasn't enough sleep to rid me of my headache or stiff neck, but it was plenty of time for the bruise on my temple to blossom into gaudy color.

"Do you know you have a dog in your back yard?" he asked as he came in.

Great. I fed and watered him, and the dog showed himself only to visitors. "No I don't," I'd grumbled. And Mike hadn't argued. The guy definitely had some smarts.

Punctuated by phone calls, we'd been at it for nearly five hours, and we were beginning to go in circles.

Mike walked back in from the kitchen. He'd made a pit stop, with a detour to the kitchen for a couple phone calls, one to let his Aunt Gee know where we were in case she discovered anything, the second one to Diana.

Getting her week's vacation lined up had been the small chore Diana had done before heading to Burrell's ranch. With two kids to feed, she'd figured it was a necessary backup.

"How is she?" I asked.

"Great. She's planning to paint a couple rooms and put up a new storm door this week. That woman's amazing."

"Because she knows how to use a paint brush and a screw driver?"

"No, because she sounds as if she's looking forward to it."

We grinned at each other. "Any news from the station?"

"Yeah, Diana said Billy, her technician friend, made two copies. He's got one squirreled away and gave her the other. Apparently he made them in the nick of time, because Thurston commandeered the camera and managed to ruin most of the original—purposely or through ineptitude, nobody seems to know."

With the copies safe I didn't spare more than a grunt for Fine.

"Okay, where were we?" Mike settled into his corner of the couch.

"Mona's murder."

Mike paled—he wouldn't forget what he'd seen in that trailer any time soon—but he nodded. "Doesn't this narrow our list of suspects?"

"Who would you knock off?" I winced. "No pun intended."

He waved that off. "I'd say this eliminates Gina, Widcuff and the Johnsons. I can see their motives for killing Redus—scorned and discarded wife, boss trying to hold off an ambitious subordinate, revenge-bent family—but how would they apply to Mona?"

"Same way Burrell's motives do—he killed Foster to protect his daughter, then killed Mona because she was a threat to his being caught. She could be just as much a threat to anyone else if they killed Redus."

I swept crumbs off a legal pad and consulted a list made the night before. "We still have the Johnsons for revenge, Gina for revenge, Widcuff to get rid of a rival and Judge Claustel to either keep his son's homosexuality quiet or possibly to get rid of a blackmailer."

"Okay, if motive's open, and means is open since every pickup in this county has a shotgun—"

"Are you sure about the gun?"

"She was shot with a shotgun," he confirmed grimly.

I wasn't going to argue. "You know there was one pickup that should have had a shotgun but didn't."

"Redus'," Paycik agreed. "So the murderer took Redus' gun last November and held onto it all this time . . ." He tapped his pen against his chin. "Actually, it wouldn't have been that risky, because there are enough shotguns around that it wouldn't stand out."

"So even people who don't own shotguns can't be eliminated because anyone who killed Redus could have used his shotgun to kill Mona."

"And that brings us to opportunity." Paycik took the legal pad off my knees and flipped over several pages.

"Gina," he read. "Says she was returning to O'Hara Hill from shopping in Sherman. She'd go right past the trailer.

"Roger Johnson. Says he was talking to a rancher near Cody about his overdue fuel oil account. The rancher confirms Johnson was there, but is vague about the time, and Johnson could have easily gone by the trailer.

"Myrna Johnson. Says she was cleaning house. No witnesses. She could have taken back roads and not been seen.

"Sheriff Widcuff." Paycik was pleased with himself for calling Widcuff and asking where he'd been when he heard the news about Mona. Widcuff had answered before a voice in the background, identifiable as Thurston Fine's, demanded to know what was going on. He'd been in Widcuff's office doing an "exclusive" and sounded as if he was about to burst a blood vessel when he realized who had interrupted. "Says he was driving back to Sherman from O'Hara Hill, where he'd been attending a public meeting on expanding the substation, and heard the news over his radio. His attendance at the meeting, which also included Judge Claustel, County Attorney Hunt, two county supervisors, three ministers, our esteemed news director and anchor, along with fifty some citizens, was captured on video by KWMT's own Diana Stendahl."

He took a bite out of a donut from the box he'd brought this morning.

"Not only did she have the presence of mind to get Haeburn to sign before coming to Burrell's, but she actually had the form in her van. I'll tell you, that woman is frightening." Haeburn and Fine had stuck around after the meeting officially ended to have Diana shoot promo stuff with them looking involved in the community. "Anyway, Widcuff's departure from O'Hara Hill, confirmed by Aunt Gee as well as Diana, would have given him time to reach the trailer, shoot Mona and get out of there before we arrived."

"It would have been awfully close." We'd gone over these calculations.

"Only if he stuck to the speed limit," Paycik said. "And he doesn't."

I spread my hands, palms up, in acquiescence, and he went on. "Judge Claustel. Same as Sheriff Widcuff."

"Except both would have run the risk of being seen by the other or anyone else coming from O'Hara Hill."

"The road curves around the base of Jelicho Mountain just before the turnoff to the trailer, so unless someone's right behind you, they wouldn't see you turn. They could have parked in back."

Something about that didn't set right, but I couldn't pinpoint it.

"Brent Hanley," Mike continued. "Says he was fishing. Alone. On Jelicho River, about five miles from the trailer."

That was new. "When did you talk to him?"

"This morning. He was as charming as ever. And kids on the track team say Hanley's beat up two kids who made comments about Rog possibly being gay. Hanley has a mean temper."

"Don't I know it." I could still hear the sound of that shot put passing through my air space.

"Plus, he admits to being in the vicinity of the trailer."

"*Everyone* was. My God, there should have been a traffic jam. With all those pickups, it should have looked like an old TV commercial with Bob Seger singing 'like a rock.' And none of them has an alibi worth even trying to crack, and that includes Burrell."

Irritation had driven me upright, but now I flopped back.

Paycik waited a couple seconds, as if to make sure I'd finished. "Okay, let's listen to the tape again."

I groaned. I'd heard Mona's voice in my dreams. I almost wished Paycik hadn't thought to copy it before handing over the original to the police.

He played it again. And again.

"*Mike? Mike Paycik?*"

"*Yes. Who's this?*"

"*Mona Burrell. I want to talk to you. You're still doing this reporting stuff on Foster being murdered, aren't you?*"

"*Elizabeth Danniher and I are looking into the story, yes.*"

"*Yeah, you and her. Well, I might have something to tell you before I go. There's something—well, I didn't get it right off. Not 'til they found Foster, but then it made sense. I thought I could . . . . But Foster thought that, too. Maybe this is better. I can still get something. It doesn't mean I can't. But this'll be my cushion. Like some insurance, you know?*"

"*What are you talking about, Mona? If there's something you want to tell me—*"

"*I'll tell you . . . I'll tell you, but not on the phone. Not now. Meet me at Tom's office. I gotta get something. It's the trailer, you know? Out Yellowstone*"

Street. You know where it is?"

"Sure. I know it."

"Okay. Meet me there. One hour."

"Okay. But, Mona, tell me what——"

Click.

"She knew something," Mike said. "That part about not getting it until Foster's body was found, but then it making sense. She had to know something."

"Or think she did. But even if she knew something for sure, we have no idea what. So we're right back where we were before Mona's death. Except . . ." I slid down until the small of my back rested on the seat cushion, despite my mother's voice echoing in my head with predictions of permanent spine injuries. "Mona was talking around town that she was getting out of here and taking Tamantha with her, and that gives Burrell another motive."

"As if the guy didn't have enough pointing to him." Paycik leaned forward, resting his elbows on his knees. "And it doesn't even seem like he's fighting for himself. Before all this, I would have said Tom Burrell was the hardest fighter I ever knew. I would have thought he wouldn't ever give up, if only for Tamantha's sake, because he wouldn't want her to have a killer for a father."

I sat up so abruptly I knocked the legal pad off the couch on one side and a depleted bag of chips on the other. "For Tamantha's sake. Of course . . . . C'mon, Paycik." I piled the pad and chips on the coffee table and tossed an extra pen into my purse. "We have places to go, people to see."

"Where are we going, Elizabeth?" he asked as I herded him out.

"To jail. Directly to jail. Do not pass Go, do not collect two hundred dollars."

But maybe we'd collect some answers.

Chapter Twenty-Six

BURRELL'S LAWYER HADN'T liked the idea of his client talking to the media, but he'd agreed to ask. The word came back "yes."

Mike had been patient while we waited for the lawyer to arrive to make sure his client didn't say anything incriminating to the media. He'd even put up with the lawyer's suspicious questions about hidden microphones.

I was the one pacing.

The lawyer, James Longbaugh, glared at me and rubbed his temples as I passed for the third time.

Mike, seated opposite the lawyer at the rectangular table in the center of the bare room, said "What makes you think he'll tell us anything now when he wouldn't before?"

The creak of the door opening provided instrumentation for the last part of his speech, and I spun around to face Thomas David Burrell, handcuffed and accompanied by a thin, balding deputy. The deputy muttered something apologetic about not taking off the handcuffs, attached in front this time, and being right outside the door, then left Burrell standing just inside the door, watching me.

I broke the silence, answering Mike by addressing Burrell. "Because there's no reason now not to tell us everything. Is there, Tom?"

He looked like a man who'd come through a terrible storm—exhausted, battered by forces greater them himself, but relieved. "No, there's no reason not to tell you everything now."

Without releasing my look, he took two steps to the empty chair near where I stood and pulled it back. I sat. His handcuffs clinked as he pushed the chair in. He went around the table and sat across from me and next to his lawyer.

"Ask your questions, E.M. Danniher."

"Let's start with an easy one. Why do you think Mona was at your office?"

One side of his mouth lifted slightly. "You want my thoughts, or the sheriff's theory that she went there expressly to be killed by me?"

"Your thoughts."

"Passports."

"Tom! Don't say anymo—"

Burrell stopped his lawyer's protest by raising one large hand, palm out. "It's like she said, James. There's no longer any reason not to tell everything."

"Even though it gives you a stronger motive?" I asked.

"You're a little late there, E.M. Danniher. The sheriff's already added that motive to his collection." This time both sides of his mouth lifted. "There's not a soul who passes through Sherman Supermarket who doesn't know Mona'd made noises about leaving town and taking Tamantha. And Widcuff tells me the passports were out of the office safe."

I nodded. "Okay. What was your real reason for telling Redus to stay away from Mona and Tamantha?"

"Tamantha saw Redus hit Mona. He'd told them both he'd beat Tamantha if she told anyone, but she told me. I tried to get Mona to press charges, but she wouldn't. He'd done it before, but she said he'd promised not to hit her again, and she swore she'd never let him hurt Tamantha. I told Mona if she kept seeing Redus, I'd go for sole custody, and I'd use his abuse as cause."

"Tom, I don't think—"

Burrell waved off the lawyer. He already knew he was describing a stronger motive for murder than any the sheriff's department had so far.

"So, Mona told Redus, and he came to your ranch to confront you."

He confirmed my supposition with a nod. "I'd counted on that. I told him to his face what I thought of a man who beat on a woman and threatened a child. That's when he swung. Everything else happened the way I said."

"And when Redus disappeared, you thought Mona had made good on her oath not to let him hurt Tamantha."

"Mona?" The shocked word came from Mike on my left, and I heard a sound from the lawyer.

Burrell met my look and nodded. "Tamantha let it slip the next day that her mother had been gone several hours that night. But after it came out that Redus was missing, I couldn't get her to talk about it. Not about that night or Redus or any of it. Mona must have told her not to talk about it, and Tamantha was being loyal to her mother. It was the only way it figured."

"And you thought that meant Mona had killed Redus." I watched him closely as I added, "But it could also figure that Mona was busy accusing you of involvement in Redus' disappearance, and it was loyalty to her father, not her mother, that kept Tamantha quiet."

He didn't look startled at the thought. I wondered if it had occurred to him before Mona's murder, or if a night in jail had done the trick.

"Maybe." His tone implied he meant to find out.

If Tamantha decided she didn't want to tell him, I would buy a ticket to that battle of wills.

"Why didn't you tell the authorities you thought Mona killed Redus?" demanded Longbaugh. "Or me, when you were charged last winter?"

Tom flicked a look at the lawyer, not quite apologetic. "I didn't have proof."

"You had this information about Redus abusing Mona, and his threats."

"I didn't know Redus hadn't just lit out for bright lights somewhere. He talked about it often enough. Besides . . ." For the first time, his eyes dropped, apparently focusing on his folded and handcuffed hands.

"Besides," I picked up, "you didn't want your daughter's mother convicted of murder."

Silence confirmed my words.

"But what if you'd been convicted?" objected Mike.

"I couldn't see how they could convict me as long as they didn't have a body. When they found him . . ." He shifted, and I figured that was probably as close to an admission as we'd get that Tom had wondered if he'd made the right decision.

"Did you have any other reason for thinking Mona might have been involved in Redus' disappearance?" I asked.

"Yes." Something too dry to be called a grin tugged at Burrell's mouth. "Why don't you just say it, E.M. Danniher? This isn't *Jeopardy*, you don't have to make everything a question."

"Okay. Redus' disappearance so soon after he'd had a fight with you seemed to point to your involvement. Presuming you weren't involved, it was either planned that way or a very convenient coincidence. Convenient coincidences aside for the moment, to plan it someone had to know Redus was going to confront you, and probably know why."

"That's how I figured it," Burrell confirmed.

"You didn't tell anybody about Redus hitting Mona?"

"No."

"Who could Mona have told?"

He sat still and calm, returning my look with his dark eyes knowing, slightly sad, but understanding. It could have been simply a smart move on his part to pick up on my theory and indicate it had been his motive all along. Someone who murdered two people sure wouldn't balk at a little opportunism.

Did I think the man looking back at me could have done that? I didn't know, did I?

"I don't know who Mona could have told," he said. "I have wondered."

"Have you asked Tamantha?"

"No." His full-force glower returned. "And I don't want you asking—"

"Don't tell me not to ask questions, Burrell." I met his look. After a few seconds, the hardness in his eyes eased slightly. "I won't scare her," I promised, trying to keep the thought that I probably couldn't scare Tamantha Burrell from showing. Maybe he saw it anyhow, because his eyes lightened.

"I'd like to see you try," he murmured.

Chapter Twenty-Seven

WE DROVE NORTH to Red Lodge, Montana directly from the jail. Longbaugh had promised to call Tom's sister and let her know it was okay for us to talk to Tamantha.

"My daddy's in jail," Tamantha accused as soon as she saw me. "You're supposed to help him."

"I'm trying. But for me to help him, I need you to tell me some things, Tamantha."

In small increments, I took her back over the day Redus disappeared—almost surely the day he'd died.

Redus had hit Mona on Sunday after she'd interrupted him watching football on TV. That's when she'd told him what Tom had said.

In a monotone Tamantha told how Redus said he had a friend who'd make sure Burrell didn't bother him. Tamantha hadn't heard—or Redus hadn't said—who this friend was or what he would do.

Tamantha also said Mona had stayed home all that Monday, preparing a special dinner for Redus. When he didn't come by five-fifteen, Mona left, presumably looking for him. Tamantha didn't know when her mother returned, because she had put herself to bed and went to sleep.

She didn't know if her mother had told anyone else about being hit.

Tamantha sat straight on the chintz-covered sofa in a glass-enclosed porch, her eyes solemn and intelligent. She shed no tears in our presence, though her aunt had said Tamantha knew of her mother's death.

As we rose to leave, Tamantha tugged at my hand. After exchanging a glance with Mike, I sat, and he maneuvered the aunt out of the room.

Tamantha's hand turned in mine, clasping it.

"My Daddy needs me." The end of the sentence lifted slightly into a question. She turned to look at me. "I want to be with my Daddy."

My throat tightened. "I know you do. He wants to be with you, too."

She studied me a moment longer, then nodded. She released my hand, and I joined Mike in farewells with Jean-Marie Burrell Watson.

Tamantha had given no orders this time. She'd asked for no pledges. But I felt her expectations and hopes more heavily than ever.

Mike and I mulled over what she'd told us as we started back toward Sherman. Mona could have spoken to someone on the phone that day, telling them about the situation with Burrell and Redus, but no one had come forward with that tidbit in the intervening months. A better bet was that Redus, who'd spent the day out and about, had contacted his "connection," which gave him the confidence to confront Burrell.

Unless all this was a smokescreen thrown up by a very clever man who knew there was no sense trying to hide what was already in the open. Burrell could have knocked Redus unconscious in that famous fight, driven him up Three-Day Pass Road in Redus' truck, arranged his victim, cracked him on the head with the butt of the shotgun, then pushed the truck off the edge, and walked home, carrying Redus' shotgun in case it came in handy later.

I shivered.

"Turn right, Paycik."

"What? Why?"

"Turn right. We're stopping in O'Hara Hill."

"MRS. PARENS, IS TOM BURRELL capable of murder?"

She shook her head and gave me that teacher look that said she was shaking her head not in answer to my question, but at my asking it.

"Elizabeth Margaret—" My spine automatically straightened. Paycik had stayed in the car, probably to avoid that tone. "—I'm surprised at you."

"I didn't mean to put you on the spot, I—"

"I am not on the spot. I could give you an answer from my observation of Thomas David." Her eyes narrowed. "Indeed, also of Gina and Roger and Myrna Johnson. But my answer would be worthless. It is not possible to look fully into another human heart. Perhaps after years of a certain type of friendship or marriage one can see a great deal, but even then there are shadows of secrets. There must be. And I believe that is what you fear, Elizabeth Margaret."

"I don't fear—"

"Yes, you do," she cut me off neatly. "We all do. You fear that the truth you seek might not be a truth you like."

For someone who'd said it wasn't possible to look fully into another human heart, she'd done an uncomfortably creditable job with a new acquaintance.

I didn't know if Thomas David Burrell was innocent. I wanted him to be. For Tamantha. For himself. Yes, and maybe a little for myself. There was something . . .

But I didn't know. And I needed to.

Or did Mrs. Parens mean other shadows? Fears beyond this case?

Shadows of secrets left despite years of a marriage? Yes, I knew about those. How could they not make me question my judgment? How could they not make me mistrust what I thought I knew—or thought I wanted?

The case. That's what mattered. That's where I had to keep my thoughts.

"What if he did it?" I said bluntly. "What about Tamantha?"

"We cannot know how Tamantha's life might unfold. But consider if Tamantha never knows the identity of her mother's killer and if a portion of her community believes her father was responsible. Would knowing a horrible truth be worse than never knowing?"

"So you're saying a bad answer's better than no answer at all?"

"On some tests it is preferable. For all concerned."

THE PHONE WOKE ME Monday morning. I don't know why I bother to own an alarm clock.

I do, however, know why I own an answering machine.

It was to capture calls such as the one that had awaited me last night. My parents and assorted family had been together for Sunday dinner and decided to call. I listened to voices coming on one by one to say hello, to the instructions and remonstrations and laughter in the background. I listened to it twice. It was too late to call back, nearly midnight in Illinois. I listened a third time.

The answering machine was also for such early-morning calls as this.

I stayed in bed and listened to my recorded voice telling the caller what it could do, though in much politer terms than I was feeling at the moment.

The beep beeped, and I waited.

Until I heard Mel's voice, I didn't realize I'd expected it to be Mike, informing me he was on his way.

"Danny, are you there? I know you monitor this thing, you antisocial hermit you." When I'd gone three weeks without answering the machine at the cottage in January, he'd come in person. That's when he'd told me I had to work out the rest of my contract in Sherman. "It's Mel. Are you there? No? Well, call me back. I need to talk to you. I know you could use a bit of good news, with no income right now, and this is good, kid."

I had a fair idea of what Mel might view as good. Sorting out what I would consider good was beyond me. I pulled the pillow over my head and went back to sleep.

When the phone rang the next time, I was ready to get up. I caught it on the second ring, answering with a hello muddled by a stretch.

Remembering Mel's call now that I was awake, I paused in mid-stretch. Wait a minute, how had he known I didn't have any income right now? I hadn't told him or any of the rest of my family about being suspended without pay. So how did he know about what was happening at KWMT?

"Ms. Danniher?"

The rushed woman's voice pulled me back to the present call. Mel, what he knew and what he shouldn't know got bumped from the lineup as long as murder was the lead story. "Yes."

"This is Myrna Johnson. Can we meet somewhere?"

I swallowed, pushing down the memory of Mona's call to Mike. "Where?"

Chapter Twenty-Eight

MYRNA JOHNSON CHOSE a pull-off overlook on Highway 27A along the Jelicho River as it rushed to meet up to the south with the Snake River.

Locals wouldn't have any reason to stop this close to town, and a hillock obscured parked cars from the road. So it was a considerably more private meeting than our talk in the park.

A blue pickup with Idaho plates was parked to one side of the gravel area, and I saw a young couple with a toddler at a picnic table near the water. As I pulled in, Myrna got out of a white Chevy and started walking toward me.

Her hands were empty.

I felt a little stupid noticing that, considering this was the woman who looked like Mrs. Claus' younger sister. But I'd rather feel a little stupid than a lot dead.

Whoever had killed Redus apparently had felt vulnerable enough to not let Mona keep living, so who was to say the same logic might not apply to me?

Myrna met me near a wooden sign explaining the geological significance of the striations in the wind-scoured cliffs across the river. She didn't glance at the sign or the cliffs. A path wound down to a rock bench at the water's edge.

I mutely gestured for her to lead the way.

When we were seated, she looked straight ahead for five seconds, then turned to me. "If I tell you something, will you swear not to use it on TV?"

"I can't swear that, and I think you know that, Mrs. Johnson." I kept my tone unhurried, in contrast to her rush of words. "Why don't you just tell me what it is?"

"I checked you out—your degrees and your awards. What I can't find out is if you are a compassionate woman, Ms. Danniher."

"Compassion only comes after the fact, it can't be dispensed beforehand. I'll tell you this, though, I do my damnedest to deliver what the public needs to know and what's necessary to see that justice is done. What the public might think it wants to know doesn't interest me much."

She turned away, facing the water and cliffs, back straight, head tilted as if examining the ragged silhouette against the blue sky. "I want you to understand." When I said nothing, she faced me. "About my husband. He told me what he said to you after they found Deputy Redus. That he—that we're both relieved—to know Redus is gone from this town for good."

Relieved and *gone from this town* were definitely understatements, but I wouldn't haggle over word choices.

"Yes, he made that feeling clear."

She winced. "You think we're vicious people for being glad of another human's death, don't you? I don't suppose you've ever hated the way we have. Not unless you've had a child die."

I couldn't argue with her there. I *could* question. "But why do you and your husband blame Redus for Rog's death? There's no question about it being suicide, is there?"

She drew in a breath on a faint rattling sound, and her eyes hazed over. "No, there's no question." And I remembered she had found her son.

"Rog hung himself in our shed. My husband took that shed apart with his bare hands. Board by board. Ripped them free and burned them. Then he stood out by that fire all night after the last spark was gone. I'm just glad I'm the one who found Rog."

I tried to come at the issue another way. Matt's information had provided a number of answers, but not all of them. Myrna Johnson, with her knowledge of the county and its people, might provide more answers. If I could get her past this huge hurdle. "Do you know specifically what about being arrested would have caused Rog to kill himself?"

She shook her head. I didn't believe her. "There was something odd about that whole night. Disorderly conduct," she said scornfully. "That wasn't Rog. And why wasn't Frank arrested?"

"That's a good question. Why do you think Frank wasn't arrested?"

She hovered at the edge, then retreated. "I don't know."

But she did. And so did I. Frank Claustel wasn't arrested because his father was Ambrose Claustel. What I didn't know was if Redus let Frank go in hopes of future favors from the judge, or for something more concrete.

"Did you ever ask Frank Claustel about that night?"

"I haven't seen or talked to Frank since he picked up Rog to go to the movies in Cody that night." I must have shown my surprise. She smiled, more sadly than bitterly. "The Judge sent Frank off to Europe the day Rog died. He didn't even come to the funeral. Just a big wreath from the Judge. Not a call, not a visit. Just those damned lilies. Frank went off to Europe, finished up his classes by correspondence we were told, and then to college. Rog isn't going anywhere."

She sucked air in through her teeth, letting it out slowly.

"Do you know anything about Frank's activities at college, Mrs. Johnson?"

"No."

I told her what Matt Lester had told me about Frank editing the gay newsletter. She flicked one look at me, then stared straight ahead. When I finished, there was silence.

"You knew your son was gay, didn't you, Mrs. Johnson?"

For a moment neither of us breathed.

"I knew he was worried about it." She shifted against the stone. "He never said anything to me, but I knew him. And I saw him with Frank. It wasn't . . . it wasn't like I was used to." She shook her head at the inadequacies of language. "I suppose the idea of a boy killing himself over being a homosexual seems strange to you, but it's different around here. The expectations are . . . different." She drew in a shaky breath. "At least the fear of the expectations is."

"Mrs. Johnson, with what we've found out about Redus, it would fit if he tried to blackmail Rog, or you and Mr. Johnson."

"I don't know. I mean, I know he never came to Roger or me, but Rog . . . I don't know." She clasped her hands. "Do you think that's why . . .?"

I could only echo her answer. "I don't know. You'd know better than anyone. Some kids from the high school said Redus would roust them and their girlfriends out of parked cars. If Redus came across Rog and Frank—" She flinched. "—he could have tried to use that information. Especially if he thought their parents would pay—one way or another—for his silence."

"Rog was trying to protect us?" She put her hand over her mouth, but I could make out the words. "Oh, God, Rog was trying to protect *us*."

"The only way you can help him now, Mrs. Johnson, is to help me find the truth. Tell me what you know about Judge Claustel and Foster Redus."

She was shaking her head before I finished. "I don't know anything."

"But Frank and Rog—"

"Were good friends. That's all. And that's all I'll tell you." She'd retreated. Back to where we'd started.

She stood, and so did I.

"How about justice, Mrs. Johnson? Don't you care about justice?" She started to walk away. "Mrs. Johnson, was Rog right? Would you and his father have been ashamed?"

"I don't know. I just don't know." Her head came up, and she met my eyes. "I would have fought for Rog if he'd let me. No matter what. But that's not how it is now. Now I only have my husband to fight for, and I won't let anything hurt him. Rog gave his life for that, if I have to give up justice in order to protect my husband, then I'll give up justice."

Chapter Twenty-Nine

"I WISH YOU were the murderer." I flipped the legal pad to the coffee table. It held only doodles. "It would simplify my life considerably."

Mike Paycik, slumped so low on my couch that his very nice butt barely clung to the seat cushion and his legs stretched halfway to the kitchen door, did not look particularly willing to simplify my life. We'd been talking in circles for two hours.

"You just want me to be the murderer because you know I want to ask you out. And if I'm in jail, I can't. That would make your life simpler, wouldn't it?"

Oh, shit.

Had I known? I didn't know any more because now I *did* know and it colored my view of everything I'd thought before. If I had sensed something beyond ambition and professional regard, wasn't it telling that I hadn't let it come to the surface? God knows I could use some ego boosters, yet had something in me held off the recognition?

And what did it say about my frame of mind that I considered having a funny, intelligent, hot guy, ten years younger asking me out an *oh, shit?*

If that didn't make it clear I wasn't ready for this, I don't know what could.

"Mike, I could give you the bad-to-mix-professional-and-personal speech, and after my experience I'd mean every damned word of it. But the truth is, it's more than that. I don't know where my life is going right now. I don't know where my career is going. Until I get those things straight, I couldn't even think about—what's so funny?"

"Sorry, Elizabeth. It's just that I've given that speech so many times. First it was because I was building my football career, and then the need to stay on top. No time to even consider a serious relationship. Then my knees went, and the speech changed to needing to put everything into figuring out what I was going to do in the next phase of my life." His smile faded. "It's strange to be on the other end of it."

I didn't know what to say.

"I'll give you time, Elizabeth. But I won't give up. That's one of the things you don't know about me . . . yet." He looked at me intently a long moment. Abruptly, he sat up. "Okay, so . . . I still think the Johnsons are the most likely candidates."

He'd been saying that with some regularity since I'd reported on my meeting with Myrna Johnson, as per our agreement. With only slightly less regularity, he'd been saying I'd been damn stupid to meet her alone.

"Everybody had the means and opportunity to kill Redus," he added, "but the Johnsons have the strongest motive—wanting revenge on the man they blame for their son's death. Otherwise, why would Myrna clam up on you?"

"Because if Claustel killed Redus to keep him quiet, *why* Claustel wanted him quiet would be sure to come out, and then the secret Rog died for would come out. She couldn't stand that. Besides, can you see one or both of them shooting Mona in the face with a shotgun?"

"Self-preservation is a powerful motivator," Paycik said.

"Yeah, but—" I started, also not for the first time, when a knock at the front door interrupted me.

It was Jenny, the assistant from KWMT.

"Hi. I thought you might want the stuff from your inbox at the station. It's just awful what they're doing to you. Hey, Mike. Everybody's up in arms. Well, not everybody. They know Thurston's just scared of you. Because you have so much more experience . . ." She looked in my general direction for a split second as her gaze bounced around my living room with the speed, intensity and randomness of a strobe. ". . . and because you . . ." A nanosecond of attention to Paycik. ". . . are an up-and-comer, and he's afraid you'll get to a Top Ten market before him, as if he has a chance," she added with a snort.

"And, of course, everybody knows Haeburn is pissed as hell that the owners said he had to take you . . ." A glance at me again. ". . . and even more pissed that he's been told to give you a free rein."

"What do you mean—"

If I'd ever had her attention, it was gone now. "Hey, neat set-up," she squealed as she spotted computer components huddled on the big walnut desk in one corner of the living room. "But you don't have it plugged in. Here . . ." I'd trailed her across the living room, and now she capitalized on my proximity by dumping two fat manila envelopes into my arms. She turned with relish to the computer. "Your cords look like spaghetti."

"That's why it's not plugged in," I muttered, tossing the envelope with his name on it in Paycik's general direction. "The laptop does what I've needed."

From the way she was slinging cords, plugs and steel gray rectangles, Jenny had trained on Bill Gates' assembly line.

"What do you mean, Haeburn's been told to give me free rein?" My ex had finagled to have my contract assigned to KWMT as the smallest speck on the map he could find, so there was no way he would have lobbied for me to be given freedom. "Who told him that?"

"Mmm. Heathertons, I guess. Here, hold this." I took the disentangled cord she handed me. "Or maybe Craig Morningside."

The Heathertons owned the station. Or, more accurately, their matriarch, Val Heatherton, owned it. I'd never met them. "Who's Craig Morningside?"

"Now if I could just . . ." Jenny dove under the desk trailing a length of black electrical cord behind her like a spelunker's safety line.

"Station manager," Paycik said.

I should have known there was one lurking somewhere. Was this part of Haeburn's *they* whose rules he was flouting by suspending us?

"Son-in-law," Paycik continued elliptically as he leafed through pink message forms from his envelope. "Val gave him a cushy job to keep him out of trouble. She's the real power. She . . ." He stood, leaving all but one pink slip on the coffee table. "I'm gonna use your phone, okay?"

Not waiting for an answer, he headed for the kitchen. I started after him to ask about the station hierarchy, but just then Jenny emerged from the nether regions of the desk. "You shouldn't let these things get so dusty." She sneezed reproachfully.

"Sorry," I muttered. Too late to ask Paycik now. He was already on the phone. I tried to listen to his end of the conversation without getting in his line of sight. I was almost certain he was talking to his Aunt Gee.

"You need a surge protector. Better yet, a UPS."

"UPS?" The people in brown trucks?

"Uninterrupted Power Source." She wiped the desk with her sleeve and began arranging components. "Around here's it's a necessity. Gives you time to save everything if the power goes off. The better ones turn off your computer before the power runs out."

In the kitchen Mike was muttering, darn him. But then I heard clearly, "Damn! They just better run the right damn tests."

Then silence from the kitchen. Not so from the other end of the living room, with Jenny's continued commentary on dust, static and smudges. When she examined my keyboard, crumbs joined her litany. She was still complaining when Mike came back.

"Well?" I demanded.

"Sure, I can get it going," Jenny said, answering my question aimed at Mike.

"Uh . . . good. Thanks." I prodded Mike again with a sharp look.

"They've run through the contents of Redus' truck. All the keys fit what they should, nothing extra, nothing missing except—"

"The shotgun."

He nodded. "Widcuff has taken Tom's shotgun from the office to run tests. He's sure it was the murder weapon—as a club for Redus and shot for Mona."

"I thought shotguns couldn't be connected to a wound that way."

He shrugged. "Widcuff seems to think he can. Another thing. Widcuff has a witness who was passing the trailer when Mona drove up and got out of her car. Alone. Her Mustang was the only vehicle there. They're thinking from the position of her body and the safe being open and all, that the killer came in after she did."

Before I could chew on that for long, Jenny came up for air. "There. It should run now."

Sure enough, with the punch of a couple buttons, the familiar hum started and light flickered across the screen.

"That's great, Jenny. Thanks."

She dropped to the floor in a graceful fold and snagged the open bag of chips off the coffee table.

"No problem. Now, where was I? Oh, yeah, the Heathertons." I wondered if she was related to Penny at the supermarket—neither dust, nor cords, nor computer disarray shall turn me from my appointed rounds of gossip. "Val told Craig, and Craig told Les that you were to be given free rein. That was about three days after you were hired. Haeburn was a real thundercloud about it, and Thurston . . . You'd think somebody had taken out all his hair with tweezers!"

"I don't know Val Heatherton." Why would she bother?

"Sheila in administration says somebody had called Val. Some guy who went to school with Honey Heatherton, who was always Val's favorite."

"Did Sheila remember a name?"

"Nah, just that he was some lawyer from Chicago."

She knew nothing more, but she'd already sent my radar for secrets into alarm mode.

The lawyer I knew best in Chicago was Mel Welch, and he was family. As in Catherine Danniher had his direct number and did not hesitate to use it.

✧   ✧   ✧   ✧

THAT NIGHT I DREAMT OF SPIDERS. Spinning webs that disappeared whenever I tried to make out their pattern.

Some maddeningly motherly spiders. Some benevolent spiders with Mel's balding head. Some with big bellies. Some wearing Stetsons, along with cowboy boots on each leg. Some spinning webs like the lace doily on the tray at Gina Redus' house. Some webs catching golden sawdust that glinted in the sun for an instant before the glinting burst into something red and wet. Too heavy for the gossamer threads, dragging them down with tears of blood.

I sat up in bed, wide awake but disoriented.

The mother and Mel spiders were the most familiar.

I'd known Mel Welch since I was nine and he became my mother's cousin's oldest daughter's boyfriend. It was instant crush on my part. He showed more tolerance than most college boys would, leaving no scars. So when, in due course, he married my mother's cousin's oldest daughter—Peg by name—our relationship settled into a comfortable, trusting friendship.

That friendship had expanded recently into the professional arena as my ex-husband appropriated sole possession of the personal lawyer and the agent we'd once shared, and I had lacked any motivation to search among the usual suspects for my own.

If Mel was weaving a web that involved KWMT's owners, the chances were excellent that Catherine Danniher was behind it somewhere.

I would need to get to the bottom of that.

But not now.

Not with the bloody web of murders to deal with.

I went to the kitchen for a glass of water. It was very early. So early, the sheer curtains that screened the bottom half of the window by the small kitchen table allowed no light through. Sunset was a battle most nights, a clash that splattered the sky in red and orange, then purple and mauve. But this was an evolution, a gray-blue limbo before day pushed on.

Shivering, I accepted that I wasn't going to sleep with spider dreams lingering. In fact, I grabbed a can of bug spray and sprayed around the front and back door and around each window frame.

Still, spider webs remained on my mind as I sat down with a cup of coffee once the coffeemaker had finished its work. Like the web I'd seen in the trees that first day at Burrell's ranch, with sawdust caught in it. And the web at his office, so thoroughly sprayed with a mist of blood that it tinted the window beyond it.

Spiders don't want their webs to be seen, otherwise their prey avoid them. But every action produces a trace of some sort. Sawdust from chain-sawing. Blood from murder. And then the spider web was revealed.

But what trace would be left if someone had set up Tom Burrell? If I knew that, I might know how to find the pattern that would lead to the spider.

If there was one.

I'd just started to wrangle with that thought when sound shattered the stillness.

Chapter Thirty

MORE ACCURATELY, a brick shattered the glass in the kitchen door's window.

But I wasn't considering accuracy at that moment. I was hitting the floor.

Seeing the brick was almost a relief, because my first thought had been that it was a gunshot. Actually, that was my second thought. My first thought was a mental scream: *Duck!*

Throwing bricks might not be friendly, but the mortality statistics aren't real high. Still, it seemed the wisest course to crawl away from the source of the brick sitting amid a glitter of glass shards on the worn linoleum.

I'd nearly reached the front door, still on hands and knees, when a second brick arrived in my kitchen, this one through the window over the sink. I stood up and quietly went out the front door. The heel of my right hand was bleeding. I dug out a tissue from the pocket of the sweats I'd slept in, and wrapped it around my hand as best I could.

For some reason, the sight of my blood soaking through the ineffectual bandage made me angry. I could have—I *should* have—run to a neighbor's house and pounded on a door telling them to call the police. The fact that the only neighbor I'd talked to for more than a do-you-recognize-this-dog conversation was an elderly woman across the street who would probably die of a heart attack if awakened in such a way was not really the reason I didn't follow that path.

Quite simply, I was angry.

What right did somebody have to come hurling bricks through my windows at this ungodly hour of the morning? This rental house wasn't much, but it was mine, by God, and I was going to defend it.

I was not, however, angry enough to be completely stupid, no matter what Paycik said later.

I skirted around the side of the house, behind the row of budding lilac bushes dividing my house from my next-door neighbor's, and snagged the shovel from where I'd left it leaning against the back of the garage. I came up behind my house-attacker as he let fly a third brick, right through the window by my kitchen table. The sky was lighting rapidly, and I could plainly see the gaping hole it left and the flutter of the curtain as a draft sucked it out.

I also could see the thrower's stocky build beneath a Sherman High School letterman's jacket.

Brent Hanley was using a pile of bricks left by a previous tenant for ammunition like a kid's stack of snowballs. He reached for another rectangular missile. Holding the shovel just above the metal part, I swung the handle like Sister Mary Robert wielding a yardstick. I aimed for his forearms. He must have caught sight of the handle just before it hit because he yanked his left hand back.

The handle thudded against the padded surface of his right jacket sleeve hard enough to make him drop the brick, but the cracking against his hand was the more sickening sound.

He bellowed, "My hand! Oh, shit, my hand!"

"Get back," I shouted while he careened around, nursing his left hand in his right. "Get away from those bricks." I used the handle of the shovel like the muzzle of a gun to line him up against the garage wall.

"You broke my hand! I think you broke it."

"That'll teach you to play with bricks." I had no sympathy. "What the hell do you think you're doing, Hanley?"

"You wouldn't stop asking questions." He seemed to think that justified heaving bricks through my windows. I didn't. "I had to show you I was serious. I could've done worse than this, you know."

"Then you would've been in even more trouble than you are now."

That didn't seem to penetrate. But then came a sound—a throaty, rumbling growl—that definitely grabbed his attention. Mine, too.

The shadow that had been slipping around the yard since I'd arrived had materialized into a matted, thin dog who stood at my hip. His lips were snarled back from an impressive set of teeth.

The fact that the teeth, snarl and growl were aimed at Brent rather than me was a major relief.

"Don't let your dog bite me. Call him off!" Brent pleaded.

I didn't let on how new—and tentative—this alliance was. "Answer my questions then."

"I did it 'cause you gotta stop nosing around. You gotta stop doing a story on Rog."

"It's not *on* Rog. I'm reporting on Redus' death." If the two overlapped . . .

"You can't ask any more questions." He'd started at threat, slid to bluster, and now he was nearer entreaty.

"Why, Brent?" I asked softly.

"They'll find out." He slumped against the garage wall.

I glanced at the dog. The snarl was gone, but he focused intently on Brent.

"Who'll find out? Your aunt and uncle?" His only answer was a muffled sound, like sorrow being swallowed whole and nearly choking him. "Brent, I think they know. At least your aunt. I think she's wondered for a long time, and now I think she knows Rog thought he might be gay."

"Not that. They'll find out . . . they'll find out it's my fault. It's my fault." He wailed the repeated words. "I told him . . ." He tried to take a deep breath. It turned into a hiccup that shook him. His face was mottled red and white with sorrow and strain.

"What did you tell him, Brent?"

"I told him to keep it quiet. I cut class and went out there the day after he was arrested, and he told me about Redus taking Frank home and how Redus and the Judge was thick as thieves. Redus told Rog it could go easier on him if Uncle Roger donated to some fund Redus had. Redus said he could make the whole thing disappear. Rog said it was blackmail, and his father wouldn't pay blackmail no matter what.

That's when Redus hit him.

"Rog said he wouldn't tell his father. I told Rog he was stupid. He had to pay up or word would get all over about . . . about him. Rog said he didn't have money and he couldn't do that to his parents. He kept saying over and over how he couldn't do it to his parents. I told him to quit sniveling . . ." Brent sucked in a breath on a sob. "I told him he had to do what he had to do. But, oh, God, I didn't mean for him to hang himself. I swear, I didn't. I swear . . ."

The sobs were stronger than his words, and Brent Hanley bent double beneath their weight, the top of his head nearly touching the hands he still held one inside the other. The dog moved, and I shifted the shovel handle, hoping I wouldn't have to use it to protect Hanley.

But all the dog did was get his shoulder between me and Brent's slumped form.

A flash caught my eye between the lilac bushes and my neighbor's house. It was a patrol car, slowed nearly to a crawl, searching out an address. Someone must have called after hearing noise—either glass shattering or Brent howling. In another minute, representatives of the Sherman police force would join us. They'd take Brent away and, in the shape he was in now, he'd talk his head off.

I hadn't met any of the Sherman police yet, but if they were as closely connected to Claustel as Widcuff and his cohorts, could the boy be in danger?

To Brent it was a side issue, but to a lot of other people what Rog Johnson had told his cousin about Redus and Judge Claustel would be of paramount interest. Maybe the judge had sent Frank away not only so his son wouldn't be exposed to talk about him, but so he couldn't talk himself. Maybe the judge was determined enough to prevent talk to resort to murder.

"Listen, Brent. The cops are coming." He jolted, and I hung onto his right arm with both hands, at the same time telling the newly tense dog, "It's okay. Brent, I'm going to let you go, but I want you to know that you might have to tell the authorities what you just told me."

"I can't," he wailed, two tears sliding from his right eye.

"Yes, you can. In the meantime, you tell your Aunt Myrna what you told me. Do you understand? Then the two of you decide if your uncle needs to know. But carrying this around as a secret has got to end. If you don't tell your aunt, I will. Got it?" He gave a wavering nod. "Okay, now get going."

His red-rimmed eyes shifted from me to the light blinking between the houses, then he took off without hesitation. I counted to twenty, then circled the back of the garage, so I would greet the cops with the building between us and Brent's escape route.

"Stop! Right there!"

I stopped.

"Drop it!"

With some surprise, I looked at the shovel I still held. I dropped it.

"And call off your dog."

The shadow seemed to have attached itself to my side, and was grumbling deep in its throat at the shouter of these orders.

By the time I had introduced myself to the police, shown them the damage to my kitchen and lamented my inability to catch the perpetrator, the sun was out in full force and so was the neighborhood. I told everyone the dog wasn't mine. Hearing how I'd been feeding it, and looking at it still on watch beside me, everyone laughed and said, "He's your dog now."

By the time the police departed, I had met the neighbors on both sides, reassured the nice old lady across the street that this probably wasn't the work of a serial brick-thrower and declined with thanks three offers of breakfast. All I wanted was to brush my teeth, take a shower and clean up. In that order.

By the time I got out of the shower, Paycik was on my front door-step.

"It's barely sun-up, Paycik. What are you doing here so early?" I scoped out his hands. No bakery bag. "And without any food or coffee."

"Aunt Gee heard a call at your address and called me." The woman must sleep with a police scanner under her pillow. "Are you okay? What happened?"

I told him—the real story, not what I'd told the police—while I swept up glass. He had several comments on my intelligence in going after Hanley, which I refuted with dignity and logic. He didn't see the light.

"You need a keeper, Danniher. And don't tell me how some wild dog was your backup. It could just as easily have attacked you. Or it could have been rabid. How could you—"

"That's it, Paycik. Out." I held the broom.

Perhaps remembering what I'd accomplished with a shovel, he held up his hands. "Okay, okay. I'll shut up. For now."

I reached toward the doorknob, and threatened, "You want to meet this dog?"

He threw in another bargaining chip. "And I'll tell you more news my aunt told me this morning. They've got the murder weapon."

I put down the broom. In tacit truce, we pulled out chairs and sat. "Positive ID?"

"Hard to get a hundred percent with a shotgun. But preliminary tests show the wadding and the chemical traces on Mona's skin and on the barrel match. Plus—" He looked a little green. "—blood and, uh, other stuff that matches Mona's was on the barrel."

I don't know how my face looked, but my stomach felt as if we'd become color-coordinated. Awaking to images of blood-spattered spider webs after too little sleep, then fending off a high school behemoth who wavered from assault to tears was not my idea of a good morning.

I thought of the gun neatly held in the rack in Tom Burrell's pickup truck. "So the gun in his truck was the murder wea—"

"Not the truck. That one hadn't been fired lately. It was the one in the cabinet in the trailer."

"The one in the cabinet? But . . . Something's wrong about that."

"What?"

"I don't know. Something."

And then I did.

The dream. "Spiders."

Mike stared at me. "What?"

"Spiders—actually their webs. That gun wasn't used to kill Mona."

"Spiders? Are you going to explain?"

"There was a spider web from the windowsill to the cabinet door pulls."

"Okay," he said slowly.

"A big, intact spider web. Don't you see? There's no way anyone could have opened the cabinet to get that gun, then put it back without ripping the web. And no spider could have completed a web that big between when Mona was shot and we found her. Impossible. So that couldn't have been the gun used to kill Mona."

"Are you sure? I mean, it was a pretty gruesome and—"

"That's why I focused on the spider web, Mike. I am sure. Absolutely sure. That spider web was intact. The gun we saw in Burrell's office couldn't have been the murder weapon."

"But the gun they found in that rack *was* the murder weapon."

"It was a different gun from the one we saw," I insisted.

"That means either the murderer risked coming back after we left or . . ."

I stared at Mike as I finished his sentence. ". . . or the murderer was there in the trailer with us and made the switch after we left."

Chapter Thirty-One

"IF SOMEONE WAS THERE, how'd they get away?" I asked that after we both pushed down the willies enough to function.

He grunted something that sounded like "parked round back."

"The window was open. We would have seen a truck there." The way I'd seen the cab of Burrell's white pickup.

"Bicycle, horse, on foot," he muttered. "But you're not asking the right question—the better question is if that would affect anyone's alibi. The rest of them had plenty of time. But could Tom have beaten us back to his ranch if he left the trailer after we did? And that answer is yes, by pasture roads through his place instead of paved roads around."

My mind snagged on his phrase about not asking the right question. *Sometimes you learn as much about the truth from the questions that don't get asked.* That's what Burrell said in the rain in Sherman Supermarket's parking lot. Questions that don't get asked. There was one that had niggled at me.

"Because there's no reason to ask the question if you already know the answer." I snagged the strap of my purse. "C'mon, Paycik, let's go."

"Where?" He was already unfolding his large frame from the couch.

"To test a theory that the question someone doesn't ask can be more revealing than the answers to questions that are asked."

✧ ✧ ✧ ✧

"GINA, WILL YOU PLEASE show us Foster's leather case?"

Without hesitation she went to the closet across from the front door, drew out an old-fashioned accordion-sided leather case that was heavy enough to require both hands to carry and brought it to her chair. She sat with it between her feet.

"The sheriff's department doesn't seem to know anything about that leather case," I said.

She still said nothing. She hadn't said anything when she opened the door for us, either. It was a nice change of pace after Paycik peppering me with questions all the way to O'Hara Hill. I told him I couldn't answer until I got some answers of my own.

"But you know about this case, don't you, Gina?"

Mike's head jerked around at my low-voiced question, but it drew no response except a neutral stare from Gina.

"You made sure to know where it was. Because you still inherit everything Foster had, don't you? A lawyer knew right away that if a man dies without a will—like Foster did—his wife inherits, even if she has sued for divorce. As long as the papers haven't gone through. The lawyer knew that right off, without having to look it up. He's not even a divorce lawyer. So I've got to believe the divorce lawyer you saw in Cody would have told you that."

Silence.

"I checked, Gina. You stopped divorce proceedings the week after Foster disappeared."

She stared at me without expression. Her hair and skin looked duller than two weeks ago, her eyes lacked even their earlier spark of anger at Mona Burrell. "Not much sense in paying for a divorce when I knew he was dead."

I swallowed. "How did you know Foster was dead, Gina?"

"Because that's the only thing that'd stop him from coming back for this damned case."

I allowed myself to look at it for the first time. A leather strap over the top ended in a mangled brass lock.

"How'd you get it?"

"I followed him to Marty Beck's that afternoon and took it. I was just so tired of him coming 'round, using this place like a motel, using me. He screwed me that afternoon, ya know. He did that a lot when he came by. Sometimes I tried to say no, and he'd rough me up. It got so it wasn't worth saying no.

"But that afternoon . . . . He was full of himself. Saying how no-body'd be able to touch him in this county. How he'd found his ticket to Easy Street." She stared straight ahead, into someplace I didn't ever want to see. "He hurt me."

It was quiet and stark and chilling.

"I wanted to get back at him. I went over there, thinking . . . I don't know what I was thinking. Maybe I'd do something to his truck. Maybe break in on him and Marty, scare them some, you know.

"But when I got to his truck, I saw that case, behind the seat. I had keys to the truck—he knew that, and he'd know it was me took the case. So I did it. I didn't know what was in it, and I didn't care. I brought it here, and I sat in that chair with the case at my feet and my gun ready. I knew he'd come for it.

"About six o'clock, I heard a car in the drive. I was sure it was him. There was no way he wouldn't come after that case. My heart was pounding so hard I thought it would burst right through my ears. But it wasn't Foster. It was Mona in that red Mustang of hers, out looking for her tomcat. Just sat there for a couple minutes, then drove off."

"Which direction?" I asked as softly as I could.

"South. I figured she musta already checked Marty's place before she came here, or she'd've gone north. She went south, toward Sherman."

Also toward Tom Burrell's ranch and Three-Day Pass Road.

"I waited all night. All the next morning, too. Until it was noon, and I was real hungry, and I made a liver sausage and tomato sand-wich. I was washing the plate when I realized Foster had to be dead. It was the only reason he wouldn't have come after me.

"So I opened the case. Only key I knew of to it never left Foster's chain, so I had to break the lock. It was full of money."

She leaned over, flipped the strap aside, and spread open the top. She was right, it was full of money. Some loose, some in rubberbands.

Mostly small bills. But not all.

"There used to be more," she said with faint satisfaction.

"Do you know where it came from, Gina?"

"No."

"But you have suspicions?"

"He was taking bribes. To let people off."

"How long did you suspect that?"

Gina Redus let out a quick breath through her nose. "Just about from the start. One time he was bragging about arresting this big person or that big person in the county, and I said real nasty that none of those cases ever amounted to anything. He smirked. Said it depends on what you mean about a case amounting to anything."

"When did he start carrying the leather case?"

"About a year after we came here."

"How about this past year, did you notice any changes?"

Gina stared, unfocused, as a spot on the curtains. Mike drew in a breath as if to speak, and I cut him a look. He let the breath out slowly. For a full minute, breathing was the only sound.

"He started talking this once about his future taking him big places. He said he'd put nickel and dime operations behind him, and now he was looking at the big picture. But that didn't mean he had to paint the same big picture somebody else was painting." Her eyebrows dipped into a frown. "I asked what he meant, but he wouldn't say any more."

"And you have no idea what he was talking about?"

She shook her head.

"When was that? Do you remember?"

"Last spring. About a year ago, I guess."

Mike and I stood.

"Gina, one last thing . . ." This wasn't nearly as off-hand as I tried to make it sound. I figured if it worked for Columbo, it might work for me. "What time did Foster get here that last day?"

"Around two."

"What time did he leave?"

"A few minutes before three maybe, something like that. I told you, he didn't stick around long. He never did. Just a wham-bam, not even the thank-you-ma'am."

"Did he say anything about what he'd been doing that day?"

"Just that he'd had a meeting that morning. He was real pleased about that. Said he'd had a good meeting and his future looked good."

I tried to keep my voice even. "Did he say who his meeting was with?"

"No."

I hadn't really expected any other answer, but I'd hoped.

"We'll have to tell Sheriff Widcuff about the case, and the money, Gina." She gave no reaction. "You can't spend any more."

"Okay."

As Mike closed the door behind us, I mentally amended my statement about telling the sheriff. We'd tell Widcuff and the state people and the Sherman police and Ames Hunt . . . just to make sure.

Back in the car, Mike didn't turn on the engine right away.

"How the hell did you know about the money?"

"Bits and pieces of things." The rumors about Redus being on the take. The pattern of his arrests. Penny's ramblings in the grocery store about the timing of Gina's new buying habits. "And Gina hadn't asked about the leather case. Mona did, remember? Now what I want to know is who told the sheriff's department that Redus was on his way to see Burrell that day. The official report simply says they learned Redus had intended to see Burrell. How'd they learn that? Who told them? Who called in the anonymous tip?"

"Gina could have. She said she followed Redus to Marty's. Maybe she kept following him. Maybe she saw him go to Burrell's and leave. Somehow she got him to go up to Three-Day Pass Road with her. Hits him on the head. Takes the case and uses her truck to push his truck over the edge."

"Thus setting up Tom Burrell as the fall-guy?" I objected.

"Maybe all that stuff about loving him is a lie, a cover-up. She had the money as a motive—she took the case, and she's been spending it for six months."

"But look at what she's spending it on—mustard, hair styling, dinner at Ernie's, lingerie. You saw that case, she's barely made a dent in it. She could have bought a new house, flashy clothes, a new car—hell, she could have left Cottonwood County. I don't think it was the money. She took the case because it was important to Redus, so it was a way to get back at him. When he didn't come for it, she kept getting back at him by frittering away his precious money."

He spread his hands—in surrender if not conversion—so I went on.

"We know from Gina and Tamantha that Mona wasn't home all night like she told us, but if Mona had known Foster had gone to the Circle B, surely she would have raised the alarm sooner instead of assuming he was with another woman. Next we find out if Marty told the police. If she didn't, it becomes a real interesting question: who was keeping close enough track of Redus' moves that day to know he'd gone to Burrell's ranch?"

Paycik turned over the engine. "Let's go find Marty Beck."

✧　✧　✧　✧

"WHY SHOULD I TELL you anything? You're the ones trying to get Burrell off."

Marty lifted her chin in a way she probably imagined was plucky, then ruined the effect by looking over Mike Paycik with avid interest from behind the counter where she served breakfasts and lunches at the Saddle Up.

Mike answered. "We're trying to get to the bottom of this, Marty. And we think you can help. Of course, it's a matter of record that he came by that afternoon to, uh, visit you. That's been in the report since the first day."

"Yeah, it has. And I don't care if Mona is dead, she was lying when she said Foster loved her and was going to take her away. It was me he loved." Some people don't know when to quit. Marty Beck was still fighting a dead woman for a dead man. "He trusted me. Not like Mona. He said she was always poking into his things, listening to his phone calls. He said it was a real pleasure to spend time with me and know I wouldn't go prying. He trusted me."

An image of Redus leaving his precious leather case in his truck available for Gina to commandeer popped into my head. And words popped out.

"Even after you opened his leather case? Did he trust you then, Marty?"

Anger blasted red up her throat and across her cheeks. "I didn't take none of that money. I don't care what anybody says, I didn't take none. And Foster knew that. When he calmed, he got over that idea. He understood I was curious was all, what with the keys right there and all, and him in the shower. And he came back, didn't he? He came back to be with me."

Before I could say anything more, Paycik, without taking his eyes off Marty, pressed his foot down on mine in a clear and painful order to be quiet.

"That's right, Marty," he said. "Everybody knows he came to see you that afternoon. All we want to know now is what time he left."

She turned away from him, then slued her eyes back, looking at him through her lashes. I would bet a lifetime's supply of Milano cookies she'd practiced that in a mirror.

"About four."

He unleashed his smile on her. "That's great. That's real helpful. Of course, if you had something else to tell us, maybe something that Redus said that afternoon about his activities, somebody he'd talked to earlier in the day, we'd be happy to hear it, too."

She gave him a direct look. "We had better things to do than talk."

I got another nudge from Paycik, and headed to the car without him.

He didn't stay long. When he slid in behind the wheel, he shook his head. "She didn't tell the sheriff that Redus was going to Burrell's, because she didn't know. And the same argument applies to her as Mona—if she'd known, she wouldn't have been so worried Mona might have Redus hidden away, and there wouldn't have been that cat-fight at the Walmart." Mike was frowning thoughtfully as he asked, "Next stop?"

"The sheriff's substation. Your Aunt Gee."

✧ ✧ ✧ ✧

"I'VE BEEN LOOKING FOR YOU, Michael." Gisella Decker glanced beyond the dispatcher's horseshoe to the deputies' desks. The only one occupied was Richard Alvaro's. He was openly listening. She frowned, then relented regally. "I suppose I can tell you, since the sheriff's setting up a news conference. Though why he doesn't wait until he knows something for a fact, I never will understand."

"Tell us what?" Mike prompted.

"The gun they found at Tom's office, the one that killed Mona . . ." She drew in a breath dramatically. "It was registered to Foster Redus."

"What?" Mike and I demanded in unison.

But it only took a second to add that to the pattern that was finally coming together.

Redus had been using his position as deputy to arrest people, then let loose the ones who could pay. But recently it had become something different. Not a simple bribe, but more elaborate schemes. The big picture. A bigger picture that someone else was painting?

So he must have been working with someone higher up the food chain. Someone who'd had his own scheme going. A scheme Redus had spotted and horned in on? Someone Redus had met with the last morning of his life. Someone who had known enough about Redus' plan to confront Burrell to make him a handy scapegoat when Redus disappeared. Someone with enough connections to law enforcement to drop the hint to look at Burrell's house for evidence of a fight. A fight he knew about because he'd seen Redus' wounds and had heard his outraged tale just before he smashed in Redus' skull with the stock of his own shotgun.

Alvaro walked over to join us. "They're checking to see if it was also the weapon used to kill Redus."

"There are marks on the stock," Gisella Decker said in a tone that made it clear this was her story to tell. "They'll test it for DNA. The narrow edge would fit the wounds to Redus' skull. And, of course, when they recovered the body and the truck, his shotgun was missing."

"Aunt Gee, do you remember where Redus was supposed to be the day he disappeared?"

"He was on liaison at the courthouse, of course, but he stopped by here, bragging about keeping his nose to the grindstone all morning at the sheriff's office in Sherman."

"What time did he get here?"

"Arrived at four-ten, left at four-thirty."

Mike and I exchanged a look, not doubting Aunt Gee's precision, but in recognition that Redus hadn't had time to do anything except go directly to Burrell's ranch, where he'd arrived shortly before five.

"What are you frowning about, boy?" Aunt Gee's question brought our attention back to Alvaro.

"Redus wasn't in the sheriff's office all morning." He looked from Aunt Gee to Mike to me. "I reported to the courthouse first thing that morning to testify, but I ended up waiting around until mid-afternoon. While I was out in the hall in the morning, I saw Redus. He went right in, and stayed there a good hour."

"Where?"

"Judge Claustel's office."

Chapter Thirty-Two

"**MS. DANNIHER** and Mr. Paycik of KWMT to see you, Judge Claustel."

His assistant's announcement was formal and strained. She'd answered the first call we'd made from the car, and had been so uncooperative that we'd called Ames Hunt, asked him to set it up, and sidestepped specifics.

"And then I'll be leaving," she added.

She did that well, with the faintly aggrieved note clearly exempting her boss and aimed squarely at Mike and me for keeping her into the evening.

"Of course, of course. And thank you." It was Hunt playing host. "Come in, Elizabeth. We were just having an after-hours drink. Since this is, as you told me, a strictly informal gathering to clear up mistaken impressions about this case."

That was a quarter turn from what I'd actually told him. And what I'd told him had been another quarter turn from the truth. That brought us all the way around to face away from where we were actually heading, enough misdirection to keep everyone at ease. For now.

Hunt waved us to the guest chairs, now facing the couch, and settled back into the chair pulled around from behind the desk. His sports jacket, neatly hung on a hanger, joined Claustel's wrinkled robe and shapeless jacket on the antler-topped coat tree.

"You know Judge Claustel and Sheriff Widcuff, of course," Hunt added with a nod to the men seated on the couch, Claustel with one arm spread across the back with a studied air of ease.

"I believe you know Michael Paycik." Nods all around.

Claustel lifted his glass, revealing amber liquid. "Would you care for one?"

We declined.

I felt suddenly edgier than I had when anticipating this meeting. And then, almost as quickly as I recognized the reaction, I recognized its cause. Just the faintest scent, like a whisper in passing. But it was definitely the remnants of Mona's strong perfume.

A surge of adrenaline tingled out to my fingers. Mona's scent clung to one of the men in this room, woven into the fabric of his clothes so deeply he probably no longer smelled it. From their last encounter, when he shot her at the trailer?

A noise at the door caught my attention. Mike opened it, revealing Diana, who'd been trying to bump it open with the camera because she had both hands on the strap of her gear bag. She'd been the second call we made from the car.

I'd asked her if she could get her hands on a camera from the station. She'd said no. But she did have one of her own, even older and bigger than the station's antiques, that she'd bought on eBay and kept running herself.

Of course she did.

"This is Diana Stendahl," I added. "She's going to record this. I'm sure you don't mind, since I'm sure you all are as eager as everyone else in Cottonwood County to straighten out the murders of Foster Redus and Mona Burrell, even if it is done informally."

"Always glad to get any unpleasantness with the media straightened out informally," Claustel said, political smile intact, as he set down his glass on a side table, out of view of the camera. "That's what's so wonderful about this part of the country. We don't have to stand on ceremony, Ms. Danniher. Or do you think we know each other well enough to use Elizabeth and Ambrose?"

"I'd feel more comfortable with Judge Claustel."

I nodded to Diana. She dropped the equipment bag and started taping—and I do mean taping. I hadn't seen one of those behemoth cameras, complete with attached tape deck, since early in my career.

"Ah, journalistic integrity."

I ignored that, instead opening with a softball question about his working relationship with Foster Redus. I listened with every appearance of great interest as he rolled on about that, then segued to his terrific working relationships with everyone in the courthouse, including County Attorney Ames Hunt and Sheriff Tom Widcuff.

He truly was a political pro. Not only had he shared the limelight, but he timed it perfectly to allow Diana to focus on each of the other men—briefly—before he called the camera back to himself by concluding, "Which adds to our determination to bring to justice the murderer of Deputy Redus."

"You would agree, then, that it is in the best interests of the community to ensure that someone who had motive, means and opportunity to murder Deputy Redus answers questions concerning the murder?"

My peripheral vision caught a small motion from Hunt's hand to my right. It was quickly stilled, and he made no sound. But I suspected the county attorney had just hit the accelerator on his brain to come up to speed.

"Absolutely, Ms. Danniher. We owe it to this fine community as well as to that young man and his family—and the law enforcement family, too."

I nodded, not quite able to bring myself to thank him. "So, the first question to clear up is if you knew Redus was taking bribes to falsify arrest reports before he used that ploy to blackmail you into giving him the job here at the courthouse?"

"I did not give him the job or arrange . . ." He'd started with the automatic denial of political wrong-doing, then he spotted the criminal wallop within the question.

He gobbled. Sounds came out, but no words.

"Redus had you where he wanted you. And he was not discreet or subtle. You had to get rid of this blackmailer—there's the motive, Judge Claustel.

"Opportunity? That's easy. You arranged to meet him on Three-

Day Pass Road to make a payment.

"Means? Redus' own shotgun. You probably casually asked to take a look at it, he handed it over, then you used it to crush his skull.

"After that, it was simply a matter of pushing his truck over the edge. Problem solved."

"This is—you can't . . ." Words were coming now, though nothing coherent.

"Except it wasn't problem solved, was it? Not when Redus' truck was found. Did Mona Burrell call and tell you she'd put together the pieces and knew what you'd done? Did she try to cash in, just as Redus had? Leaving you right back where you were before.

"That must have been a bad moment. But now you knew how to handle a blackmailer, and you acted quickly. At the trailer. With Redus' gun."

"Wait a minute," Widcuff said, a plea rather than a command. The sheriff definitely wasn't up to speed yet.

But Judge Claustel was getting there fast.

"Are you—you can't be accusing *me*?" He gave it the full judicial treatment.

"I am."

"That is outrageous! You cannot make such accusations with impunity, reporter or no reporter." Not bad. That almost sounded genuine.

"Of course you will say that." I nodded understandingly, then hit him fast. "Do you also say you didn't attack me in the KWMT tape library?"

"I have no idea what you're talking about." Weak—the weakness of a guilty man.

"I suppose it was Thurston Fine who told you I was looking up the arrests Redus had made. You wanted to prevent me from finding out—"

"You are making totally unfounded accusations."

"Would you care to show us your shins, Judge Claustel? Whoever attacked me will have spectacular bruises from crashing into the file cabinet drawers."

"You're crazy." That sounded as if his lips had gone stiff.

"It was little things, including the attack on me in the library. A scattering of chips that only formed a mosaic after a good bit of moving the colors around. One of the last pieces came an hour ago. The morning he died, Redus met with you in your office, didn't he? That's when he told you about his plan to confront Burrell. He was sure you'd protect him from any consequences of a run-in with Burrell. That's probably when you saw your opportunity."

"That proves you're crazy. Redus was in my office that morning, but just to bring me papers from Ames, here. Ask him, ask my assistant."

Moving only my eyes, I saw Hunt, staring at the judge, give a short, jerky nod. "I did ask Redus to drop off some papers after he said he was going to the judge's office next. I don't know how long he stayed."

That still left the door wide open, yet Claustel seemed to take energy from it.

"Redus never mentioned Burrell," he said strongly. "And you will regret this absurd grandstanding. I've given you enough rope, and now you've hanged yourself, just as I knew you would. You went too far back east—I knew that must be why they drove you out. And now you've done it here. This is the end of your career."

I didn't let him throw me off my narrative.

"You were patient. Careful. Never greedy. You didn't want money to throw around. You wanted the control. For your career. For your prestige. You never made anyone feel pressured. Just a political ally repaying a favor.

"I'm talking about the selected, subtle manipulation of the law that you practiced in order to have important people in the county owe you big favors, so you were sure to continue as political kingmaker. Maybe add a little extra income to your judge's pay. Help pay college tuition for Frank. The trip to Europe."

"More accusations with no proof. I hope you are getting all this on tape, young woman," he said to Diana, "because it will make a defamation case laughably easy."

I cocked an eyebrow. "I'll agree, you were very careful. But Foster

Redus wasn't. That's why I can't believe you voluntarily took him in as a partner. No, he must have caught on to what you'd been doing, yet lacked the proof. Then, once he came across your son and poor Rog Johnson, he had you. And he was going to ruin it all, wasn't he? Because he didn't want just a little power among political allies, he wanted money. A lot of money. So you shut him up. Permanently."

"I did no such thing!" Claustel turned to the man beside him. "Bob, I demand you do something about this."

"Before you do, Sheriff," I said, "answer one question. Did Ambrose Claustel order you to burn Foster Redus' files?"

Widcuff's mouth closed, then opened again. It remained that way for a full three seconds before a sound came out. "He said . . ." The sheriff swallowed. "He said it'd be better politically to bury those ashes."

Now Widcuff was staring at Claustel, too.

I added more pressure on the judge. "Redus squeezed you for all he was worth, didn't he? And he used the one pressure point you couldn't withstand—your son's homosexuality."

"You shut up! You shut your damn mouth, you bitch!"

Wheezing, he started to rise, but Sheriff Widcuff put a beefy arm across his chest like a bar. The judge seemed to shrink, but the sound of his labored breathing remained. The same sound I'd heard in the KWMT library.

"Turn that thing off!" He stabbed a finger toward the camera.

I nodded to Diana. She nodded back, as arranged.

She turned off the camera, took it down off her shoulder, then fiddled with her bag on the table, switching on the small camcorder she'd carefully arranged inside. The quality wouldn't be much, but the content might make up for that. Even if we couldn't ever use it on air.

"I know you've been asking questions about my son." No political smile now. "Asking your dirty questions. Trying to dig up dirt. You have no right to bring your sleazy muckraking here. My boy's done nothing wrong."

"I agree he's done nothing wrong, but you were afraid other people wouldn't agree if they knew Frank is gay, so you did something wrong. Very wrong. Redus came across Frank and Rog Johnson. When he brought Frank home that night and said he'd tell the world that your son was gay unless you danced to his tune, you agreed."

Claustel stared at his hands, clenched hard on his knees. He said nothing.

"Rog Johnson's father couldn't offer Foster Redus anything he thought was worth taking except money. Rather than have his family be blackmailed and fearing they'd be shamed if Redus talked, Rog killed himself. He thought it was the only way to keep from hurting his parents."

I leaned forward, trying to see the man's face. "I don't believe the Johnsons would agree that that was a secret worth their son's dying for. Was it a secret worth killing for, Judge?

"The secret Redus discovered and used to blackmail you into taking him in as a partner. Until you killed him up at Three-Day Pass in November. You thought that was the end of it, but it wasn't, was it?

"Mona was out looking for Redus that night. She'd have driven right by Three-Day Pass Road at least twice. She saw something—saw you. Not enough to realize right away. But then, when Redus' body was found, it was enough, wasn't it? Just enough to try blackmailing you, and there you were, right back the way you'd been with Redus. So you used the same solution. Scheduled her right in after your appearance at O'Hara Hill, and killed her, too."

His hands opened from fists and he straightened his back. He'd been near the breaking point, but now he was backing away from it, gathering himself.

"All to hide your son's secret."

Damn. *Damn, damn, damn.* I'd counted on hitting him between the eyes and having him go down for the count.

"I won't stay here and listen to this."

He stood, and so did I, then everyone else. I took a step closer to the door. I couldn't stop him from leaving, but I could slow him long enough to take one last swing.

"Bank accounts will show the money trail. And there'll be physical evidence. Nature took away a lot of the evidence at Three-Day Pass, but there's a lot for the forensics guys to work with on Mona's murder."

Just the words conjured up the image. The blood stiffening in the blonde hair, the spattering across the spider web, the reddened reflection in the glass of the open window. And that scent of her perfume. Stronger now.

His face was pale, except for his bulbous nose. But Judge Ambrose Claustel hadn't given up. "This would be laughable if it weren't so serious. But it *is* crazy. *You're* crazy. You have no proof."

"There'll be proof. You know what they say—that no murderer can help leaving something of himself at the scene or taking something away. And you were stuck there longer than you'd expected, weren't you? Because you had to hide when Mike and I showed up, hoping we'd leave so you could get away. Were you planning how you'd kill us, too, if we found your hiding spot? After two murders, what's two more? But every second you stayed there added to the evidence the experts are going to find. Fibers and threads and dirt and fingerprints and residue from—"

"I have never killed anyone in my life."

It stopped me for an instant, that judicial voice ringing out in the small room.

"Yet you're not denying the official misconduct or—"

"You will never make that stick." His gaze swept the room in an echo of his magisterial command. "You don't think I'd survive this long as a politician if I didn't take precautions, do you?"

He strode to the door, then faltered at the sight of Deputy Richard Alvaro on the other side of the threshold. "You need to come with me, sir."

Claustel spun back to face us. "Hunt?" he demanded.

Ames spread his hands. "We can't just ignore this, Judge."

Claustel squared his shoulders and marched off, with Alvaro just off his shoulder.

As I turned back, I caught a speculative gleam in Ames Hunt's expression as he gazed around the room, following the same path Claustel's gaze had.

Possibly sensing my attention, Ames met my look. He tilted up one eyebrow, and I was certain he was wondering the same thing I was— what precautions might the judge have taken?

"I'll be damned," Widcuff told the room. "I'll be damned to hell and back."

Chapter Thirty-Three

"ALL RIGHT, everybody out," the sheriff ordered.

"Aren't you going to secure the office?" Paycik demanded.

Widcuff's face turned red. "Don't you try to tell me my job, young man. I'm going to take this key—" He turned the large old-fashioned key and put it in his breast pocket. "—and keep it right here."

"That's all? You're not going to—" I'd gotten close enough to Paycik to elbow him in the side.

He glared at me, but he shut up.

I wish I could say the same for Ames Hunt. "He's got a point, Sheriff. You really should call the state boys in immediately. There's no way you can handle this case. Why the evidence . . ."

"This is my county. My county!" The sheriff's face would have done a pomegranate proud. "I'll handle this case. And every bit of evidence. Just you wait and see."

I don't think any of us jammed in that hallway doubted that Widcuff would *handle the evidence.* The question was what would be left when he was done.

✧ ✧ ✧ ✧

WIDCUFF AT LEAST KEPT UP appearances to the point of having the courthouse locked up behind us as our group trailed along the path to the jail, with Diana filming all the while.

When Widcuff barred Diana, Paycik and me from entering the jail, we went into overdrive. With the light fading fast, I did an off-the-cuff setup in front of the jail so we had it in the can . . . in case.

The *in case* was if Haeburn was too stupid or too pig-headed to send a decent station camera for Diana to use. We debated long and hard about how best to handle it. A two-thirds majority (Diana and I) voted Mike should be the one to pitch the situation to Haeburn, while we covered the jail.

He gave in with ill will. Then proved us right by returning within an hour with the camera, plans for a live shot via point-to-point wireless—no satellite van for KWMT—a field visit from Audrey Adams (who would oversee the live shot at the studio end), bags of takeout to sustain us, and entertaining descriptions of Fine's epic hissy fit.

Mike also had a couple of tidbits only for Diana and me—he'd gotten hold of Diana's trusted tech Billy, so there were Fine-proof copies of all the footage from inside Claustel's office, and he'd called a contact with the state bureau of investigation.

Audrey was nervous, but competent. We hashed out the details the best we could without knowing what was going to happen. When she returned to the station, she sent Jenny to us as a runner for whatever we might need.

The next three hours were typical reporting: Extended periods of boredom while we made dozens of phone calls that garnered no new information, interspersed with rare, frantic bursts of activity. The bursts of activity included, first, the arrival of a lawyer Mike recognized, and, second, a man we filmed entering the jail on general principle, and discovered later was the judge for a neighboring county.

"Why a judge?" I demanded. Not for the first time. "It's double murder—Claustel's got to be held without bond."

"Don't count anything out in Cottonwood County," Mike said.

We set up lights and did our checks before ten to be ready for the live feed. A dozen or so citizens gathered around, attracted like moths by the lights.

Needham Bender from the *Independence* arrived with plenty of questions, which we did not answer—not until after the live shot—and news that he'd been called and told to be at the jail for a big story.

Then, three minutes before the hour, a deputy I didn't recognize came out and said the sheriff would be making a statement in a few minutes.

So, Widcuff wasn't as stupid as he sometimes seemed. We'd have to play his statement live. We certainly couldn't go on with our live piece in front of the jail while he was standing on the steps making his statement.

He emerged two minutes after the hour. He started on a preamble about justice, Cottonwood County and a boy who'd grown up to be sheriff of the greatest county on earth. Not only was it the worst bit of live TV news ever, but it threatened to cover our entire newscast.

Mike was on the phone. Diana was shooting. Bender was watching Widcuff with the amused tolerance of a journalist whose deadline was days away.

Oh, hell.

I stepped into the glare of the lights, snatched the microphone clipped to a stand in front of Widcuff, and cut in, "Sheriff Widcuff, is it true that Judge Ambrose Claustel has been charged with the double murders of Deputy Foster Redus and Sherman resident Mona Burrell?"

I don't know which flustered him more—the question or the gasp from the spectators. I pushed the mic up toward Widcuff's stuttering mouth.

"That's . . . I mean to say. Charged? Very serious . . . Investigating. Looking very closely."

From the corner of my eye, I saw Mike coming, turning off his phone with one hand and reaching for the microphone with the other.

"Sheriff Widcuff, KWMT has learned that you are releasing Judge Claustel on his own recognizance tonight despite these desperately serious accusations and growing evidence against him."

This time the gasp came from me. "Releasing!"

"Is this true, Bob?" demanded Bender.

"How do you explain this to the citizens of Cottonwood County, Sheriff Widcuff?" pursued Mike.

Widcuff might have melted into a stuttering mass right there on the jail steps if not for an alert citizen among our live audience.

"There he goes!" shouted this unidentified observer. "It's Judge Claustel going out the back of the jail!"

Sure enough. There was the bulky form of the judge, accompanied by the lawyer who'd arrived earlier, scuttling across the grass toward the parking area that served both the courthouse and jail.

The chase was on.

To her everlasting credit, Jenny grabbed the stand of lights, and ran with them as far as the tether would let her. Which wasn't far. Bender huffed along, but had the presence of mind to keep snapping flash photos. Diana did a sprint that no human being carrying a TV camera should ever have to do. I stayed with her.

But the honors went to Mike Paycik. Despite his bum knee, he actually had his hand on the car door before Claustel pulled away.

Still, not even Paycik was a match for a six-cylinder engine, leaving us only a shot of departing taillights.

"The sheriff," I managed.

But Widcuff had taken the opportunity to retreat inside the jail, and he wasn't coming back out.

We all started back toward the jail, but Jenny met us partway, aiming the lights at us and pantomiming live air. Mind you, I couldn't see her against the glare of the lights, but I could feel the breeze from her gestures, and I could smell the desperation.

I will never know what I said—or wheezed—over the next sixty seconds. I refuse to ever watch it.

THE SPECTATORS QUICKLY dispersed after that.

We decided to divide in hopes of conquering.

Mike and Jenny went to the station and traded the camera for Jenks, then went to check out Judge Claustel's home, south of town. The camera's return to the station was a Haeburn edict, since Diana was still on vacation—and who knew what might happen to it left in my officially suspended hands?

Diana and I stayed at the jail. Widcuff had to come out sometime, didn't he?

Although the fact that at midnight all the exterior lights except a solitary security light behind the jail turned out, and that only the dimmest glow came from a couple windows of the jail seemed to indicate Widcuff and his deputies had called it a night. Of course, that could be a ploy, just as his *statement* on the front steps had been.

But for now, it was dark, quiet and boring.

I wondered if Tom Burrell, in his cell inside the jail, knew what had been happening tonight.

To pass the time as we sat in the front seat of my car, Diana played back what she'd shot in Claustel's office.

We'd just finished a second playback from the camcorder. The quality looked like a sting operation from the 1980s. Come to think of it, that was probably the vintage of the first camera Diana had used to tape Claustel.

"Let's see just that last part again," I said.

Diana nodded, rewound it to where Claustel said he'd never killed anyone in his life, and started it again.

Precautions. What had that meant? And that look around the room—had he been looking from face to face? Sending a message to one person in particular? Was it the instinctive checking of a hiding spot? Or the bluff of a desperate man.

"Again?"

I nodded.

If precautions meant something physical, it could wrap up the whole case.

On the other hand, if there was something up in the office, with Claustel free and Widcuff apparently snoozing, what were the chances it would ever be found?

A flicker beyond the windshield caught my eye.

I ducked my head for a better angle and stared, as I asked, "Did you see that?"

"See what?"

"A shadow. Like the back door of the courthouse opening." I shook my head. "Maybe nothing."

She'd dutifully peered out the windshield, but even the dim light of the camera screen made it hard to see into the layers of dark beyond us. "Probably nothing, since we saw Widcuff lock that door, and nobody's around."

"Probably," I conceded.

But I kept staring.

Oh, hell.

I got out of the door, closing it quietly behind me.

"What are you doing?" Diana demanded, out of her door now, too.

"I'm just going to check. If it's locked . . . well, it's locked. But I want to *know* it's nothing."

"Not without me you're not. Wait up."

I turned back and saw her hoisting the big camera into place on her shoulder.

"What—"

"If it *is* something, the camcorder will never pick it up. Old Faithful here just might."

"EBay, really?"

"Sure. Why not? Got a great deal. Can pick up spare parts the same way. And it comes in handy sometimes, as you saw."

"Yeah, but it must weigh—"

"Less than a bale of hay."

She'd caught up with me, and I shrugged. A gesture she probably didn't see now that we were in the total dark beyond that solitary security light, with even that partially blocked by a corner of the jail.

We were silent as we reached the door. I found the knob by feel more than sight. It turned.

"Open," I breathed.

The silence continued as we headed for the staircase, tacitly ignoring the noise of the elevator. The stairs creaked a bit under our feet, but they also creaked a bit where we weren't walking, so I hoped our ascent wasn't noticeable.

On the third floor, faint light from the open outer door of Claustel's office formed a dim trapezoid in the hallway. I felt a reluctance to step into that light, but there was no way to see inside otherwise.

From the hall doorway, I looked past the assistant's dark space and into the judge's office, lit only by the lamp on his desk.

As I eased into the assistant's office and could see into the room, the first thing I noticed was that whoever was in there hadn't bothered to close the blinds on the side window. But there was no one to see the light, not from the deserted streets of Sherman, Wyoming at this hour.

A man's sports jacket was folded over the back of one of the leather chairs, while the jacket's presumed owner leaned over the other chair at an odd angle. Only when I stepped inside the office could I see that his hand was down in the crevice between the seat cushion and the side of the chair.

And that the man was Ames Hunt.

Behind me, Diana emitted a faint sound—a breath more than a gasp. But it was enough.

He spun around, jerking his hand free from the chair, and took an awkward step backward, his eyes wide behind the lenses of his glasses. "Elizabeth."

"What are you doing, Hunt?"

His lips lifted slightly, clearly recovered from the momentary fright. "You mean until you and . . ." He peered past me. "Ms. Stendahl scared a couple decades off my life? I would imagine the same thing you came to do. Looking for whatever it is Claustel hid away as his insurance."

"Shouldn't you leave that to the sheriff?"

"Shouldn't *we*, you mean?" he asked sweetly, then exhaled a cynical huff. "Not if we hope to find it. You're thinking about not interfering with the crime scene? The experts getting a second chance? Sure, that was true of the trailer. Like you said, a crime scene entirely different from Three-Day Pass. But that was a crime scene Widcuff couldn't ignore. This isn't. He'll ignore it just fine. And with Claustel free . . ."

Having echoed my own earlier thoughts, he shrugged, then added. "So it's up to us to find . . . well, whatever it is."

"And what *is* it?" Diana asked him.

"I have no idea. Do you, Elizabeth?" he added to me.

"Not a clue. Guess we'll know it when—*if*—we see it."

"Then we better get started. When the judge looked around earlier, I thought he focused on these chairs, but I haven't found anything. I'll try the cabinets." He tipped his head toward a double-wide set of filing cabinets near the side door.

"We'll take the desk."

Diana and I skirted the chairs and the desk. She deposited the camera on one corner, then pulled open the lap drawer. I opened the top drawer on my side.

The third time I moved a tin holding paperclips, I realized my mind wasn't on this task.

I felt like I had when I was a little girl watching *A Wonderful Life*, when everyone's feeling so sentimental about his friends helping George Bailey, and nobody's paying attention to what Mr. Potter got away with. "Hey," something in me kept shouting, "Look over here! Look at the spider web instead of the flies caught in it."

Frustrated, I closed the drawer and moved to the bookshelves by the side window. A spider web connected from the frame of the window to the edge of the case.

It felt like Mr. Potter and fate, laughing at me.

With my body blocking what little of the lamp's light reached this corner, I blindly reached for a book with some notion of starting to shake them out one by one, and caught a flash of color from the corner of my eye.

"What?" Diana demanded.

"What what?"

"You made a sound." She straightened, stretching her back. Across the room, Hunt paused, too.

"Sorry. I thought I saw something, but it was just a reflection in the window. My sleeve, I guess." I moved my arm again to show her.

She and Hunt grunted in unison, returning to their tasks. Diana opening the bottom drawer, Hunt moving the chair holding his jacket to give him better access to a drawer.

But I kept looking at the window. I'd seen a flash of red. Not the blue of my jacket.

Red. Like the car spotlighted by that solitary security light behind the jail. Spotlighted, yet unlikely to be seen, since the corner of the courthouse would hide it from the jail and a stand of pine trees screened it from the deserted side street.

I moved my arm again.

No blue. Just red.

Which came from outside, not inside the window.

"Wait a minute," Diana said. Her voice suddenly seemed far away.

"What?" Hunt responded from that same distance.

The trailer. The blood. The gun cabinet. The spider web. And the window.

The window wasn't red from the blood inside. It was red from outside.

Yes, there'd been blood on the spider web, but not enough to flood the surface of the window with red the way it had been.

The window was cranked open, tilted.

"What's that?" Diana asked. "That shiny thing by your foot, Hunt."

"I don't . . . oh."

And the scent. That lingering scent of Mona's. Along with a faint undertone of acrid smoke and another, even less pleasant odor.

A waft of it had just reached me—a memory stirred by thinking of the trailer that day? Now it was fading.

I turned my head and saw Ames Hunt's well-tailored jacket folded over the back of the chair nearest him. The chair he'd been bending over, sliding his hand into the crevice . . .

"It's a key," he said.

I watched him open his hand, displaying the small silver key he'd retrieved from the floor.

"It's small," Diana said. "No way would that open a door."

"Maybe a cabinet?"

The gun cabinet.

The spider web.

The window.

I'd kept thinking there hadn't been a vehicle behind the trailer because I hadn't seen it through the window the way I saw Burrell's white pickup the first time I was there. But a sedan wouldn't have been visible from the window, yet the sun hitting its roof could reflect into the tilted window. A sedan parked behind the trailer. A red sedan.

Like Fine drove in emulation of the man whose coattails he expected to ride. Like the one out in the parking lot right now.

"Maybe. Have to be an awfully small cabinet. It's too small for a safety deposit box."

Just right for a leather case, though.

I felt as if my mind had split in two, remembering words that now belonged to parallel universes. The words I'd spoken earlier this evening, the words I'd just listened to again in the car . . . and words about preserving the crime scene at the trailer for the forensics experts.

Like you said, a crime scene entirely different from Three-Day Pass.

Yes, I'd said that. I'd said it when only Mike and I were in the trailer. Mike and I—and a murderer who'd been interrupted before he could place the murder weapon in Tom Burrell's cabinet.

"What do you think, Elizabeth?"

And I was seeing in parallel universes. Seeing the spider's web *and* the flies, but still searching for the spider.

Then I saw it.

The same facts, a different view. The picture clicked into sharp, cold focus. The entire spider web.

I stared into the face of the spider at the center of the web.

Ames Hunt.

Who was between Diana and me, and our way out.

Who was looking at me with sharp eyes.

Who still held the small silver key in the palm of a hand he'd covered with the handkerchief.

A handkerchief to prevent covering fingerprints. Or to avoid leaving them.

Of course. He'd been *planting* that key when we interrupted him. The key to Foster Redus' leather case that Mona had to break open to get the cash for her Grey Poupon. The key taken from Redus' chain, while all the rest of the keys were tossed into the truck before it was sent over the edge.

The key that being discovered here would not only tie Judge Claustel to Redus' scheme—as accomplice, victim or both—but also tie a bow onto his motive for murder.

"I think this is just what we were looking for." I forced the words out. "We should call the sheriff right away. And the state folks."

"But we don't know if it's really anything at all," Diana protested. "It could be entirely innocuous."

"Why take the chance on compromising important evidence?" I dug in my pocket for my phone, at the same time trying to edge Diana out from behind the desk and toward the hall door. "And we should leave, so Widcuff doesn't have a fit."

I had the phone. Still in my pocket, I was feeling for buttons.

"Get the camera, Diana." She'd protest leaving without it, so we'd just have to take it.

"But—"

I overrode her voice. "So you make the call, Ames, and we'll—"

"Put down the phone, Elizabeth."

Since he knew what I was doing, there was no point not going for speed. I pulled it out. "Pick up the camera, Diana," I repeated, and she hoisted it up.

He reached toward me. Before I could pull back, he'd knocked the phone out of my hand to the floor. That was because his reach was longer than I expected—by the length of a handgun equipped with a silencer.

"What the hell?" Diana started. "What's going on?"

"Your friend is a little too smart for her own good. And yours." He turned to me. "Aren't you, E.M. Danniher?"

He'd never buy a lie. What I had to do now was play for time.

"I understand about Redus." Without taking my eyes from Hunt, I made a slow small gesture to Diana to start the camera resting on her shoulder. "He was going to ruin your careful plans, wasn't he?"

"He was a moron," Ames Hunt said, the bland features showing no emotion. "He started hinting that he knew how I was building my political capital, as if that were all I had to offer. Then, he said he'd cut me out by not arresting prominent people in exchange for money. He practically dared me to complain. I could have called his bluff, but it could have been, shall we say, inconvenient? I had him transferred here to limit his opportunities for arrests, lulled him into thinking I'd accepted him as partner and bided my time for a permanent solution."

It couldn't be good that he was telling us this. Or that he had a gun.

Don't think about that. Just keep him talking. And think—think.

"But Redus wasn't the only enemy, was he? *The way years of frustration could build up in a man.* You said that. You meant for me to think about Tom Burrell, but it was really yourself you meant.

"It was bad enough when you were kids," I said. "Then later, when he didn't even get a degree, and you came back as a lawyer, but people still thought he was special. And, the final straw, when Claustel talked about nominating Burrell for the state legislature—well, that must have been hard to take. They were practically begging him to take what you had earned. And then you saw a way to eliminate both irritants at once."

Keep him talking. Keep him talking.

I saw a glowing satisfaction in his eyes. "It had to be both. I knew Burrell would play knight in shining armor, even for Mona. Really, what did it matter if Redus beat her? But Burrell was as predictable as ever. I could get him to do battle with Redus any time I wanted. But if he brought Redus down, Redus wouldn't have hesitated to bring me down, too. Yes, it had to be both."

With a hand behind my back, I gestured to Diana, who stood enough to the side to not catch his attention, to start backing toward the hallway. She did. Slowly.

"I was glad of the opportunity to get rid of Redus. But Burrell . . . that was the beauty of it. Thomas David Burrell." He smiled. A sweet, genuine smile that could win many a vote.

My stomach heaved. I masked the reaction by shifting my weight, ending a few inches closer to the hall.

"I planned that. Just as carefully as I've planned my career. I'll win that race for the state senate, you know. I've built a base of power. I know the right people. And nothing can change that Redus is dead and Burrell knows what it's like to no longer be the favorite son."

If Diana could get out, she could get help. If I could stall him. If he was so wrapped up in what he was saying. If . . .

"You did that very well," I said, softly. "What about Mona?"

He chuckled a little. "Ah, Mona. Mona was true to form. Not as stupid as she acted, not as smart as she thought, and greedy to the end. And a liar, of course. She said to meet her at the trailer at five. I went straight from the meeting in O'Hara Hill and arrived an hour early so I could do everything in an orderly manner. But she was already there, pawing through Burrell's safe."

Diana was about two feet from the hall door.

Hunt never took his eyes off me. "Mona said she'd seen my car coming out of Three-Day Pass Road the day Redus, uh, disappeared. It's possible. But then, she said Redus had told her I was his protector and she had proof. *That* was a lie, and I told her so. She said I wouldn't dare risk it, so I better hand over money to give her a start in Mexico. Said she was going to tell Paycik the whole story as her insurance when he showed up at four thirty—the stupid bitch didn't even realize she'd let it out that she hadn't told anybody yet." He shrugged. "I shot her. It was tidier that way."

Diana took another step toward the hall door.

Hunt brought the gun up in a professional-looking two-handed grip to aim at my forehead. His hands didn't shake at all.

"Oh, no, that's not a good idea," he said in exactly the same voice he'd used to say that shooting Mona Burrell in the head with a shotgun was tidier. "Move back toward the center of the room, Ms. Stendahl. I will shoot Elizabeth if you take another step toward the door, and then I will shoot you. I'm an excellent shot."

Diana looked at me, I knew that, but I couldn't take my eyes off the gun.

"Move!"

Diana came away from the door.

Still with his eyes on me, Hunt stepped to the other door, the one I'd guessed was a private entrance. Even at this time of night, could he really get away with leading two women out of the courthouse at gunpoint? The jail was so close . . .

And then I remembered the utter quiet, the sense of desertion as we'd slipped into the courthouse. No one had noticed that.

"I don't believe either of you has seen all the features of our court-house, have you? It was built in the nineteenth century, you know." He opened the door, and used the gun to gesture first Diana, then me toward it.

Diana took a step in, then looked up, before she looked back to me and Hunt, lined up behind her.

"Go ahead," he ordered.

Diana shifted the camera on her shoulder, and I realized it was still running.

As I followed her through the door, I saw why she'd glanced up. Inside the door was a two-and-a-half-foot square landing, then a steep, narrow stairway up to the left. Diana was about four steps up, listing slightly as she struggled with the camera.

Not out of the courthouse, but up. Up to the top of the tallest building in Sherman, overlooked by nothing but a dark Wyoming sky.

Lulling hadn't worked. Try something else. Anything.

"To the roof? That's stupid, Hunt." Provoke him. Unsettle him. "Somebody will see us."

He chuckled. Unprovoked, totally settled. "In this town? At this time of night?"

He was right. If we screamed, who would hear us? The nearby businesses were deserted. Maybe someone inside the jail . . . . Not likely. And even if someone did hear and reacted immediately, less likely that they'd be in time. We were on our own. With a double murderer who'd come equipped with a silencer.

As if he'd heard that thought, he said, "I brought the gun in case Ambrose happened to come to his office tonight, and I decided he needed to commit suicide. It's his, you know. Took it at his annual Christmas party as a precaution, and now it's come in quite handy. In fact, everything's worked out very well. Took some doing to get Widcuff to let Ambrose out tonight, but it was worth it."

The thought came to me that if Hunt succeeded, Diana's two children would be orphans. And the shadow dog—would anyone feed him?

"Go on." Hunt jabbed me in the back with the gun.

Starting up those stairs, my throat closed at the anguish my family and friends would feel. *Mom, Dad, I'm sorry to do this to you.*

Other voices echoed in my head.

Sometimes you learn as much about the truth from the questions that don't get asked.

You fear that the truth you seek might not be a truth you like.

Mrs. Parens was right. I had feared the truth. And that was one of the truths I should have learned about myself by following Tom Burrell's advice and looking at the questions I wasn't asking.

Not about the case, but about myself.

Five months I kept telling myself—five months before I reclaimed my old life. But I'd never asked myself what I wanted from my future life. No more than I'd asked myself why my marriage had gone wrong, and why I'd stayed in it so long after it had. Because I'd focused on the professional fallout of my divorce while I hid away from the emotional ones. In fact, I had a whole pile of questions I hadn't asked.

They wouldn't get asked or answered if I died now.

"They'll find us," I tried again. "They'll figure out it was you."

"Don't be modest, Elizabeth, I doubt anyone else will put it together. As for finding you, there's a shed up on the roof that won't be used until they pull out the Christmas decorations. By that time, what with our hot summer sun, there won't be much of your bodies for forensics to bother with.

"But if you two are found sooner, no one will believe any alibi Ambrose might have. Not in his desperate situation, and with you shot by his gun and found where only his office has access."

So maybe the window blinds had been open not because nobody would see the light but because he hoped someone might—and report there'd been activity in Claustel's office tonight.

He'd thought of everything.

Diana stumbled slightly as she reached the top, balancing the camera with difficulty as Hunt ordered her to open the door there.

We stepped from the dim light of the stairwell into the dark of a moonless Wyoming sky that seemed to wrap around us like cobwebs.

No ambient light from the town pierced it. When they rolled up the sidewalks in Sherman, they took all the light with them.

We were on a narrow portion of the roof, a slice of horizontal between the four-story drop to the ground and the rounded base of the conical tower that peaked thirty feet above us.

"Here, let me take that camera, Diana." She started to protest, but I jostled her to hide a low growl of "do it," and she handed over the lump that I cradled like a load of firewood.

"Easing her burden, Elizabeth? How thoughtful." Hunt moved around us. "Though soon you both will be eased of all burdens. Stand over there." He gestured with the gun farther around the curve of the tower, to a narrow opening between the tower and a metal box atop the addition's roof. The shed.

He was right that nobody would find us here by accident. Although Hunt probably had thought the same thing about Redus' body. The chance of our bodies being found someday was not, however, a major consolation.

"You know, I almost had to do this at the construction trailer when you and Paycik blundered in. Maybe I should have."

"What about Claustel?" I asked desperately. As a kid I used to try to extend my bedtime by asking my parents all sorts of questions. Mom never fell for it. Dad did. I prayed it was a gender thing.

"You really were quite amazing in his office earlier, Elizabeth. Although you had a few little things wrong, like that Redus came up with the idea of going after the Claustel boy. That was me—redirecting his greedy attention so he didn't ruin everything. And of course thinking Claustel had the brains to be running things."

"Were they in on it—Claustel and Widcuff?"

He tsked. It echoed eerily against the wall behind us.

"Those buffoons? They weren't in on anything. Claustel swallowed having Redus as liaison like a lamb. He thought it was his idea, because Redus had caught his son with another boy in a backseat. And all I had to do with Widcuff was drop a hint here and there, and he held off searching for Redus. I will say his making a mess of the investigation was mostly on his own, though I dropped a word about how he wouldn't want the state guys coming in and taking all the glory. But arresting Burrell too soon—I will take credit there. A nice touch, don't you think? Burrell got to squirm in jail, then I come back and look like the even-handed voice of justice and let him free. Of course by then, everyone thought he might be a murderer."

He raised the gun. "No more delaying."

"Hunt . . ."

"Please, Elizabeth, you're not going to say something clichéd like I'm not going to get away with it, are you?"

"No." I shifted the camera.

A voice echoed up the narrow stairway like liquid up a straw. It was Mike, calling my name, then Diana's.

Ames Hunt's eyes flickered to the open door. His arm straightened in front of him and his finger stretched toward the trigger as he turned to us.

That flicker wasn't much, but it was the only opening I had. I hefted the camera higher, and as Hunt turned, I threw it at him with all my strength.

The man had no reflexes. Any normal person would have dropped the gun and tried to catch the camera. He did neither.

The camera hit him high on the chest and the right shoulder. He staggered back a step from the impact, trying to twist around to keep the gun on us. Fighting for balance, his left foot crossed over his right. His left shin cracked against the low edge of the stone railing. He seemed to hang there an instant, then he tipped like a falling tree and disappeared.

His scream echoed in the man-made canyon where we huddled, long after Ames Hunt had come to earth.

Chapter Thirty-Four

THE JOCKEYING FOR POSITION was something to behold.

Sheriff Widcuff kept trying to get a hand on the side rail of the gurney carrying seriously injured Ames Hunt to make it look as if he had the murderer in custody. He succeeded in looking superfluous, since Richard Alvaro and the state investigators already flanked the EMTs. The Sherman police chief had better luck by walking ahead, pretending to clear away the swarms.

There were no swarms, but there were a pair of interested bystanders from the jail, along with Needham Bender, his photographer from the *Independence* and Diana—operating a spare camera from the van Mike had driven back—Mike and me. We trailed behind in a strange procession to the ambulance.

Thurston Fine showed up as the ambulance doors closed.

"There's been a mistake," he proclaimed.

He tried to open the ambulance doors to be sure it was truly Ames Hunt, the owner of the coattails Thurston had intended to ride, who was in there. Finally, Widcuff convinced him, adding that Hunt had still been clutching the gun when the medics got to him. Fine turned his back on the departing ambulance and shifted the gears of his ambition. Mike had to physically block him out of Diana's shot of Widcuff's statement.

Fine was still wailing about that when we all arrived back at the station.

"They had no right. My contract clearly says I have the lead story. Five and ten, Monday through Friday. I get that story. I get that story!"

Haeburn stepped in. "Give it to me, Diana."

He meant the camcorder. Diana had told me there was a chance the tape from the camera that went over the edge with Hunt could be recoverable. We'd decided to tell no one beyond Mike until we knew for sure.

I'd told her I was sorry about her camera, and I'd get her a replacement—a modern, compact, top-quality replacement.

She'd given a wry smile. "We'll be lucky if Haeburn doesn't claim that since it saved our lives, we have to go back to using those all the time."

Not if I had anything to say about it. And I intended to start saying things. Right now.

"Not yet," I told Haeburn. "We have some things to decide, then we—"

Haeburn's face went red—all over, all at once, as if someone had put a red filter over a lens. "I make the decisions here." He tried to snatch the camera from Diana.

Mike stepped in.

What little Mike had said in the past hour had been to blame himself. He shouldn't have left Diana and me. He should have known Hunt was the killer. He shouldn't have asked me to get involved. He should have returned to the square earlier when there was no sign of Claustel. He should have thought to try the courthouse door sooner when he found my car empty. He should have run up the stairs faster. He should have prevented every evil in the world.

Someday we'd have to talk about his megalomania. Mike Paycik might have great shoulders, but Atlas he's not. Now, however, wasn't the time for that talk.

With Haeburn trying to dodge around Paycik, I picked up as if he hadn't interrupted. "Then we can start acting like real journalists. We'll give Fine the story for the newscasts, but Mike's on-camera stays, and we—" I gestured to include Mike, Diana and myself. "—do the editing. That doesn't interfere with his contract. And—"

"She can't, she can't," Fine spluttered into Haeburn's face, sending a fine spray across his glasses, "dictate to me."

I easily hurdled this interruption. "And the three of us get a free hand for a half-hour news special to go on at ten thirty tonight, after the early news tomorrow and to be repeated at least twice this weekend."

"What makes you think you can dictate the coverage by this station?" Haeburn's face went from rose to cherry. "What makes you think—"

"We have the story. If you want it, you take those terms. Or no story."

"You are employees, you have to—"

"You suspended us, remember? This was done all on our own time. For that matter, Diana did most of the shooting with her own equipment. Which reminds me, that's another condition: reinstatement." I considered. "And veto power on assignments for Mike and a raise for Diana."

"You can't . . . she can't . . . they can't . . ." Fine kept sputtering.

"How about you?" Diana asked.

I considered asking to be left in peace, but letting Fine and Haeburn know what I most wanted didn't seem like a good idea. "I want twice weekly promos for 'Helping Out' for the next six weeks."

Les Haeburn is a lot of things, but he is not totally stupid. "Okay. Get busy on that damned wrap-up show."

We left him wiping his glasses. And Fine still sputtering.

THE CLIP OF THE STRETCHER holding County Attorney Ames Hunt being escorted by law enforcement officers as it was put into an ambulance made a great teaser. It drew interest from several tabloid TV shows. When Hunt died on the operating table, the networks got interested. None of them could resist the idea of a murdering elected official killed by a TV camera. Haeburn, naturally, handled all dealings with them.

Mike, Diana and I, with assistance from Jenny and Diana's cronies on the technical end, slammed together the wrap-up show. The only timeout I took was a quick call to my family. I don't know if they'll ever get over the shock of my calling just to say I loved them all.

We slept about three-and-a-half minutes, then, fueled by caffeine and adrenaline, tore apart the show and with the help of other reporters, editors and photographers, updated the version that ran after the next day's early news.

The updates included that the gun registered to Tom Burrell and kept at the office of Burrell Roads was found in the shed on the roof of the courthouse. Presumably Hunt had taken it when he put Redus' gun in the cabinet, then stashed it as another link to Claustel. Also, Gina, in exchange for agreeing to tell everything she knew about Redus' schemes, would get probation for spending ill-gotten money.

The judge who agreed to that deal was not Ambrose Claustel. Claustel had resigned.

Richard Alvaro and Aunt Gee didn't think Claustel would be charged, because there was insufficient proof he'd dismissed any cases so Redus could benefit financially. I'd been wrong about that—there was no money trail, because Claustel had gone along with Redus only to keep the deputy quiet about Frank Claustel's sexual orientation.

No reports surfaced on KWMT, the *Independence* or the radio about Frank Claustel's role in his father's downfall, but I wondered how long it would take to circulate through the grapevine. And I wondered how Roger and Myrna Johnson and Brent Hanley would deal with it when the talk included Rog Junior.

But those were thoughts for lying awake and staring at the ceiling, not for the frenetic activity of putting together that wrap-up show. We were still applying finishing touches when the five o'clock news started, but it wasn't quite as close a call as the obstacle-course-running character had in *Broadcast News* to get a story into the network feed on time. There are shorter halls and fewer obstacles to hurdle at KWMT.

No one left the newsroom. Staff clustered around the TV monitors and watched in near silence. I think I held my breath through the full half-hour—including commercials. When it was over, they didn't applaud. They did better. They wandered past where I sat and said good night, or gave me a wave, or passed an every-day comment. You don't do that to a shark or a queen.

"C'mon, Elizabeth, let's go." Mike held out my purse to me.

"Go? Where?"

"Your house. Some folks are getting together."

"At *my* house? But it's awful."

"Sure, makes everybody comfortable. Nobody has to worry about spilling anything."

Diana laughed—she could. She hadn't seen my place yet. "Wasn't it nice of Paycik to volunteer you to have us all over for dinner?"

"Dinner?" I hadn't even had time for medicinal grocery shopping lately.

"Quit looking panicked," Mike said. "I ordered pizzas. All you need to provide are napkins. Now, c'mon, or we'll be the last ones there."

Mike, Diana, Jenny, Smitty, Billy and Jenks came from the station. Needham Bender, his wife Thelma, and Cagen from the *Independence* and, to my surprise, Mike's Aunt Gee, Mrs. Parens, and Deputy Sheriff Richard Alvaro. My next-door neighbors stopped by, as did the nice elderly lady from across the street, too. Several guests had brought wine. Beer appeared (the elderly lady from across the street knocked one back in record time.) Someone else brought a case of soft drinks. The pizzas arrived in good order. I had no napkins. Paper towels did just fine.

"What I don't understand," Jenny said into a hush of people lulled to silence by full stomachs and empty glasses, "is how you knew it was Hunt and came up with that great bluff of accusing the judge."

"That was no bluff. That was stupidity. I thought it *was* Judge Claustel." I twirled the inch of ruby liquid remaining in my glass. My ex had insisted on using Baccarat for wine. I'd discovered that knowing a glass would line up nicely in the dishwasher added a certain sweetness to its contents. "It was only when I was hearing my own words that I realized they could apply another way."

I explained about the spider webs as best I could, and in the process reminded myself I had a call to make to a certain distant in-law lawyer who'd spun his own benign web around me at KWMT. "If

Claustel had been the murderer, it would have meant that Tom Burrell was just a handy scapegoat. But the sort of web I kept seeing had been spun around him as much as around Foster Redus."

"But how did you know Hunt hated Burrell?" Jenny pursued.

"Oh, Mrs. Parens got me started on that, because she told me how long Hunt had been coming in second to Burrell. If it had been anybody else who was being touted over him for the nomination, Hunt probably wouldn't have framed him for murder." Noting the look Mrs. Parens sent toward Aunt Gee, I quickly added, "Of course, there never would have been a solution without Aunt Gee. Or a lot of other people."

As Mike filled in some of the information we'd gotten from Gina, Mona, Marty, Tom and others, I remembered the first morning he'd come to pick me up to drive to O'Hara Hill. I'd been thinking then that the small evening-ups in life like the teenage bitch queen who'd been the bane of your adolescence getting wrinkles brought the truest satisfaction in life. After seeing Ames Hunt, I'd changed my mind.

Letting go was, by far, the saner course.

Was I ready for some sanity?

"Here's to a wonderful addition to our little community of journalists," said Needham Bender, raising his glass. "Who was instrumental in finding a murderer in our midst."

While everyone else drank, Mike leaned over and added quietly, "And who made a little girl happy."

Later that night, I watched a copy of the wrap-up show. The segment I kept replaying was a shot Diana had taken that morning, with the eastern sky igniting clouds into puffs of flame, and the western sky grudgingly relinquishing its purple velvet. Amid golden light and long, lush shadows softening the stone of the courthouse, Tamantha Burrell walked down the front steps, holding her father's hand.

It was the first time I'd seen Tamantha Burrell smile.

I WAS AWAKENED by the phone the next morning.

It was Mel.

"Danny? You wanted firm, I got firm. Political talk show in St. Louis. Every Sunday. And consulting with the political reporting team. It's not the big bucks you were making, but—"

"No."

"No? But—"

"I'm going to finish out my contract here, Mel. I need these months. To think and plan. Come next fall . . . . Maybe then I'll be ready to sign off news for good. I don't know. But I know I'm remaining KWMT's 'Helping Out' reporter E.M. Danniher until then."

It took more than that to persuade him I was certain, but when I did, he accepted it, even supported my decision. That's one of the benefits of blending personal and professional, I thought as we hung up.

As for the drawbacks . . . I would tackle him later about exactly what strings in his spider web he'd pulled to get me to KWMT-TV. To get me exiled instead of executed, so I still had the chance to make choices about my professional future. And the chance to ask myself questions about my personal future.

I filled the bowls on the stump with food and water for the dog, then sat on the steps by the back door. He came from behind the garage and looked at me for a long time. Slowly he advanced to the stump. He ate hurriedly, drank deeply. But when he was finished, he didn't slide back into the shadows. He stood and looked at me. And I talked to him, soft and slow. He came toward me.

He didn't come close, and he didn't stay long. But I looked into his melting chocolate brown eyes and knew Brent and the police and the neighbors were right. He was my dog. That morning, I named him Shadow.

That afternoon, I answered a knock to find a tall, lanky man who looked like Abraham Lincoln's good-looking cousin standing on my doorstep—my front doorstep, in full view of anyone who might be watching.

"Thank you, E.M. Danniher."

And then he kissed me.

For news about upcoming "Caught Dead in Wyoming" books, as well as other titles, subscribe to Patricia McLinn's free newsletter.

Don't miss any of the Caught Dead In Wyoming series:

SIGN OFF

With her marriage over and her career derailed by her ex, top-flight reporter Elizabeth "E.M." Danniher lands in tiny Sherman. But the case of a missing deputy and a determined little girl drag her out of her fog.

Get SIGN OFF now!

LEFT HANGING

From the deadly tip of the rodeo queen's tiara to toxic "agricultural byproducts" ground into the arena dust, TV reporter Elizabeth "E.M." Danniher receives a murderous introduction to the world of rodeo.

Get LEFT HANGING now!

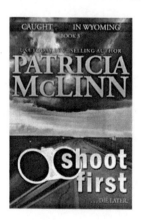

SHOOT FIRST

Death hits close to home for Elizabeth "E.M." Danniher – or, rather, close to Hovel, as she's dubbed her decrepit rental house in rustic Sherman, Wyoming.

Get SHOOT FIRST now!

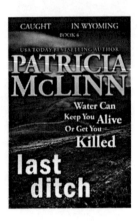

LAST DITCH

A man in a wheelchair goes missing in rough country in the Big Horn Basin of Wyoming. Elizabeth "E.M." Danniher and KWMT-TV colleague Mike Paycik immediately join the search. But soon they're on a search of a different kind – a search for the truth.

Get LAST DITCH now!

What readers are saying about the "Caught Dead in Wyoming" series:

"Great characters" … "Twists and turns" … "Just enough humor" … "Truly a fine read" … "Exciting and well-crafted murder mystery" … "Characters and dialogue were so very believable" … "Couldn't put it down" … "That was fun!" … "Smart and witty"

For excerpts and more on the "Caught Dead in Wyoming" series books, visit Patricia McLinn's website.

Dedication

For Mom & Dad, who taught me to read, told me the stories, bought me the books, and let me read just a few minutes longer so many nights.

Your love for each other has taught so many so much.

Acknowledgements

The author gratefully acknowledges

—William Beagle, who answered many questions about TV news and reminded me when I was wondering why on earth I hadn't just written about newspapers that it's because I like to learn things. Oh, yeah.

—Bill White, who continues as a timely resource on things Wyoming. As I've said before, after he stops laughing, he answers all my questions.

—Pat Van Wie, who has fulfilled two roles in bringing this story to life, both amazingly well.

—TV journalists Patrick Comer, Steve Trainer, and Samantha Kozsey, who answered many questions when this story was barely a seed.

—Shirley Rooker of CallforAction.org and WTOP radio, whose generous sharing of her time and information sprouted that seed.

—Brian Wagner of WHIZ, who answered last-second questions with aplomb.

—Coworkers in the newsrooms of the Rockford Register-Star, Charlotte Observer, and Washington Post. Some of you are among my favorite people on earth. Others, not so much. The former I thank for your friendship. The latter I thank for being great fodder for fictional murders.

About the author

USA Today bestselling author Patricia McLinn spent more than 20 years as an editor at the Washington Post after stints as a sports writer (Rockford, Ill.) and assistant sports editor (Charlotte, N.C.). She received BA and MSJ degrees from Northwestern University.

McLinn is the author of nearly 40 published novels, which are cited by readers and reviewers for wit and vivid characterization. Her books include mysteries, contemporary western romances, contemporary romances elsewhere in the world, historical romances, and women's fiction. They have topped bestseller lists and won numerous awards

She has spoken about writing from Melbourne, Australia to Washington, D.C., including being a guest-speaker at the Smithsonian Institute.

She is now living in Northern Kentucky and writing full-time. Patricia loves to hear from readers through her website, Facebook and Twitter.

Dear Readers: If you encounter typos or errors in this book, please send them to me at: Patricia@PatriciaMcLinn.com. Even with many layers of editing, mistakes can slip through, alas. But, together, we can eradicate the nasty nuisances.

Thank you! – Patricia McLinn

CPSIA information can be obtained
at www.ICGtesting.com
Printed in the USA
LVOW08s2315160417
531052LV00001B/186/P